HIDING

LIES

HIDING

The Eleanor Ames Series

LIES

JULIE CROSS

Entangled Publishing, LLC
2614 South Timberline Road
Suite 105, PMB 159
Fort Collins, CO 80525

Entangled Teen is an imprint of Entangled Publishing, LLC.

Visit our website at www.entangledpublishing.com.

Edited by Liz Pelletier and Lydia Sharp
Cover design by Bree Archer
Interior design by Toni Kerr

ISBN: 978-1-63375-816-2
Ebook ISBN: 978-1-63375-817-9

Manufactured in the United States of America

First Edition April 2018

10 9 8 7 6 5 4 3 2 1

entangled teen
an imprint of Entangled Publishing LLC

To my readers: thank you for sticking around.

CHAPTER
1

It's been nearly a year since I decided to give up my conning ways for the honest life. But here I am again, hiding up in a tree, studying an asset. I lift the binoculars to my eyes so I can get a better view of the hot guy walking toward me. Despite the chilly, December night (why in the world did the Founding Fathers consider Virginia "the South"? It's freakin' cold here!), he's not wearing a coat. Probably because one of his arms is in a sling. He approaches the building slowly, carefully, his gaze never holding one place but scanning the area.

I shift my binoculars toward a car in the distance. The headlights are off, so I can see a man and a woman inside. They're sitting in the dark, looking perfectly comfortable. Nothing exciting. I go back to spying on the dark-haired hottie, but I'm distracted. My butt is painfully going numb. The tree branch I'm sitting on is covered in snow. I shift, trying to find a dry spot. The hot guy stops, holds perfectly still, and then tilts his head upward. His beautiful, blue eyes seem to land on me. This is confirmed a second later when a dimple appears on each cheek. I used to never trust anyone with dimples. Recently, I've become more flexible with this rule. But even so, my heart plummets to my stomach at the sight of them.

Caught.

My feet have been dangling. I start to lift them up, attempting to conceal myself. But I'm not fast enough. Warm fingers wrap around my ankle.

"Got you," the guy says. "How long have you been up there spying on me?"

"Spying? On you?" I shake my head. "Don't know what you're talking about. I'm waiting for someone. He'll be here any second."

The hot guy takes the binoculars and looks them over, analyzing the zoom-in and recording switches hidden on the underside. "Fancy. Not exactly for recreational use."

That's because they're Aidan's. My sister's boyfriend. Up until two weeks ago, when he was forced to resign, Aidan was a Secret Service agent. He used all kinds of spy gear in his former job—like these high-tech night-vision binoculars.

I hop down from the tree, assessing the intruder, searching for body language that says friend or enemy, even though I already know the answer. No harm in having a little extra practice. Role-play is definitely a skill of mine, but it's also a muscle that must be worked regularly. "Just so you know, I *am* trained in self-defense. Wouldn't try anything if I were you."

"Yeah?" He lifts an eyebrow. "That's good because this place is sketchy as hell."

We both glance around the deserted warehouse building beside us, the vandalized lumberyard nearby, and the questionable items strewn across the walkway leading to the giant warehouse door—condom wrappers, broken beer bottles, cigarette butts.

"You're right, it's sketchy," I say. "I better take off before something bad happens."

"Wait…" Hot Guy reaches for me, his fingers curling around my waist. He tugs me until my back rests against the tree and we're hidden from anyone on the street. "Tell me about this other guy you're waiting on."

I stare up at him, taking in the cocky smirk, perfectly messy dark hair, and blue eyes that hold dozens of secrets. "What other guy?"

He grins, showing off two perfect dimples to go with the rest of his perfects. "Good answer."

Then, before I can refocus on the role I've been playing, he leans down and kisses me. It's only been a week but feels like a month. Maybe longer. His cheeks are cold, but his lips are warm and tender. I bring him closer and closer until his slinged arm is lodged between us.

"Miles," I mumble against his lips.

"Uh-huh."

"Miles," I repeat, too caught up in this kiss to celebrate the slip he just made. "That's *his* name. The guy I'm waiting on."

"Miles. Sounds like an asshole. Forget him." He pulls away just enough to see my face. His good hand rests against my cheek. He looks like he's about to dive into kissing me again but hesitates. "It's really cold out here."

"And sketchy," I add. "Why would you pick a place like this? You can't coast forever on the whole mysterious-hot-guy persona. So if that's your plan, I'd rather meet at the Y or Planet Fitness like a normal person."

He rolls his eyes. "Yes, that's my goal in life. Devote all my time to training to be a spy so I can impress girls."

"Doubt you would be the first." I plant one more kiss on those warm lips, and then step around him and head for the door to the warehouse. He really does need to get out of the cold. "Hopefully someday you'll be able to wear a coat again."

"And dress myself," he agrees. "My mom had to button my shirt today."

"And drive you here." I nod toward the parked car where his parents, Agent Beckett and Agent Beckett, are waiting. "How much longer with the sling?"

"Another week or two," he says with a hint of longing in his voice. Not surprising. Since the day I met him last September, I've watched him swim thousands of laps in our apartment complex's pool, go for runs and not come back for two hours. He's good at concealing his frustration most of the time, but without those outlets he must be so restless right now.

We enter the warehouse, and Miles flips on the lights, revealing the large square of blue mats covering part of the floor, a weight bench beside the mats, and a punching bag dangling from the ceiling. Like a good student, I kick off my shoes before stepping onto the mats. When we're in this building, like we've been for the past three Sundays, the kissing gets left outside along with sarcasm, whining, and pretty much any talking on my end. And considering Miles's personality invites constant opportunity for sarcasm, this is no easy feat. But after Miles and I were kidnapped two weeks ago and nearly murdered, I've decided it's probably a good idea to take these self-defense lessons seriously.

He can't drive until his shoulder fully heals (an injury obtained during the previously mentioned kidnapping incident), so the Becketts have been nice enough to make the drive from their house outside of Baltimore. Every Sunday.

"What have you worked on this week?" Miles asks.

He's all business now, too, though his eyes roam over me when I toss my coat aside and reveal a skin-tight workout top. It's a reaction I expected and even planned for. What kind of partner would I be if I didn't test his strength of focus every once in a while? I stand there for a long moment, making eye contact but not moving a step toward him. Sure enough, his feet shuffle my way, his good arm rising a few inches, as if his hand is planning to land at my waist.

My mother told me something years ago, when I first began helping out with the family biz. She said, "The ability to command the attention of others is mastered through actions, not words, through the way you walk, the way you hold yourself. The very air you exist in must bleed charisma, confidence, and believability. That skill will be your greatest weapon."

If I can distract a military school–trained, compulsive rule-follower like Miles, even for a few seconds, that means I've got at least one weapon on me and ready to use at any time.

Miles stops, the movement abrupt and deliberate, his good arm falling back to his side. He shakes his head and his lips twitch, fighting a smile. Caught me for the second time tonight. "So…what have you worked on this week?" he repeats.

I laugh under my breath and then grant him a response. "Lots of cardio, weights, and a little bit of work on escaping a chest mount."

During the week, I have training sessions with a woman who is a friend of Aidan's from his days in the Marines. She does a good job, but she approaches our lessons like I'm a girl who wants to avoid sexual assault in college—which I definitely am. But I'm also a girl who might need to escape highly trained assassins. Everything that happened a couple of weeks ago, though, is top secret, so I can't exactly ask her for more offensive tactics without raising questions.

"Good," Miles says. "Cardio is good. Running away is often your best defense."

Okay, maybe my weekly instructor isn't the only one focused on defense. "*My* best defense or anyone's?"

"Anyone's," he clarifies, putting a note of finality to this conversation.

I asked my mother the same question when she gave me her "greatest weapon" advice, worried that she was really trying to tell me that all I had going for me were my looks. She answered exactly the same as Miles just did.

"Start on the bag," Miles commands.

I retrieve my gloves from a storage closet and approach the punching bag. I keep one gloved hand close to my face and use the other to strike the bag. This exercise used to be nearly impossible for me. Now it's not so bad.

"Don't let your elbow lock out," he says. Then with his good arm, he demonstrates a punch. "You're making yourself vulnerable to having that arm twisted behind you."

I do at least a dozen more punches with my left arm until I've earned Miles's approval and he orders me to switch hands. After a while, my arms begin to feel like Jell-O and sweat trickles down my face. Whenever I start to get tired, I imagine being locked in that cold, dark room where Miles and I were held a couple of weeks ago. I visualize the door opening, offering me a chance to escape, but first I've got to get past Agent Jakowski—Jack—who was Aidan's boss and a trusted friend turned murderer.

The bag morphs into Jack's face. I clench my jaw and strike harder, devoting every ounce of strength in my arm to that punch. And the next one. And the one after that.

"Hey…" Miles's hand wraps around my wrist, holding it in place. "I said stop."

"Sorry, I didn't hear you." I tug my hand away from his and loosen the Velcro on my gloves, preparing to take them off. "Weights next?"

He just stands there studying me, his forehead wrinkled. "What were you thinking about just now?"

"Not locking out my elbow, keeping my front foot planted, using my hips, protecting my face," I rattle off, but I can't look at him. Instead I focus on unfastening my gloves.

Unfortunately Miles isn't buying it. "Maybe we should call it a night? Head over to Clyde's early?"

Miles's uncle lives in the apartment beside ours. Clyde and Miles's parents are hosting an early Christmas dinner at Clyde's tonight, and they invited my sister, Aidan, and me to join.

"Can we finish, please?" I need this. I really do. But *he* needs honesty from me and won't go forward without it. I drop my arms and turn to face him. "It feels good learning this, but at the same time…" I release a breath and force out the worst of my current fears. "I hate imagining situations where it might come in handy."

Miles is silent for the length of several heartbeats but finally says, "Me, too."

In those two simple words, I can hear his own fear, can feel it pulsing in the space between us. It's both a comfort and a source of anxiety.

"So you think it might come in handy?" I chew on my left thumbnail, a clear sign of doubt, my father would tell me if he were here. "In the near future?"

I know Miles's parents (and possibly Miles, too) have far more information than I do about what happened to us a couple of weeks ago. About the rogue group of assassins and whether or not the organization is still intact. Part of me wants to push for details, and the other part would love nothing more than to return to being just another student at Holden Academy, oblivious to the world of secret government agents gone bad.

"I hope not," Miles says, and then he breaks his own all-business-on-the-mats rule, moving closer to me and laying a hand on my cheek. "But it's definitely possible."

My stomach twists with fear, and my heart picks up, but I give one sharp nod and clap my hands together. "Okay, what's next?"

I just have to hope the near future allows time for me to learn enough to stay alive.

CHAPTER

2

A shirt-size box wrapped in red paper printed with Santa heads all over it lands in my lap.

"That's from us, Ellie," Mrs. Beckett says, resting a hand on her husband's arm.

My face warms, though I don't know why. Guess I'm not used to people just giving me things with no strings attached. I tear the paper carefully and slide the lid off the box. Inside is a very old book, worn from years of existing and likely multiple readings. My fingers brush lightly over the leather cover. I've assessed enough valuables in my lifetime to guess that this is a first edition. It's also a story so familiar to me, if I close my eyes and draw it from my memory, entire sentences will leap out at me.

"'I could tell you my adventures—beginning with this morning,'" my mom read from the worn book in her hands, the paper cover hanging by a thread. "'But it's no use going back to yesterday, because I was a different person then.'"

"Like us," my five-year-old self said. "Yesterday Daddy had a mustache and you had black hair."

Mom laughed, the sound ringing with truth and etching itself into my memory. "Yes, just like us."

I rub the goose bumps on my arm, willing them away. It felt real. Her voice in my head. I haven't heard it in nearly a year.

"Saw you admiring that book when you and Miles came for the weekend," Mr. Beckett says, referencing the two-day vacation Miles and I took last month at his beautiful house in the woods near Baltimore. I'd almost refused to go. The idea of meeting CIA parents freaked me out a little. Especially since my own identity and criminal past had still been a secret then. Now Miles, his parents, and his uncle all know. But not anyone else, like the kids I go to school with.

"We're gone more often than we're home," Mrs. Beckett adds. "Figured we should find a safe spot for some of our valuables."

"Who better to keep your precious items safe than a skilled con artist?" I tear my eyes from the book and look at Mr. and Mrs. Beckett. "Sure you don't want to rethink that?"

They both laugh. So does Clyde. My sister, Harper, looks like she's not sure how to react. I'm not the only one who's still adjusting to the idea of people knowing our family secrets.

Miles, who had been in the bathroom, returns to the living room and glances around, picking up on the weird tension. "What'd I miss?"

He plops down on Clyde's couch, beside me. I offer him the box, and he lifts the book from it. "Wow, guess I know who my parents are leaving all the good stuff to. Clearly not their only son."

My face flushes again, even though I know Miles is joking. He's not at home much, either. His school, Marshall Academy, is a military boarding school. One he's been attending since the sixth grade.

With Simon Gilbert, I can't help thinking.

As much as I try not to think about Simon, it's hard

whenever I see Miles. Simon's death was the reason we met. Long before I came to Holden Prep and became Simon's friend, he and Miles were best friends and roommates at Marshall Academy for three years.

Miles's hand brushes my shoulder, and I try to shake off all thoughts of Simon. Miles and I did what we'd set out to do—prove that Simon's death wasn't a suicide. Now I just need to figure out how to put it all behind me. Would probably be easier without the revenge of the Government Agents Gone Bad hanging out in the near future.

But it's Christmas. It's only December tenth, actually, but we're celebrating Christmas. Which means I need to shove all that future crap to the side for now and enjoy the last few hours I get to spend with Miles until the middle of January.

My sister offers the Becketts and Clyde the tins of cookies we made for them. Well, mostly Aidan and I made them and assigned Harper as many fireproof tasks as we could think of to keep her busy.

"I have a present for you." Miles leans in closer, his lips resting against my temple. "Leave your window unlocked, okay?"

I turn my head toward him and whisper, "I've kept it unlocked since the first time you climbed up my balcony."

He grins at that memory, but the smile fades quickly. "You should definitely lock it. After I leave."

The happy Christmas bubble pops. My stomach twists and knots all over again.

After we leave Clyde's, after Aidan and Harper turn in for the night and I'm left alone with thoughts of agents gone bad climbing into my window instead of Miles, I turn to my gift from the Becketts for comfort. I flip to a random page, then drop into my desk chair, allowing the small built-in lamp to illuminate the words. My insides warm more and more with each familiar name or place. But then I remember that the person who brought these words to life for me is currently locked up in prison, and the warmth turns to cold dread.

It wasn't supposed to be her. When I made that deal with Agent Sheldon and the FBI team, it was supposed to be *him*... my dad. The man who kept me from seeing my sister for five years. The man who wouldn't allow even so much as a mention of Harper after she left. A small part of me is still stuck there, in that bank parking lot with half a dozen FBI agents.

"Eleanor," Sheldon said, approaching me slowly. "We had a deal. One that involves you handing over that piece of evidence."

"This evidence?" I pressed the point of my black heel deep into the flash drive resting beneath it on the bank parking lot. "These files are important? I had no idea."

One of the two male agents behind Sheldon drew his gun. But Sheldon stopped, turned to the guy. "Seriously? She's a sixteen-year-old armed with a pair of heels. Put away your service weapon."

"This was not what I agreed to." I lifted a finger, pointing in the direction in which the unmarked car had just fled. "Bring my mother back and the evidence is yours."

Agent Sheldon shook her head, her tightly woven dirty-blond bun never slipping. She reeked of by-the-book agent, from her hairstyle to the pressed button-down white blouse and black dress pants—not the outfit I'd wear to take down a bank investment fraud operation. Before I'd seen it with my own eyes mere minutes ago, I'd have never been able to conjure an image of this woman throwing someone like my mother to the ground, straddling her, yanking her arms practically out of their sockets behind her to get on those cuffs. My legs shook, tears threatening to form.

"So you didn't know?" Sheldon asked. "That they switched?"

"No, I didn't know." Had she thought I was playing her? That I'd rather send my mom to prison? I closed my eyes, trying to shake off the image of my mom's face, pressed against the tile floor of the bank. She'd turned to me, trying not to make it obvious, since she believed I was playing the part of an innocent bank customer. The look she'd given me said, *"It's okay. I'm okay."* She was worried about me. After what I'd done. And like a coward, when she'd mouthed, Run, seconds later, I did just that. Though unfortunately, the FBI had the place surrounded and needed the evidence my mom had slipped me earlier.

Sheldon held perfectly still, studying my face, my body language, clearly trying to decide if I was lying. If I had actually known who I'd really be turning in.

"Okay…okay," she said finally. *"Let's sit down and talk this through, you and me."*

"Your case is thin without this evidence," I reminded her. *"Bring my mom back, and I'll tell you exactly how to find my dad. I'll tell you everything you want to know about my family."*

A hint of greed flickered in Sheldon's eyes, but it vanished quickly. *"The testimony of an undocumented con-artist teenager is hardly hard evidence for a real case. And you're dealing with the law, Eleanor, not some rich businessman you can coerce. Even if I wanted to bring your mom back, to let her go free, I can't."*

It was in the air between us—truth—but I didn't want to believe it yet. *"You're letting me go free—why not my mother?"*

"You and I made a deal," she said. *"We put it in writing beforehand that you entered the crime scene as our informant under the direction of the FBI."*

Guilt burned in my chest. What had I done?

"How long before she's released?" I whispered, afraid my voice would shake.

"That's difficult to predict —"

"How long?" I demanded.

A hint of anger or frustration finally broke into Sheldon's robot face. "Twelve to fifteen months."

"Will she know?" I asked. "That it was me?"

"Not if you don't want her to," Sheldon said, still in her unkind manner but also sounding truthful. "Now can I have the flash drive?"

"Put it in writing." I made sure my heel continued to hold the flash drive captive, threatening her entire operation.

"Here?" Sheldon said, looking mollified by the suggestion.

"It should say that she won't be sentenced to more than fifteen months and…" I thought carefully about what I needed to feel better about today. "And that I have permission to see her before she gets out."

"I promised your sister that you wouldn't be allowed to —"

"Allowed to see my father," *I corrected. "Those terms are invalid now."*

The three FBI agents all exchanged looks. I tapped my heel against the drive and said, "What are you waiting for? Grab a pen and paper."

I open the desk drawer that I installed a false bottom into and remove the folded McDonald's receipt Agent Sheldon had scribbled our contract on, promising my mother no more than fifteen months in prison and promising me a visit with her the day before release. My plan that day in the parking lot with the flash drive and the FBI had been to tell my mom the truth right before she got out and to convince her to come live with us—though Harper would likely have many objections to this—but life was so different with Harper and Aidan. Everything was good. And then I got caught up in Simon's death and Miles. For a while, I thought I could just let it go, move forward, and not look back. But with the one-year mark approaching and lots of feelings stirred these past few weeks, I'm not sure I can do that.

Needing a break from these thoughts as well as the Agents Gone Bad worries from earlier, I tuck the book away and go in search of a tin of cookies I hid way, way in the back of the freezer. But when I reach the kitchen, I spot Aidan's broad shoulders, his head buried in the freezer.

"What are you doing?"

At the sound of my voice, he jumps, banging his head on the freezer, but quickly emerges, cookie tin in hand. "Look what I found way in the back."

I snatch it from him and open the lid, admiring the peanut butter fudge I made yesterday. After I take a few pieces, I finally offer him one.

"Miles not here yet?" Aidan says, his back to me while he grabs two glasses and the carton of milk.

I stuff my mouth full of fudge. "It's after midnight. Why would Miles be here?"

"Why indeed?" Aidan leans against the counter, watching me. The teasing grin falls off his face. "What's wrong?"

It used to be only Harper who could do that—read me without trying—but now Harper has taught Aidan some of her tricks. I slide onto the counter and balance my glass of milk on my knee. Believe it or not, there are some things I can talk about with Aidan that I can't with my sister. Our mother is one of those things. "Where's Harper?"

"Passed out." He reaches for another piece of fudge. "Lost count of how many glasses of wine she had."

"Clyde just kept pouring and pouring," I agree. Then, after taking another bite of fudge, I brave the Mom topic. "Have you heard anything from Agent Sheldon? Anything about the sentencing?"

He hesitates and then nods. "Yes, but not about the sentencing. It hasn't happened yet as far as I know."

"I can't believe it takes this long," I say, shaking my head.

"But they'll do that time-served thing, right? All these months count?"

Aidan nods again. "Agent Sheldon says they're moving her next week."

"Where?" The fudge tumbles around in my stomach. Texas is already far enough.

"Near Raleigh," he says.

I look up at him in surprise. "Raleigh? That's only, like — "

"Less than a four-hour drive," he finishes.

For several seconds, I don't know what to say. Next week, my mother will be only a few hours' drive from me. It feels like a sign, like she wants me to come and see her.

Aidan leans closer, his voice low. "I get why Harper feels the way she does, but you aren't your sister. I know you worry about your mom, wonder how she's doing. Maybe it would be easier if you just…saw for yourself?"

Nerves course through me. And excitement, if I'm being honest. *Yes, it would be easier, Aidan. You're not wrong. But what would I tell my sister? What would I tell Miles? Remember my criminal mother? The one whose case you studied in your white-collar-crime course? I'd like to see her again and maybe keep in touch, but don't worry, I know you'll love her.*

Sure, that'll go over well.

Aidan is busy wiping down the stove with a sponge, deliberately not looking at me when he says, "Harper has the ski trip early next month."

Harper is a nanny to toddler twins during the week and sometimes travels with the family or stays overnight at their house when the parents are gone. This plan is quite devious for Aidan, doing something so big behind my sister's back. It should make me feel guiltier, more reluctant to say yes, but it doesn't. If Aidan is willing, he must believe that it's okay, maybe even a good thing for me to see my mother.

I don't get to offer a response because the bedroom door flies open and my sister bolts like an Olympic sprinter toward the bathroom. Aidan drops the sponge and takes off after her.

"I'll get water and Advil," I call after him. "Let me know if you need the mop."

I set water and two pills on the nightstand in Aidan and Harper's room before heading back to my own. I pace back and forth for a few minutes, processing everything that Aidan told me. Mom won't be all the way in Texas anymore. That felt like a gazillion miles to someone who has never flown on a plane, only used cars, buses, and trains to get around. Not like I could have snuck off to Texas without my sister finding out. But a less than four-hour drive…it's very possible.

And without telling Aidan, without even forming an official answer in my head, I know I'm going to do it. In January. While Harper is off being Ski Nanny in Vermont or New Hampshire, I can't remember.

I shake out my arms, my hands already trembling just thinking about this plan. And I still have to decide what to tell Miles. If anything.

The only problem is that Miles wants honesty. He needs it, actually. It's kind of his thing, when it comes to us anyway.

Telling him might mean his telling me not to. Or losing his trust. I did promise him that I was done with my criminal family. My past has already put a thorn in our relationship. Visiting my mother in January could mean the end of Miles and me.

CHAPTER
3

Cold fingers pry the book from my hands, and I immediately jolt awake. I blink a few times, trying to focus on my alarm clock: 2:22 a.m.

"God, what happened?" Miles says, taking in the books spread all over my bed. "Some nerdy kid must have broken in, solved a bunch of algebra equations, read some US history, and highlighted Gatsby's worst lines. Are you all right? Did this person knock you out?"

I roll my eyes at him but quickly gather all the schoolbooks and notes strewn across my bed. Studying provided a great distraction and got me to quit pacing around my room. "Unlike you, I have to take finals after winter break."

"Oh, I'll have finals," Miles says, bitterness in his tone. "Just not history or algebra or anything like that."

I'm about to ask for more details, but I catch a whiff of him when I walk past to drop my books on the desk. "Have you taken up smoking?" I press my nose to his shirt and inhale. "Cigarettes *and* weed?"

"I was with Dominic," he admits. "That's why I'm so late. He wanted to talk."

Dominic DeLuca is one of our Holden Prep classmates.

He was also the guy Simon Gilbert liked to make out with when no one was looking. Dominic and I aren't exactly friends, but he did help Clyde a couple of weeks ago and came to our rescue during the whole kidnapping thing.

"So…you and he are still in touch?" I ask.

"He needs a friend. He's still pissed at Bret." Miles shrugs, and then his hand is on my waist, his slinged arm between us. "Let's not talk about Dominic."

"Or school or finals," I add, laying my ear against his chest. *Or my mother.* "Let's talk about Turkey. Do you really have to go?"

All three of the Becketts are boarding a flight from DC to Turkey tomorrow afternoon for what they're calling a Christmas vacation. CIA agents are all about the globe-trotting. I feel his lips in my hair, his warm breath against my scalp, and I'm already sizzling. He hesitates, then says, "You want me to stay, I'll stay."

Yes. I should tell him yes. Stay. But Needy Girlfriend isn't my style, and besides, this thing with us is still so new. Miles has a million reasons not to trust me, and I have a lifetime of conning to shake off before I can fully let someone in. And yet here we are, trusting. But how long will it last? Until I tell him about visiting my mother in prison? Until he finds out how badly I want to see her? That she's the reason the book his parents gifted me is so valuable?

"You should go with your parents," I say. "I don't want them to start calling me names like *that girl.*"

"That girl?" Miles laughs against my hair. "Doubtful. But just say the word and I'll come back, okay?"

I tilt my head up, wanting to get a good look at his face. I won't see it for a while. My eyes shift to his mouth after only a moment, and soon he's kissing me with much less inhibition than when we were outside the warehouse with his parents in the car nearby. Okay, now is definitely not the best time to mention what may or may not happen in January. We haven't really been alone like this since before the kidnapping, so both of us dive in, wanting to take full advantage. But there's no denying the struggles of making out with someone who has an arm in a sling. Miles tries to take off my shirt one-handed, and I end up with my head caught in it. His shirt, a button-down, hangs halfway off, leaving part of his chest exposed.

Both of us start laughing, me with my head still caught inside a T-shirt. When I try to wiggle free of it, the shirt falls down into place.

"Back where I started again." Miles steps away from me, shaking his head. "This sling is so inconvenient."

"Starting over is not a bad idea." I keep a few feet of distance between us and study Miles. "I have a plan."

Wordlessly, I move toward him, and my fingers wrap around the strap of his sling. Gently, I tug it over his head with one hand, and the other supports his arm, holding it against his chest. The sling falls to the ground, and Miles draws in a breath when my hands glide over his shoulder, sliding off his shirt.

"Does it hurt?" I ask, pausing my movement.

He fixes a heated stare on me that warms every inch of my skin. "No, not at all."

Excited nerves course through my gut. I fumble a little with putting his sling back in place, but by the time I'm turning him around, nudging him until he's seated on my bed, my hands are steady again. I grip the hem of my T-shirt and slowly, deliberately raise it higher and higher until it's off my body and on the floor beside Miles's shirt.

"Okay, I like this plan," he mumbles, his gaze never leaving me.

I inch closer to the bed, and Miles scoots farther away, eventually leaning against the wall. Then he reaches for me with his good arm, tugging until I'm seated on his lap, one knee on either side of him. He kisses my lips, then all along my jaw while his good hand glides up my now-bare back, making my skin tingle. I tilt my head up, and his mouth moves to my neck, his hand gently gripping the back of it, holding me in place. Not that I plan on moving away. I reach both hands behind me and unhook my bra, loving the sound of Miles's breath catching in the back of his throat. He continues to kiss my neck while his hand roams around to my front, his thumb teasing the bottom of my bra cup before sliding beneath it.

My mind turns completely fuzzy; I forget to do anything with my own hands, forget my worries over my mom and over Miles leaving the country, over him going back to his school and all the distance between us. Or maybe I *am* thinking about those things and that's why I catch myself pressing closer to Miles, closing all the distance I can without reinjuring his arm.

"Am I hurting you?" I ask, worried for a moment over the pressure of me leaning onto his shoulder.

"Even if you are," he says, breathless, "you're not moving."

I pause for a second, committing all of this to memory. Sometimes I wish for a pen nearby to record the perfect, perfect words Miles utters, especially in these moments when he's speaking without thinking. Because he's a guy who thinks things through.

"Okay," I reply, my mouth on his. "I'm not moving."

A round four in the morning, I wake up with a jolt, blinking in the now-dark room. I was dreaming about Jack, the Secret Service agent who murdered Simon Gilbert. I was back at the cabin in the woods with Jack's rifle pointed at me. I screamed for help, and then Agent Sheldon burst into the cabin like she was there to help, but she looked at me and shook her head.

"Oh, it's only you," the Dream Agent Sheldon said. "I thought I was here to save a real civilian. Not an informant."

And then she just left me there. To die, if the dream version had gone like the real one.

"Hey…" Miles rolls onto his back and uses his good arm to feel around for me in the dark until his fingers find my cheek. "You okay?"

I catch my breath and collapse back onto the bed beside Miles. I curl into his side and bury my face in his neck before spilling all the details of that weird dream. If it were daylight and I had time to put up my defenses, I'd likely have held back some of it. But the fresh fear and the confidence a dark room provides leave me vulnerable.

"He's gone," Miles says after I finish talking. "He can't hurt you again. And this Agent Sheldon, she's all black and white, no gray."

I laugh at that last part. "All black-and-white? Like someone else I know."

Miles doesn't offer a comeback, but I can practically hear him rolling his eyes. "My dad says that attitude is common for a lot of FBI agents. The bureau is trying to diversify their trainees to avoid having so many similar personality types."

"Good," I say, faking calm. "That means I might have a chance. I mean if the Secret Service lets in murderers, the door has to be open a crack for a non-murderous former criminal like me."

"Ellie," Miles says, not buying my sarcasm. "No government agency willingly hires murderers."

"Except the secret league of assassins," I argue, because I'm feeling conflicted about too much to agree on anything.

"Aren't they a government group? But maybe they don't hire killers, they just make them?"

Jack was part of a very old and secret organization of assassins, one Miles and I accidentally uncovered in our search for Simon's killer. They call themselves St. Felicity's Shelter. According to Miles, they're a noble group that seeks to take out the next Hitler before he or she becomes an evil dictator. St. Felicity's is comprised of individuals in nearly every type of government operation—CIA, NSA, FBI, Secret Service, politicians. But Jack decided nobility wasn't for him, and he wanted to use the depth and secrecy of the organization to make money. Hired hit men to begin with. Apparently the plan was to recruit me, and since I'm no hit man (hit woman? hit person?), I have to believe there were non-murderous plans in the works.

Were or are in the works.

"St. Felicity's is aware that members of the organization went rogue for cash," Miles says, employing more of that logic of his. "They came in and cleaned up, so we know they know. They'll dig deep and clean up things from the inside. They have to. But in the meantime—"

"Keep your windows and doors locked," I interrupt, flopping back onto my pillow. "And take self-defense lessons four times a week."

"I've been taking self-defense six days a week since I was eleven," Miles says, trying to smile. But I don't miss the hint of worry in his eyes, that maybe it's all too much for me. It is and oddly it isn't. I'm someone who has had to grow up fast. But that does raise an interesting question. "Do you think Jack was telling the truth about Simon? That he'd joined St. Felicity's Shelter? Why would they put a seventeen-year-old kid on their roster?"

"I asked my dad about this." Miles pulls his good arm around me and strokes my hair. "Invitations happen practically from birth, but you don't accept until you're old enough to make a pledge of loyalty for life."

"For life?" I repeat, though I had heard this from him before. "What exactly does that involve?"

"It means you go about your life, just as anyone would, and if you're needed for a job, you drop everything and accept the call of duty." His voice has taken on an eerie tone, or maybe I'm imagining it because the explanation is so creepy. "When asked to, you put the organization above anything else—family, job, religion. Always and forever."

"I wish we could have protected Simon," I say. "He was digging for information on Jack's rogue group, and that got him killed. What if we had known and could have helped him solve everything without…"

"Murder being involved," Miles finishes, and he's now very tense. "I think about that every single day."

A mixture of grief, sympathy, and affection for this boy who I may be falling in love with hits me. I lift my head and kiss his cheek. "You are so not a normal boyfriend. What am I going to do with you and all your save-the-world ambition?"

He looks at me, and that heat flares in his eyes all over again. "Sure I can't talk you into joining military school with me? I can teach you shoe shining, ironing, rope climbing—all the basics."

"As romantic as that sounds"—I kiss him again, wanting to take all I can while he's here—"I would miss my sister too much. I waited five years to see her again."

Miles is an only child, so I know he doesn't fully get the sister bond, but he tries. "I got permission to keep a car on campus and leave on weekends."

I rest my head on his chest again. "So after the holidays, when you get back from Turkey, Sundays will be our day. I can live with that."

"Me, too," Miles says.

We doze off for a while, and then right before the sun comes up, I help Miles back into his shirt and out the window again. My heart breaks seeing him leave for what will be the last time in weeks. He won't be my neighbor or classmate anymore.

Everything will be different.

Before I climb back into bed, I spot an envelope on my desk. My name is written on the front in Miles's handwriting. I open it carefully and smile at the sheet of paper. The last present he gave me was a social security card. Today he's given me a learner's permit so I can get my driver's license. I have no idea how he does this stuff, but I'm not complaining.

There's a soft knock on my bedroom door, and before I can move to answer, it swings open. My sister stands there, attempting to look stern, her blond hair falling around her face, her satin robe hastily tied. She looks surprisingly perky for someone who should be hung over.

"Did I just see a boy climb out your window?" she demands.

Even though Harper left my family when I was only twelve, she had plenty of time to acquire the observation skills we're known for. Very little gets past her.

"It was more of a stumble out the window. That sling is a pain in the ass," I say, still staring at my learner's permit. "Did you know about this?"

"The permit? Yeah, I got one, too. Isn't it awesome?"

Due to our grifter family ways, Harper and I were both undocumented Americans born and raised in this country with virtually no proof of that fact or any footprint whatsoever. Apparently the Becketts are helping turn this around for us.

Harper enters my room, buries herself under my covers, and says, "Come on, tell me everything that happened with Miles. Are you guys going to do the long-distance thing?"

Worry creeps over me, but I join her under the warm

covers and prepare to indulge my nosy sister in some TMI details. "Think that's a bad idea?"

"Normally, yes," Harper says. "But with Miles, no. He's loyal down to his core. I doubt he'll look at another girl ever again."

"Don't get carried away. We're still in early relationship territory. Very early."

But as I glance at the window again, replaying Miles's departure, I can't help but get carried away. Can't help but want his skin on my skin all the time.

Maybe, somehow, it will work out for us.

And maybe this is all enough for me—my school, Aidan, Harper, Miles. Maybe it's enough even without my mom?

But that cold dread from earlier returns just thinking about the idea of never seeing her again. Of not seeing her in the near future. I can accept never seeing my father again, but is it so wrong to want my mother in my life?

I can't convince myself of this, which is why, later that afternoon after Miles sends me a text saying they're boarding their flight to Turkey, I get Aidan alone long enough to tell him yes. I want to see my mother next month.

He just looks at me like he'd been expecting this and then says, "I'll take you."

"No." I shake my head, then glance over my shoulder, checking for Harper. "I wouldn't do that to you."

"We're going to tell her eventually," he says in a firm tone. "And when we do, she'll be way more pissed at me if I'd let you go alone."

I swallow back the lump in my throat. Harper just talked about Miles being loyal, and look at me. Lying to both of them. Taking advantage of their trust. Bringing Aidan down with me. "Okay," I tell him, feeling like we should shake on it or something. "It's a date."

CHAPTER

4

"Maybe you should use cruise control," Aidan says for the third time in the last three hours. He keeps glancing at the GPS, pretending to check the directions. "You're seven miles over the speed limit."

Almost a month with my permit, almost a month with this plan. And here we are, middle of January, last day of winter vacation, on our way to visit my mother in prison.

I give him a sideways glance and try not to roll my eyes. "I have a permit now. It's legal for me to break the law."

"Nope," he says. "Speeding is always illegal."

"You know what I mean. It's like normal illegal. Not"—I conjure my best impression of a North Carolina police officer—"oh wait, you're driving without a license, have no identity, and hey...I think your father stole my wallet last week. Was he downtown at the Silver Bullet over on Main Street Friday night? Handsome fellow with a killer smile? Thought he was kinder than butter, invitin' me to supper after church, huggin' me goodbye. Then I get home, and my wallet's gone, walked right outta my pants."

Despite his taking this permit stuff way too seriously, Aidan laughs loudly, breaking some of the tension that's followed us during the majority of the drive. "In that case, I hope we do get pulled over, because I'd love to hear you charm the North Carolina state police."

With a sigh, I ease my foot up on the gas and click on the cruise control. I definitely didn't wear the right outfit for manipulating law enforcement.

I check the mile marker and see that we're less than ten miles from our exit now. My hands tighten on the steering wheel. I still haven't told Miles. Haven't told my sister. Haven't decided what I'll say to my mom. Does she already know that it was me who turned her in? Agent Sheldon promised she wouldn't tell her, but why would she be obligated to keep that promise? A dozen other people could have told her.

And if not, maybe I should? Maybe I should own up to it? I don't regret working with the FBI, because it gave me my sister back. But had I known it would be my mom instead of my dad…I wouldn't have gone through with it. Like me, my mom wanted to find Harper after her huge fight with my dad, when she left the family. I was only twelve but still old enough to hate him, to know that he could have told her, *Be whoever you want to be; you don't have to choose our way of life.* But that isn't what he said. For a month, neither my mom nor I would talk to my dad.

I thought she would come back, and when she didn't, a silent anger grew in me, slow and burning, until Agent Sheldon caught me and offered me the chance to lock up my dad and get my sister back. That or be placed in the hands of Child Protective Services. Maybe if I just explain all this to her she'll understand?

"Have you heard from Miles lately?" Aidan says, probably sensing my stress over the upcoming visit.

"Yeah," I say right away. "Well, last week. Not sure what he's been doing the past bunch of days, but he seems to be

out of cell reception and wifi. But they should be back from
Europe. We're supposed to meet tonight for a lesson."

"I wouldn't worry," he assures me. "The Becketts are a
strange family, probably go off the grid for fun."

I toss Aidan a smile. "For fun? Like that trip to the Grand
Canyon you're always talking about dragging Harper on?"

"Harper and you," he reminds me. "And there is wifi in
Grand Canyon National Park."

Aidan points out the sign for the exit, but I've already
seen it. Soon we're parked at the medium-security prison and
heading for the visitor entrance.

"You may not get a long time with her," Aidan says,
holding the door open for me. "It depends on their rules
and behavior of inmates."

I nod, swallow back a dozen fears, and plaster on my
game face. Aidan steps up to an information desk where an
old woman sits behind it, her glasses perched at the end of
her nose. She's wearing a uniform like the other guards but
no service weapon.

"We're here to see Lenora Hayes," Aidan says.

The old woman straightens, shoves up her glasses.
"Family?"

Aidan nods in my direction. "She is immediate family."

"One moment." The old woman lifts the receiver, holding
the phone to her ear. Before punching in numbers, she adds,
"Have your IDs ready, please."

Aidan removes his license and I dig for my Holden
Academy Student ID because I don't have anything else. My
driving permit is just a piece of paper, no photo.

We wait as the woman gives my mother's name to
someone on the other line. I glance back at the door we
came in and debate making a run for it. Maybe this was a
bad idea? Maybe she doesn't even want to see me? Or maybe
I'm too different now?

After the woman hangs up, she looks at both of us and says, "I'm sorry, but Inmate Hayes left early this morning."

"Left?" I say at the same time Aidan says, "How?"

The woman flips through pages on a clipboard, finally landing on the right page. "Ah…okay…her sentencing is in Charleston tomorrow."

Her sentencing? Maybe she'll be released soon? "But she'll be back after the court thing, right?" I ask.

The woman shakes her head. "Looks like space became available in Charleston, so she was moved again."

"Charleston," I mutter.

"I talked to someone three days ago," Aidan said. "No one mentioned any move or that today might not be a good day to visit."

He's pissed. I don't blame him. We lied to Harper. We drove all this way. For nothing. I don't know what to feel. Shock. Sadness. A tiny bit of relief because someone else made the choice for me.

I tug on Aidan's arm. His arguments are appreciated but pointless. "Come on, let's just go."

He hesitates but eventually follows me out the door. I hand over the keys, allowing Aidan to drive back. For a while, we don't say anything. Both of us just stare out at the road.

"Are you still going to tell Harper?" I ask Aidan after a while.

He shakes his head slowly. "I don't see why we need to now. Nothing happened."

I wait for him to change his mind or deliberate more about this, but instead he jumps into a new subject.

"So…Miles's dad got me a job," he says in a tone that hints at forced enthusiasm. "A good job."

I straighten up in my seat, suddenly alert. "Sounds like there's a 'but' missing from that statement."

"It's a private security gig," he explains. "Great company,

good benefits…*but* they have a mandatory six-week training program in Georgia."

"Six-week training program? Like Quantico or The Farm?" Yes, I've been reading up on government agencies over winter break. Recent events have sparked my curiosity.

"Quantico is in Virginia, and The Farm is at Camp Perry," he says. "But yes, I guess it's similar. The facility in Georgia is actually where I did my Secret Service training. They offer packages to private organizations as well."

"Do you miss it?" I ask him after hearing the wistfulness in his voice.

"Yeah," he admits. "I miss the Marines, too. I always felt proud doing work that offered direct protection for our country. It's not easy telling people I was discharged from the Secret Service."

My heart breaks a little for him. "I'm sorry."

"Don't be," Aidan says firmly. "I made a mistake. I covered for someone who I thought was trustworthy. If I had done things differently, maybe you and Miles wouldn't have had your lives threatened."

I'm momentarily stunned to silence. I hadn't thought at all about Aidan drawing that conclusion, blaming himself for what happened. He's not completely wrong, but had I been honest with him about my mission to uncover a murderer, maybe Miles and I wouldn't have been kidnapped. It's all a bunch of circular arguments leading to the same conclusion.

The real blame has to fall on the kidnapper. Jack.

I sit for a bit, trying to think of something to say, but end up landing on, "When do you leave?"

"Tonight," Aidan says, then offers a sad smile at the look on my face.

Six weeks without Aidan? "But Harper gets back tonight. Will you see her?"

"I might. Depends on when she's home and how early I

want to leave for the airport."

"Jesus," I mutter to myself.

"It all came together over the last two days," he explains. "Your sister is gonna need your help; you'll take care of her, right?"

"Of course." It's a promise I intend to keep, but still…six weeks without Aidan. Can we survive? Who will cook?

My phone vibrates in my purse, forcing me to set aside these new worries. No number is offered on the screen, just the words: UNKNOWN CALLER.

My heart picks up, hoping and hoping that it's Miles, finally out of the wilderness or whatever has made him MIA for… I do the math in my head, counting the days since I last heard from him. It was after New Year's, so…

Six days. That call had been short, not even five minutes, with no mention of meeting up tonight. The call before that, we'd talked for more than an hour. Miles called me when it was the New Year in Europe, hours before Virginia celebrated. During that call we'd made our plan for tonight. Self-defense lessons at the warehouse. Plus dinner and a movie, like normal people.

"Hello," I say.

"Ellie," a voice says on the other end of the line. Not Miles. His dad, Agent Beckett. "Are you alone?"

"No," I answer. My stomach knots. "But I can be — give me a minute?"

"Great," he says. "I'll call you right back."

I try my best to stay calm, keep my voice even. He asked if I was alone and didn't offer any exceptions to this, not even Aidan. I have to assume that was deliberate. I have to assume every move a CIA operative makes is deliberate.

Aidan is already looking very curious. I cover the receiver with my hand and say in a low voice, "Can you pull over at the rest stop in half a mile? Justice says something is happening between Bret and Dominic… It sounds bad."

Aidan follows directions, not asking questions. Of course later that will likely change. And it wasn't completely a lie. Last night one of my sort-of friends at Holden did text me because she was worried about a fight Dominic and Bret had a week or so ago, something to do with shrimp and a country club.

I hop out the second we're parked, head for the women's restroom, and check all the stalls. I answer the unknown call before the first ring finishes. "Okay, I'm alone now."

"Great," Agent Beckett says. "An issue has arisen."

"An issue?" I ask, already panicked inside.

"I need you to scrub Miles from the Holden school records," he says.

"Uh…o-okay," I stammer. "How exactly do I do that?"

"Listen carefully because we only have sixty more seconds before this call is traceable."

As if my mind would just wander off at this point.

"Unfortunately the school has phenomenal security," he tells me. "It'll have to be done from the inside."

"You want me to break into Holden?"

"Yes," he says like this isn't insane. "Preferably tonight."

Guess that means my date with Miles is canceled. Are they even back in the country? He didn't say.

"Tonight," I repeat.

"Miles's mother and I have already mapped out a plan," he says. "I'll email the details to you; memorize them and remove the footprint, got it?"

Um, yeah, definitely not, but still I say, "Sure, I got it. No problem."

The conversation ends so abruptly I'm left staring at my phone. When I return to the car, it's clear Aidan wants something from me. Some bit of info. I wasn't given permission to share. I value the Becketts' trust too much to ruin it. Miles has done a good job drilling into me the meaning of need-to-know and why following it saves lives.

I have to tell Aidan something honest, something not so simple. But not the truth. "Things are kind of bad between Bret and Dominic," I say, not even needing to force worry into my voice. It's there all on its own. "They keep getting into arguments about what happened with Simon. They're like a national security risk."

Worry creases Aidan's forehead. He puts the car in reverse and then says, "You're right, they know too much to be hotheaded about it. I'll pay them a visit this afternoon, help them remember what's at stake."

Their lives. Those idiots. "That's a good plan, thanks."

You do that, and I'll just study up on how to break into my school on a Sunday night, the last night of winter vacation to be exact.

What did I get myself into?

CHAPTER

5

Cold, bitter wind smacks my face. I rub my hands together and blow on them. The gloves Harper gave me for Christmas prove that pretty and functional are rarely synonymous. I peek around the corner; only a small streetlight illuminates my view of the building entrance, but the golden letters above the front doors spelling HOLDEN PREPARATORY ACADEMY shine bright even in the dark.

Instead of having a hot reunion with my boyfriend, I'm spending my last night of winter vacation breaking into my school. But when an international spy asks you to perform a very important mission, you don't say no. At least Aidan had already headed to the airport and wasn't around to catch me sneaking out.

My watch gives a gentle beep. One a.m. I conceal myself behind a tree and wait anxiously for the doors to the school to open. Any minute now.

At exactly 1:04 a.m. the two-man maintenance crew exits Holden Prep and heads for the parking lot. Their animated voices burst through the dark silence. I stay concealed behind a tree until headlights shine in my direction and then fade down the road. Soon, the only sound left is the frantic thud of my heart. Nothing about tonight's activity is outside of my skill level. I mastered breaking and entering before I learned to read. The nerves tonight have more to do with who put me up to this task—and all the "why?" questions left after our thirty-second conversation.

I couldn't even ask if they made it back into the country, if everything is okay, if *Miles* is okay. I have to trust that they told me everything I needed to know, trust there's a good reason why Miles couldn't call me himself and ask me to do this. Now it's up to me to not let either of them down.

After we ended the call, an email popped up in my inbox, giving me a map of the surveillance cameras in the school and a brief lesson on how to evade human surveillance, as in people who might be following me. I thought I knew everything about evading people following me, but the techniques they sent were more thorough and much more advanced.

With the late-night maintenance crew gone, I make my way to a side entrance, following an indirect route. After checking the area, I retrieve a tool from my pocket to pick the lock. Seconds later, I'm slipping into the school, hopefully unnoticed, and deactivating the alarm system. The halls are dark and empty, the scent of floor polish thick in the air, burning my nose. But the heat is heavenly. I wiggle my toes inside my boots, waiting for feeling to return. After spending more than an hour in the dark, the emergency lights lining the ceiling of the hall are more than adequate to guide me to the office. Soon I'm opening the ancient cabinet in the office of the guidance counselor, Ms. Geist, and scanning the drawer for Miles's file. Last semester, he and I broke into this same cabinet during the homecoming dance. That job led to us sneaking away and making out in a classroom, then later in a girls' bathroom. Unfortunately tonight is all business. And solo. No hot boy to kiss.

My fingers land on the correct folder, and I tug it from the drawer, then stuff it beneath my sweater. After Geist's office is back in perfect order, I head for the computer Agent Beckett told me to use to access the school records system. Apparently, there is one computer in this entire building that doesn't leave a trail. Don't ask me how two people who have likely never stepped foot in this school know all this. Then again, they did allow their son to spend a semester here. Surely, they checked out the place beforehand.

The door to the IT guy's tiny office isn't an easy lock to pick, but I manage after several failed attempts. I'm not a complete idiot when it comes to technology, but I wouldn't exactly call "tech jobs" a specialty of mine. Scrubbing Miles from the school's computer system is definitely the most challenging part of this job for me. Because writing anything down would have been too risky, I had to memorize the complicated password Miles's dad dictated over the phone. I type it in quickly, then sigh with relief when I'm granted access on the first try.

I slide into the desk chair and take a deep breath, forcing calm, forcing the plan to repeat itself inside my head. *Come on, Ellie, focus. It's beginner stuff. Get this done and then you can worry about Miles.* Miles, who promised me he'd be back in this country meeting me tonight. Miles, who has never broken a promise to me thus far. There's a lot that I don't know, but I do know the Becketts wouldn't have asked me to do something like this—something illegal—if it wasn't important. Of course, for them, important means life-threatening, which brings me right back to worrying about Miles.

One problem at a time. *Tackle A before Z*, my father always said, ironically in situations similar to this one, often involving breaking and entering.

The cursor blinks at me from inside the search box, and I

finally come to life, typing in MILES BECKETT. His information loads onto the screen instantly. Miles's schedule from last semester at Holden Prep sits just below his basic personal information.

```
AP CHINESE MANDARIN
AP CALCULUS
AMERICAN LITERATURE, HONORS
LATIN IV
US HISTORY, HONORS
PHYSICS, HONORS
ECONOMICS
```

This isn't the first time I've seen his schedule, and still, it's a shock. No wonder Harvard already accepted him. Not that he'll go to Harvard. Not with the FBI, CIA, NSA, and whatever other three-letter acronyms for secret government organizations are fighting over him. Probably him and all the other McCone honors program students at Marshall Academy. What happens to those guys after graduation? Do any of them just become regular people, like doctors or lawyers or waiters at Applebee's? Or are they all destined to become invisible to anyone who knew them?

I shake off thoughts of Miles erasing his fingerprints and disappearing from existence. And then I begin deleting from this school's history all traces of the boy I fell for last semester. *He's not disappearing for real*, I tell myself. Tomorrow morning he'll be back at Marshall Academy, climbing ropes or army-crawling under things, assuming he's been cleared by a doctor to use his shoulder again. Doesn't matter that I haven't heard a word from him in six days.

Fear knots the pit of my stomach, but I continue the job, forcing my finger to click the delete button over and over again until he's gone. I know how to compartmentalize, and it's coming in handy tonight, allowing me to zero in on the computer screen and tune out everything else. Minutes later, I'm preparing to shut down the system.

A soft *pat, pat, pat* echoes from down the hall. My fingers freeze over the keyboard. Before I can even think the words, *someone's coming*, the beam from a flashlight hitting me right in the face, blinding me.

CHAPTER

6

With the bright light blinding me, concealing its owner, my first thought is, *Jack's group*. They've come to finish the job he started.

"What the hell are you doing?"

With my heart now up in my throat, I lift my gaze to meet the face of my classmate Dominic DeLuca. He might be friendly with Miles, but he and I haven't really spoken much since school let out for winter break nearly a month ago. It's possible he's still harboring ill feelings toward me because I broke into his house and stole all the files from his laptop, for starters. But to my credit, at the time I'd thought he might be a murderer, so…yeah. "Hey, Dominic, how's it going? How was your New Year's?"

No one plays innocent better than I do, but given the circumstances, I doubt the act will work tonight.

His dark eyebrows push together as he studies me. "What the hell are you doing here?"

I look him over, taking in his tortured-boy expression, which is up a few notches from its normal level. "What are *you* doing here?"

"Don't turn this around on me. I followed you here. It's

bad enough I have to come back tomorrow—definitely not interested in breaking in a day early to..." He waves a hand at the computer in front of me. "To hack into the school system or whatever."

"Bothers you, huh?" I hit a button on the keyboard, shutting down the screen before he can walk around the desk and get a peek. "All the rule breaking?"

Dominic is a party boy who survives solely on his family's reputation and money. He's got drug dealers on speed dial. But I feel guilty pointing this out after everything that happened last semester. My invading his privacy. Miles and I both accusing him of murdering Simon Gilbert, who, it turns out, he was in love with.

My jab at his party-boy, pay-someone-to-do-my-homework lifestyle seems to roll right over him. "Honestly, Ellie. You, messing with the school's computers in the middle of the night...it's creeping me out."

New cover story, Ellie. Fast. And don't underestimate Dominic. He's not an idiot. You need something good.

The Becketts are counting on my discretion.

"Have you ever paid someone to do your homework?" I walk around the desk and stand in front of him. "Ever bought a paper online?"

He runs a hand through his dark hair and folds his arms over his chest. I smirk at him. The silent confession was too easy. "How much did you pay for a good paper? An untraceable one. A couple hundred?"

Dominic drops his arms and shrugs. "So you're messing with your grades?"

"Um, no." I laugh at that. There are few things in my life I've done the honest way. But my grades at Holden? I've earned those. "I'm making bank helping the academically less fortunate." I hold a hand to my heart. "Holden has done so much for me. It feels good, giving back."

He stares for a long moment, and then I swear he looks relieved. God, what had he thought I was doing? Planting a bomb to blow up the school?

"We should get out of here before we get caught." He nods toward the door and clicks off his flashlight. "Hopefully you avoided the cameras on your way in?"

I brush past him and head for the hall. "Do I look like an idiot?"

"I don't know what you look like," Dominic says, and there's honesty to his voice, the words laced with fear and suspicion. "I don't know anything about you."

I swallow back a dozen conflicted feelings. Keeping my conning past a secret had been the hardest part of my relationship with Miles. Knowing that he knows is such a relief, but it's not like I can tell everyone. It's need-to-know. Plus, I like being the good girl. Even if it's mostly a lie. Or was a lie. The new me is determined to be good.

"What is there to know?" I say, not braving facing Dominic. "I follow the rules. To a point. But in case you forgot, my sister's boyfriend, who paid most of the monthly bills, lost his Secret Service job—"

"Because he covered for his murderer boss," Dominic snaps. "I remember."

Aidan loved his job as a Secret Service agent. He won't say so, but I know it broke his heart to be fired. "The only mistake Aidan made was putting his trust in the wrong person."

Dominic is silent, tense, making his way out of the school all while avoiding the security cameras. Once we're outside, I turn to face him.

"Do you follow me all the time? Or did you just have a hunch that I was up to no good tonight?"

His eye contact wavers, his gaze drifting over my shoulder. "I went to your place. I wanted to ask you something, and then I saw you take off into the night—on a bicycle—and that seemed strange. Especially in January."

This is the longest conversation Dominic and I have ever had. He spent all of last semester glaring at me, saying no more than one word with each interaction we had.

"Not all of us have a garage full of vehicles at our disposal. Or personal drivers." I head for the bike he mentioned, hidden near the tree I tucked myself behind for more than an hour. "I don't have my license. Buses don't run this late on Sundays."

"If you want a ride, the bike should fit in the back of my—" Dominic's eyes widen, staring at something over my shoulder.

In the milliseconds it takes me to spin around, I rewind the past few seconds, trying to remember if I'd heard footsteps, leaves rustling, anything…but I hadn't. And then I'm whispering inside my head, *Please let it be Miles.*

But it isn't Miles.

"Well look at you, Miss Eleanor." The boy—who is now more man than a boy—leans against the tree standing between my getaway bike and me. "You're not an easy girl to track down, you know?"

For several long moments, I'm rooted to the spot, unable to move or speak. It's been nearly a year since I've seen anyone from my family.

"Oscar…" I breathe out his name, my voice barely a whisper. I'm scrambling to cover my ass, but I can't think about anything except the fact that everything is about to change. *Everything.*

Behind me, Dominic shifts and then moves closer. "Ellie?"

He's clearly scared. After what happened last month, the whole kidnapping thing, I don't blame him. But Oscar is harmless. I think? My gaze sweeps over him. He's grown a couple of inches, probably pushing six two or three. He's still rail thin with that goofy face and wild sandy-colored hair. It isn't him or even the situation right now that worries me; it's what's to come when he reports back to the others.

Before I can open my mouth to respond to either guy, Oscar grins, flashing his goofy smile at me, and then seconds later, he's rushing forward, crushing me in a giant bear hug.

"What the—" Dominic starts.

Oscar notices him, quickly sets me down. He straightens his shirt and sticks a hand out to Dominic. "Should probably introduce myself. I'm Oscar. Ellie's"—he clears his throat—"cousin."

"Cousin" is a very loose term in my family.

Dominic hesitates, glances at me, and then finally shakes Oscar's hand.

Oscar grins at me again. "I should have known it was a boy. Your daddy hinted at it enough, I shoulda guessed that's why you ran off."

For almost a year, I've wondered what my family thought happened to me. I figured someone guessed that I'd been helping the FBI, that I was a traitor who tried to hand over my dad in exchange for my and Harper's freedom. But it's possible they simply thought I caught sight of the FBI and took off, wanting to save my own ass. It's kind of how we do things in my family.

It's possible Oscar doesn't even know about—

"Oh shit, Ellie," he says, glancing around. "You're working a job here, aren't you? I'm screwing it up right now. God, I'm an idiot."

He swears again under his breath, his eyes dropping to the grass. Despite his upbringing being identical to mine, Oscar never could learn to master many con skills. He's good at only two things: tracking people down and walking without making a sound. Clearly both of those skills came in handy tonight.

But I don't have time to explain my intentions tonight.

Right now, my priority is finding out exactly how he tracked me down and how much he knows. I glance back at Dominic, giving him a pleading look. *Please, please just go with it.*

I grab Oscar's arm, tugging him toward the back of the school. "We should go somewhere. To catch up." I rack my brain for a place that's the opposite direction of home. "There's a diner about ten miles from here."

I give him quick directions and watch him pull keys from his pocket. "So I'll meet you there? Or do you want to ride—"

"We'll meet you there," I interrupt.

Oscar looks at Dominic again, something protective in his eyes. "I'm sorry, I didn't get your name…"

My gaze meets Dominic's. *Lie. Please lie.*

"Fred," he chokes out. "Freddy, actually."

"Huh." Oscar narrows his eyes. Then finally, he turns back to me. "See you in a few minutes."

The second he's out of sight, headed toward whatever covert location he hid his car, I start to panic. I look around for Dominic's car. "Where the hell did you park?"

"In the parking lot," he says.

We stare at each other for several seconds, and I can see the wheels spinning inside his head. We're practically strangers, and I've just led some random guy to believe that I ran away with Dominic…er, Freddy. And now I'm about to take this near stranger along to hear all my family secrets. And that's just the beginning of this nightmare. I touch my phone in my pocket, debating whether or not to warn Harper.

I'll find out what he knows first. Information now, panic later. *A before Z.*

Dominic is still standing there, like he's waiting for me to explain. I don't know what to tell him. So I just head for the parking lot, abandoning my bike.

If only I'd been caught with Miles instead. But a tiny voice inside my head protests this. Despite his acceptance of my past and me, I'm still embarrassed, ashamed of myself and the things I've done. I glance at Dominic, and some of my worries are eased. Not like he hasn't done some things, too. He has a drug dealer on speed dial. But still, this is a mess already.

"Next time, don't follow me," I call over my shoulder on the way to Dominic's car.

"Noted," he says, appearing at my side. "But just so you know, there will be questions later."

My stomach drops. "Yeah, I figured."

Questions that I either don't want to answer or can't. Because the possibility of the return of the Agents Gone Bad is enough to scare me into keeping silent about my reasons for being at the school tonight.

CHAPTER

7

Oscar's fingertips tap a familiar beat against the plastic diner table. He refuses eye contact with the waitress but instead follows each of our drinks from her tray to the cheap cardboard coaster she rests them on. The waitress narrows her eyes, suspicion in her expression. Clearly the added stature did nothing for Oscar's conning skills.

To cover his nervous behavior, I flash the waitress a grin. "Beautiful women frighten him."

Pink creeps up the neck of my "cousin," helping the lie. The waitress relaxes her shoulders and seems at ease taking our orders. The second she's out of sight, it's clear Oscar's ready to spit out some big secret, but he seems to second-guess himself, his gaze bouncing between Dominic and me. "So, Freddy…how long you two been an item?"

"We're not—" Dominic starts.

I pinch his knee from under the table, and he stiffens beside me. "What he means is that as far as his family is concerned, we aren't a thing. They don't approve of girls like me."

A boyish smile erupts on Oscar's face, sending a surprising pang of homesickness through my gut.

"Well. Can't really blame them for that. I've seen you in action, Eleanor." He offers Dominic a sympathetic look. "Be afraid, man. Very afraid."

This is too much. Seeing Oscar again. Giving Dominic DeLuca, of all people, a window into my past. I need to be done with the formalities.

"Okay, Oscar, spill." I lean back in the booth and fold my arms over my chest. "What are you doing here? And where is the crew I know you brought along?"

He holds his hands up in surrender. "No crew, I swear to God, Ellie."

I read his body language. Truth.

"It's your daddy." He stares down at his thumbs resting on the table in front of him. "He's in junky mode. Bad."

"Drugs or booze?" Dominic asks smoothly, like he finally feels comfortable with the conversation topic.

I shake my head. "Neither."

"Gambling?"

Confused by Dominic's questions, Oscar's forehead wrinkles. "This job he's working on? It's not... We haven't done nothing like this before. There's risk and then there's *risk*. There's greed and then there's *greed*, you know?"

Yeah, I know. My jaw clenches, holding back those words. But I do know. That kind of greed apparently makes you forget that your wife is in prison. Anger at my dad and his ability to move on clouds my own guilt over what happened to my mom. I'm the one who cut a deal with the FBI. I'm the one who played informant, knowing they would trap at least one of my family members.

I tear open three packets of sugar and dump them into my coffee. "Oscar, if you came looking for me so I could talk my dad out of whatever scheme he's trying to pull, you wasted your time. He never listens to me. I'm taking a sabbatical from that."

Not completely untrue. The sabbatical anyway.

Oscar's face falls. I replay how excited he'd seemed to see me in the school parking lot, and I almost feel guilty for stomping on whatever hope he'd had left. Things must be really bad with my family.

"Sure," he says quickly. "'Course you got your own life, and your daddy's a grown man. He's the best in the biz, no doubt about that. It'll work out fine."

Lie. If I hadn't already caught the fib in his tone, I'd have seen it through the tensing of his right pinkie finger.

I debate asking him more about this big job, but Dominic's presence combined with the fact that I refuse to get sucked back into my family's world stops me. Harper would kill me, especially after everything Aidan's done for me. And what would I tell Miles? I shudder at the thought, remembering how he'd looked at me right after I told him the truth—disgust, disappointment. I unroll the paper napkin and extract a spoon to stir my tea. There is something I need to know. "Are they asking about me?"

His eyebrows shoot up. "You're kidding, right? 'Course they're asking about you. But your daddy always says the same thing when someone asks where you went. 'Let her be. Every great con tries their hand at going solo.' It's part of nature or natural selection or whatever."

If the waitress wasn't heading this way, carrying our food, I would have sworn out loud. Dominic isn't an idiot, but for some reason I was hoping the word "con" would remain a silent presence here.

"Sure miss having you around," Oscar says, likely just to make conversation while plates of food are set in front of us. "Think you might come home for a visit anytime soon?"

Not a chance. Assuming I even know where "home" is at the moment, which I don't. "Maybe? If I get bored around here."

He seems pleased with this. Or maybe with the giant double bacon cheeseburger resting in front of him. But instead of diving in and taking a bite, he slides out of the booth and stands. "I'm gonna wash up before I dig in, if you don't mind?"

I shake my head and watch him walk toward the back of the diner. Dominic is surely about to spew questions at me, but I hold a finger to my lips, shushing him. I feel under the table until my fingers land on a tiny piece of plastic stuck with a weak adhesive to the underside of the table. That little sneak. I wiggle the listening device until it's unattached and pull it to my lap, looking for an off switch.

"So…" I say to Dominic. "How are the onion rings? I should have ordered those instead. My fries are soggy."

I glance up from the device long enough to see Dominic's challenging look. He's likely reached his limit of playing along. But after several seconds of hesitation, he slides his plate closer to mine. "Here, have some."

My fingernails dig into the plastic, prying the casing open. "Can you pass the ketchup?"

"Sure." He sets the bottle in front of me with a loud *clunk*.

The outer case finally pops open. I turn off the device and quickly put it back together, then stick it to the table again. My hands are suspiciously emerging from beneath the table as Oscar strides back toward us, but I reach for the ketchup bottle, hoping he doesn't notice.

Oscar devotes most of his attention to his burger while Dominic and I both watch him and pretend to eat. I force down a couple of onion rings over the next twenty minutes, and soon we're paying the bill and heading for the exit.

Outside, Dominic treats our goodbye as a private family moment and leaves us to wait in his car.

"I really do miss you at home," Oscar repeats. He glances across the diner parking lot at Dominic's car and then turns back to me. "Guess this is goodbye?"

All these feelings I can't quite identify swirl around inside my head. I don't want this. I don't want to be back in Oscar's world, yet the nostalgia is undeniable, even for me, and I'm awesome at denial.

"You didn't forget your bug from under the table, did you?" I ask, and am rewarded instantly with his trademark grin. "Might want to up your game, get a little more creative than planting it under the table. Everyone looks there."

"Nothing gets past you, Ellie. Haven't changed a bit." His smile fades slowly and he's wearing a super-serious look. "New York City. That's where we're headed. In case you change your mind about visiting."

My poker face is in place, but inside I'm mulling that over. New York City? My family drifts all over the place. It's what we do, but never as far north as New York City. We tend to fit in better and gain trust easier in the South.

"You're thinking it, I know you are," Oscar insists. "We got no business in a place like New York City. And this job—your daddy is so far in over his head, and no one will tell him. That was your mama's job. And yours."

"I told you already that he never listens—"

"But you could try?" Oscar pleads.

"Why? So I can get thrown in jail like my mom?" Cold wind hits me square in the face. I tug my zipper up to my chin. "If you were smart, you'd walk away, too, before he gets you in trouble."

There's that disappointment again. He didn't like my answer. He expects more from me. He expects me to care. Well, I can't. I won't. Not anymore. I have Harper and Aidan. I have Miles. I don't need them anymore. None of them.

Except my mom.

God, I need to shut that voice down. Kill it permanently.

"Well, that's that, then." He tugs keys from his pocket and

gives me a nod, no giant bear hug like earlier. "Take care of yourself, Eleanor."

"You too," I mumble, genuinely meaning it. Wishing I didn't.

He heads toward a gray truck, and I cross the lot and slide into the passenger seat of Dominic's SUV. Dominic puts the car in drive and pulls out of the parking spot. I keep my eyes on the side mirror, watching for the gray truck. "We can't go home."

He glances sideways at me. "Why not?"

Before answering him, I punch in a quick text to Miles.

ME: Need to talk asap. Kind of an emergency.

"Get on the interstate, head west," I order, holding my phone like a lifeline. *Please be available and okay, Miles.* "We'll pass a few exits and then get a hotel room somewhere cheap."

"Seriously?" Dominic asks. "This is crazy. Let's just go to my house. I don't care if he knows where I live. The dude seems harmless."

Oscar may have found me tonight, but I'm nearly positive he doesn't know where I live. Or who I live with. Harper left our family under some controversial conditions, and her name became taboo. If my dad knew I lived with her, he'd come pluck me from Virginia himself.

"Oscar is harmless," I agree. "But the rest of my family isn't."

CHAPTER

8

I'm staring at my phone, willing Miles to text or call, when Dominic taps on the passenger window and gestures for me to hop out. I step carefully onto the ice-covered parking lot of the Roadside Inn and follow him up the steps to the balcony level. Once inside the economy room, he hands me a key card.

"So you do have a fake ID?" When we arrived, I had been worried about how we would book this room without either of us being eighteen. I'd asked him if he had a fake ID, and he just said not to worry, he'd take care of the room.

Dominic plops down onto the double bed nearest to the door. "I slipped the guy a fifty. He didn't ask any questions."

Guess conning is kind of obsolete when you have a near-endless supply of cash and Mom and Dad's credit cards. But where's the creativity in that?

Dominic stretches out on the bed, his long legs crossed at the ankles. His designer jeans still hold their perfect fit even while lounging. His sandy-colored hair is a bit disheveled, adding to his cool-kid persona. But unlike the other cool kids I know, like Chantel's boyfriend, Jacob, or Bret, Dominic doesn't have any of that boyish charm. He's all sharp angles and serious looks. I can't think of any time I've seen him smile or heard him laugh. Even now, from the neck down he's the picture of lazy teen, but his face is the complete opposite—tense jaw, pinched forehead, vacant eyes like he's deep in thought. I'm not sure who the bigger mystery is anymore, him or me.

I watch him for a few more seconds, allowing myself to process the events of tonight. After forcing calm at the diner with Oscar, panic begins to roll over me in waves. I shake my arms out and pace the hotel room. In a few hours, Dominic and I are supposed to be in school. Oscar probably followed us here, will probably follow us to school if we let him. Harper is going to freak if she wakes up and I'm not home. I'm stuck here for a while. With Dominic DeLuca as my sidekick.

I can't do anything about Dominic right now, can't undo what he's already heard and seen. But we are hiding out in a cheap motel. I haven't let Oscar follow me home. And my original mission tonight was successful. Miles is gone from Holden records. Maybe everything isn't ruined. Yet.

So Harper. She's my first order of business.

I yank my phone from my pocket and call my sister. She answers on the third ring. "Ellie? I swear to God, if you're in jail—"

"Not jail," I say quickly. "A hotel room. With a boy."

Dominic looks over at me and shakes his head. I roll my eyes. *Don't worry, I get it. I'm not your type.*

"But I thought Miles had to cancel," Harper says.

Practicing those need-to-know skills, I hadn't told her about the assignment the Becketts gave me, but I had told her I wouldn't be at the warehouse tonight. "He did cancel. I'm not with Miles. I kind of ran into Oscar tonight and—"

"Oscar? Who is—" The grogginess drops from my sister's voice, and I can tell she's now upright in bed, probably fumbling to turn on the light. She ran away from our family five years before the FBI reunited us, and Oscar was much younger then, but I'm sure she remembers him. "Oh shit. Are you with him now? Did he—"

"I'm not with Oscar anymore. I don't think he knows where we live. Or that *we* live together." I glance at Dominic, who is listening intently. I give Harper the details of what happened at the diner in as few and as vague words as possible. But I can't explain why I broke into Holden Prep tonight, so I lie and say I met up with Dominic as a favor to Miles.

"Just stay where you are," Harper says when I'm finished with the rundown. "I need to call Aidan."

I consider protesting. Aidan's had so much shit to deal with lately, and he's far away in Georgia and believes we can take care of ourselves. Clearly I can't.

"Promise me you'll stay put? You won't do anything yet?" Harper insists.

What exactly would I do? "I promise."

When I hang up, Dominic swings his legs over the side of the bed, sitting upright. He stares at me, his eyebrows raised. "Time for you to answer some questions."

"Fine," I agree.

It is fine. Completely fine. This isn't an inquisition from Miles Beckett Jr., CIA operative in the making. This is Dominic DeLuca, just one of many spoiled, privileged kids at Holden Prep. Whatever he thinks he knows about my family or me can be undone with a little persuasion. I unzip my coat, kick off my shoes, and take a seat on the empty bed.

Dominic rests his elbows on his knees and tangles his fingers together. "When was the last time you heard from Miles?"

Wait...what? "Miles?"

"Yes, Miles," he says, annoyed. "Your boyfriend? The one kidnapped from my house last November and nearly murdered?"

"We were both kidnapped and nearly murdered," I remind him.

"When was the last time you heard from him?" Dominic repeats, more slowly, deliberately.

My stomach twists. Is this what he came to ask me tonight? *You talked to the Becketts less than twelve hours ago*, I remind myself. If anything had happened, they would have told me. And what could happen? He was on vacation in Europe with his family and is now likely back at his very secure military school. It's not like he's still out chasing drug dealers like he'd done during his semester at Holden. Dominic's dealer, Davey. Maybe I should tread carefully with this question. Maybe Oscar isn't the only one I should be worried about.

"Why do you ask?"

Dominic scrubs a hand over his face and sighs. "Can you just cut the act for, like, five seconds?"

"What act?" I say. I can't help it. Old habits and all. He glares at me for the first time tonight, and I'm reminded how that look is like ice in my veins. He spent months glaring at me. During most of which I had no idea why.

I retrieve my phone again and scroll through text messages as if I don't know exactly how many days it's been. "He called me six days ago—seven now actually—then he texted me a picture of a turkey leg that said, 'Eating turkey in Turkey, cool huh?'"

A hint of a smile appears on Dominic's face, but it's gone in a heartbeat. "Is he in the picture?"

"Jesus," I mutter under my breath. "Didn't know you were a conspiracy theorist."

The glare is back.

"Okay, okay." I examine the photo closely. There's a hand attached to the turkey leg. "That's his hand. I recognize the scar by his thumb."

The relief that washes over Dominic is so obvious I make a note to hustle him into a poker game in the near future. God knows he's got plenty of money to lose. I might as well be on the receiving end.

"So a week ago." He stands and strides across the room toward the door then pivots and heads toward the bathroom. "If that's what we have to work with, then."

Despite the caution I'd planned to exhibit moments ago, sympathy bubbles over in me. I know exactly how Dominic feels.

"I talked to his parents earlier today, or yesterday technically," I admit with a sigh. "I think he's fine. They would have told me if he wasn't."

As fine as anyone can be who suddenly needs to be erased from school records. My phone is still clutched in my hand when a text comes through from Harper. Both Dominic and I jump at the sound.

HARPER: Sheldon is on her way.

ME: Wtf???? Why??

HARPER: She has questions

ME: Oh, I'm sure she does. Wtf???

HARPER: Sry. Srsly. I had to call her

I refrain from tossing the phone at the hotel wall. "Great, just great."

"What?" Dominic says, alarmed.

I force a smile. "Help is on the way."

"Who?"

"The FBI." I flop back on the bed and wait for Dominic to look panicked. He's been in the interrogation room more times than I have. His eyes widen, and I feel a sense of accomplishment having at least been able to predict his reaction. "Bet you're wishing you'd picked another night to follow me, huh?"

CHAPTER

9

The knock on the hotel room door comes just as sunlight peeks through the olive-green window coverings. I give the mattress on Dominic's bed a light kick, rousing him. Through the peephole, I immediately recognize Agent Sheldon. She looks exactly the same—dirty-blond hair tied in a perfect bun, black dress pants, white blouse, black blazer, service weapon no doubt concealed beneath that blazer. Kind of hard to trust someone who can't leave her firearm out of any conversation. I don't recognize the guy behind her. He's younger than Sheldon, maybe fresh out of Quantico.

I open the door, and Agent Sheldon starts to walk in but then stops short when she sees Dominic. "I thought you were alone?"

"I thought your office was in Charleston," I say, gesturing for them to come inside. "I'm trying to figure out how fast you would have to drive to get here in less than four hours."

The guy with Sheldon closes and locks the door behind them. He's covertly checking out the window while Agent Sheldon speaks. "You should have asked to see my badge before opening the door."

I shrug. "I know what you look like."

"But—"

"Do you have an evil twin? Or was the government supply of Polyjuice Potion stolen and now ordinary people are posing as FBI agents?" I ask, because seriously, she came all this way to lecture me on safety?

The guy scoping out the window snorts a laugh and then turns it into a cough when Sheldon glares at him. Sheldon is clearly all business. After I introduce Dominic, who looks like he's in complete hell, she drills me with questions.

"Where were you when your *cousin* found you?"

My gaze bounces to Dominic for a beat, hoping he can handle this. Sheldon is kind of a robot, but they do teach their fledglings how to spot a liar at Quantico. Unfortunately. "We stopped at a gas station near Holden Prep, the Wawa on the corner of—"

Sheldon holds up a hand to stop me and turns to the guy by the window. "Pull up video surveillance."

His shoulder bag is plopped onto the table and a laptop emerges. Internally, I start to panic.

"We only drove around the back," Dominic says. "I needed air in one of my tires."

Look at you, Dominic DeLuca, telling lies to the FBI.

We wait a beat for any counterarguments, but Sheldon plunges forward. With some selective omissions, Dominic and I relay our adventures with Oscar while Agent No Name continues to study surveillance footage of a gas station that has no record of our visit.

I join Dominic, sitting beside him on the hotel bed while Sheldon passes along information to someone on the phone. When she hangs up, the usually stiff look on her face changes to something like sympathy, and my defenses go up. She exchanges a look with Agent No Name. He shuts his laptop and turns to face us.

"What?" I demand.

"I was planning on getting in touch with you today, actually. Aidan called me after you two got back from Raleigh," Sheldon says. She sucks at sympathy. Her inflection is all wrong. "Your mother's sentencing is this morning, as you already know. I talked to the judge making the ruling, asked about her transfer, and there have been some big changes."

My stomach twists. This doesn't feel like good news.

"She's not getting out in February, is she? She has to wait until April? Or is it longer?"

"It's longer," Sheldon says. "The judge is sentencing her to ten years."

For several seconds I don't move or speak. The air deflates from my lungs and pressure fills my chest. I can make the number ten fit into any reasonable scenario, but not this one.

"You promised me," I say, barely above a whisper, not wanting my voice to shake. I refuse to cry. Refuse to let them see me cry. "You put it in writing. Twelve to fifteen months."

"I told you twelve to fifteen months for the crimes at the bank," she argues. "It turns out the prosecution was able to dig up quite a bit of financial fraud with your mother's name attached. Two witnesses in Phoenix identified her, and then another two in LA with the Doctor Ames con…"

Her voice falls into the background. I can't listen or think or hold onto any of the covers I've perfected. Ten years. A decade.

What have I done?

All the energy I'd devoted to stewing over what to do when my mom got out was pointless. Because she's not getting out. Not until she's old enough to be a grandmother. Several times over. In my most private thoughts, far into the back of my mind, I've had fantasies of my mom being there to see me graduate from Holden, go to senior prom. To help

Harper plan her inevitable wedding to Aidan. I know these aren't things someone like me usually wishes for, and I know getting any of this was near impossible. But now it's actually impossible, and I can't help feeling like I've lost something important, something I truly need. I push away the lump in my throat, but I can't stop my eyes from burning.

"An appeal?" I croak out the words and then clear my throat. "She can appeal, right?"

"Yes," Sheldon confirms. "But she'll lose."

I stare at the woman who turned me into the world's biggest snitch, and pure hatred boils inside me. "You knew, didn't you? You wanted to use me just so you could close that case."

The sympathy drops from her face, the stiff, pencil-up-the-ass expression back on. "I wanted your father, the ringleader, if you remember? That case is nowhere near closed thanks to their last-minute job swap. And if I knew what the prosecution knew by trial time, I wouldn't have needed your help to convict her or your father."

With no clear target for my anger, it falls away as quickly as it hit. Even if she had manipulated and deceived me on purpose, I can't hate her for that. Manipulation and deception basically sum up my life's work prior to helping the FBI. And after, if I'm being honest. Identifying Simon's killer required manipulation and deception in dozens of assorted colors.

I clamp my jaw shut, forcing myself to think first. She didn't come here just to deliver this news (that's what cell phones are for) or simply to rescue us (she could have sent a local agent). She wants something. My father's face pops into my thoughts, the patient sound of his voice when he explained our way of life to me years ago. I was only seven or eight and already a master of the basics—creating covers, lock picking, and planting audio surveillance devices.

"Why are we listening to these people?" I asked my dad

while we sat in an old Bronco hearing the voices of a woman and her husband broadcast from an apartment across the street.

"Why do we listen to anyone?" he asked. "To get to know them."

"You mean like their favorite color?"

"Maybe that," he agreed. "But more than that."

My dad turned down the volume on the receiver and angled himself to face me. "Do you remember a few months ago when you went to that doll store in Atlanta?"

I nodded, twisting my hands in my lap. American Girl. I'd never seen anything so beautiful as the dolls in that store and their clothes and shoes and furniture. We'd gone inside only because my "uncle" had just swiped credit card info from half a dozen people and thought he was being followed. He had wanted to hide out in the sea of families and their little girls.

"You wanted one of those dolls," he said simply. Not a question.

"No I didn't," I protested. "They're stupid."

"You could have had one," he said. "Uncle Milky needed a cover, and snagging a doll for you to take into that doll salon would have been perfect."

I looked down at my hands, then selected a nail to chew on—I hadn't perfected lying without a tell yet.

My dad narrowed his eyes at me, giving me another second to come clean, and then he turned his attention out the windshield. "You didn't want Milky to ask Oscar to steal the doll, thought he might get caught. And you thought I would be mad that you like that kind of thing."

"If it doesn't teach you anything, then we don't have room for it in the camper," I recited from hundreds of paternal lectures.

"I heard you talking to your sister that night," he continued.

"I didn't tell Harper—"

"That you want an American Girl doll?" He smiled,

knowing he'd caught me. "You didn't tell her, but I listened to how you described the store, and it wasn't hard to figure out."

I tugged at my seat belt and leaned back against the chair. I had nothing to say.

"Because I listened in that night, I know what you want more than anything in the world," he said. "And that is what a good con treasures. More than cash under a mattress, more than rare jewelry or baseball cards. And what would a good con do with that valuable information?"

"Use it," I whispered.

"That's right." He opened his hand in front of me, palm up, revealing a tiny plastic device. "Plant this inside the silver Lexus two cars up without setting off the alarm and the doll is yours. Your mama's going to Miami tomorrow, and they've got one of those stores."

He set the listening device in my hand and opened his wallet. "Will this cover it?"

I looked at the six twenty-dollar bills in his hand and slowly nodded. "But it's a trick, right? You're supposed to get what you want and then trick me."

"For a job, yes," he said. "But for my daughter? No trick."

I hesitated, watching his face for signs of teasing or deception. But there weren't any. I glanced at the cash one more time and conjured images of the dolls in that store—I definitely wanted one. I reached for the car door handle, tugging it open.

Shaking off the memory of my father—it's his fault I'm in this mess right now—I replay Agent Sheldon's words inside my head, flipping them around for more careful study. What can I use? What does she want more than anything in the world?

I wanted your father.

The case is nowhere near closed.

No. I can't. Not anymore. I'm not that girl anymore.

Unless…it could be done quickly. In and out, no strings attached. Oscar provided me with a smooth transition back inside. The weight of my sister's reaction to this potential plan already presses down on my shoulders, and I circle back to the "no, I can't" argument.

But ten years. Ten years until I see my mother again. I can't let that happen. Just move on with my life and not think about her and my part in her sentencing. My insides fill with resolve. I could live with fifteen months, but not this.

Both agents look startled when, after standing in silence for so long, I turn sharply to face them. "If you want the ringleader, then let me help you catch him."

CHAPTER

10

"We're talking about your mother right now, Eleanor," Agent Sheldon says, like a question, like she's worried I might be in shock.

"Yes, my mother," I confirm. "Who is very much a follower, a puppet in my dad's lifetime of games."

"What are you trying to say?" Agent No Name asks.

I cross my arms. "I'm saying tell the judge in Charleston, the DA, whoever you need to that you've got an offer that you can't refuse. Release my mom in exchange for my dad."

Agent No Name looks impressed, whether it's with my level of insanity or with the idea itself, I'm not sure.

"It's not that simple, Eleanor," Agent Sheldon says.

"Sure it is." I lean against the door and look between the two agents. "Would you cut a deal with my mother? If she gave you enough information to put my father away for a decade? Would you offer her immunity?"

"Your mother won't give us anything," Sheldon says.

"That's because she's more loyal than I am." And blinded by love.

Agent Sheldon stands there between the tiny table and the bed nearest the door studying me. I can practically see the wheels spinning inside her head, the arguments she must be having. Just when she starts to shake her head, Agent No Name clears his throat.

"Judge Kimball owes you a favor," he says. "And remember the Livingston case? Same thing."

"Except that the informant in that case was a thirty-two-year-old man," Sheldon says, a bite to her tone. She doesn't like this guy calling her out.

I happen to love it.

"Oh," I say. "So men make better informants? I never thought of you as sexist, Agent Sheldon."

She rolls her eyes.

"So we get consent from her legal guardian," Agent No Name says.

My legal guardian is Aidan. He'll love this. *Not.* But problem A before Z.

"Don't get sucked down the rabbit hole of masterful teenage manipulation," Agent Sheldon warns her partner. I offer both of them a grin. She did call me masterful. Sheldon glares in return. "There are several flaws in this plan. With the prosecution pinning all the past jobs on her mother, we'd need new evidence of her father's illegal activity. Plus, she never told us where her father is," Sheldon says. "She might not really know."

Hello? I'm right here. "Yeah, I probably don't know."

"I probably don't know, either," Dominic says.

All three of us turn to look at him. In all my panic and plotting, I seriously forgot he was here. And despite the mischievous look he's now wearing, I know Dominic doesn't know anything. He was in the car when Oscar mentioned New York City.

I watch Sheldon watching him, both greed and concession alive on her face now. She's cracking. She's almost there. Her gaze shifts from Dominic to me and then back to him. "What exactly is your relationship?"

Yeah, that's so not an easy question. "We go to school together."

"Dominic DeLuca," she says, her forehead wrinkling. "Did I see your name somewhere in the Simon Gilbert case file?"

The mischief and coolheaded attitude are lost in Dominic's renewed panic. I look at him, trying to send a telepathic message. Miles told me, during one of our last defense lessons, that unless Sheldon had a valid reason for exploring his case, she wouldn't have access to all the details of Simon Gilbert's murder. It was outside her field office, outside her specialty, which are financial fraud and white-collar crimes not homicide. She might know some details, but she won't know Dominic's direct involvement.

"We're classmates," I tell Sheldon before Dominic either shuts down or confesses everything. "We have English together this year, biology last year. Sometimes we hang outside of class. Like last night. And we were both friends with Simon."

I hold my breath while Sheldon rolls that around her big FBI brain. Finally she turns to Agent No Name and says, "Agent Sharp and I will take your proposal higher up and get back to you."

"Agent Sharp, huh?" I say, looking at the No Name guy who now has a name. "I should probably ask to see your badge, since it's our first meeting."

"Next time," Sheldon snaps, back to business. "We need to try to tail Oscar. Will you two be okay here?"

"Well, we're supposed to be at school today—" Dominic starts, until I send him a look and he backtracks. "Forget school. I have no problem hanging out here all day. Tomorrow, too, if needed. Happy to serve my country."

"Good," Sheldon says. She gives Agent Sharp a nod, and his laptop is packed up seconds later. "We'll be in touch."

Once they're out the door, I head over to the window and watch them leave. "I can have Harper call in for us at school in a little while."

"Whatever," Dominic mumbles, like he doesn't care either way. "We're not even doing anything today. I checked all my class syllabi online. Just assembly and review sessions for finals."

I'm sort of impressed that he checked his class info, considering he's kind of a slacker at school. And I was looking forward to those review sessions. "It's probably best. Don't think we can risk cramming you and Bret into the same hallway without compromising national security."

Speaking of national security…

I drop to all fours on the ratty hotel carpet and search for listening devices Sheldon or Sharp may have left behind.

Dominic stares down at his hands. "Miles already gave me the same lecture before he took off for Turkey. And then Agent Lawren—Aidan stopped by yesterday… I'm trying, okay?"

My head bangs against the table, and I suppress a yelp before tilting the table to check the underside. After I deem the area clear of FBI surveillance, I take a seat at the table and try not to panic over the fact that I just made an offer to go undercover for the FBI. Not that it's a sure thing. But Miles is going to… Well, I don't know how he'll react. He hates the part of my life that involves my family. It goes against everything he believes in. The worst thing I can do right now is try to keep this from him.

I grab my phone, find his number, and hit call. It goes straight to voicemail. He's supposed to be back at school by now, so that means he's probably in class. Can't have cell phones in military school classes, I'm sure. But couldn't he have answered my emergency text from earlier? "Hey, it's me… Give me a call when you have a minute. It's kind of important."

"So what's the deal with your dad?" Dominic prompts. "Where is this big job happening?"

I place my phone on the table and look over at him, debating whether I can trust him or not. He definitely proved trustworthy, surviving Sheldon's visit.

"New York City," I say before I can talk myself out of it.

He hesitates for a beat and then starts laughing. Like really laughing. Something I can't remember ever hearing from him. "Seriously? Your dad is pulling a big con in New York City?"

"I mean, it's definitely not our typical location, and I don't know if he's there yet—Oscar didn't say." I stare at him, bewildered. "Why is it funny?"

I'm sure plenty of cons happen in Manhattan. Just not by my family. Yet, anyway.

"You're going on the trip, right?" He sits upright, his feet hitting the floor with a soft *thud*. "For January Session?"

January Session is a longtime tradition at Holden Prep. Last year, I didn't start at the school until right after the January course, so I haven't participated before. After fall semester finals prep week—this week—we won't jump right into spring semester. Instead we have a three-week immersion course. All day, every day.

"No trip for me," I tell Dominic. "I opted for 'Holden a History.' I've always wanted to learn more prep school ghost stories. I mean, who doesn't?"

For juniors, there were thirty courses to choose from. Only ten of those are held on campus and don't require an additional fee. I only briefly glanced at the off-campus options before ruling them out.

Dominic stares at me. "You're kidding?"

I roll my eyes. "No, I'm not kidding. I opted for a free course that doesn't require a passport. Because I have no money or passport."

"Right." He shakes his head, looking a little embarrassed. "I just thought—I mean Justice and Chantel are doing the Manhattan Arts and Culture Experience. Jacob and me, too. And Bret, I think."

There's a scowl on his face when he says Bret's name, and I'm back to worrying about national security violations if the two of them don't quit fighting in public.

"You don't need a passport for this trip," Dominic adds. "And I think someone canceled recently. That girl Eliza Shepherd? Her GPA isn't high enough or something."

"And yours is?"

He shrugs. "My dad donates to Holden all the time. They turn a blind eye more often than you know."

More often than I know? What other trouble is he getting into?

And God, wouldn't that be perfect? If I were in New York for the next three weeks. But every single one of those off-campus courses is at least three thousand dollars. It might as well be a million, because I'll never get that kind of money without stealing it. Doubt the FBI would approve of me using stolen money in order to work for them.

We sit in silence for a while, but then just when I'm about to nod off sitting upright at the table, Dominic speaks. "What if I could get you on that trip? For free?"

"It's likely more complicated than you think," I say through a yawn. He starts to protest, but I stop him. "Were you thinking you could put it on your credit card and then deal with your parents when the bill comes back after the trip is over? Because Holden isn't going to accept your paying for me without asking your parents."

"Okay, let me clarify," he says, all serious. "I was asking you what you would do if I could get you on the trip, like what is the next step, assuming you had the option to be in New York next week?"

Too tired to argue, I humor him. "I would say that we should leave this dump and let Oscar follow us so I can find out more from him. Manhattan is a big place, so I've heard. I'll need him to tell me where my family's home base is there."

"Let Oscar follow us?" he repeats. "I thought the Feds were tailing him?"

"Nah, he's too good. They won't catch him. But he'll find us quickly. There's a tracker on your car." I ignore the alarm on his face after hearing this. "I was planning on removing it before we went anywhere else. Disabling it right away only adds suspicion that we're hiding out rather than just being where we planned to be."

"Which would make him think that home is somewhere else and it's a secret," he says, understanding now.

"Exactly."

"Okay, then." Dominic jumps to his feet and reaches for his jacket at the end of the bed. "Let's get out of here so Oscar can follow us. If we're gonna get you on that trip, I've got lots of work to do to make that happen."

I don't leap to my feet as quickly as he did. There are still some looming questions. "What's in this for you? Why are you helping me? I can get your scent off Oscar's trail. You can go back to your life and forget this."

He pauses near the door, scratches the back of his head. This seems to puzzle him as much as it does me. "I...I don't know. Just want to help, I guess. It's kind of my fault your boyfriend got kidnapped before, and then you got kidnapped trying to find him."

Truth.

Confusing truth but still, he's being honest.

"Plus," he adds with a grin, "I've got a few tricks up my sleeve, too, and I wouldn't mind showing them off."

"I can't pay for this trip with stolen money or drug money or anything in that family," I warn him, trying to guess all his possible tactics. I shake my head. "Never mind. As long as I don't steal it, I don't care what you do."

A hint of a smile touches his mouth. "How about I just don't tell you? Need-to-know or whatever?"

"Deal." I reach for my own coat, nerves fluttering in my stomach. I'm really doing this. Assuming the FBI agrees to the deal. If I'm already in New York, I know they'll agree. Sheldon wants my dad so much she was practically foaming at the mouth.

I don't know what scares me more—getting inside this big con or seeing my father again.

CHAPTER
11

"No," Harper says sharply to both Aidan and me. Though Aidan is here via Harper's phone lying on the coffee table. He's between classes in his first day of the training program in Georgia.

Through the speaker, Aidan's voice overlaps my sister's. "How did you get away from this Oscar guy? Have you checked to make sure he didn't tail you home?"

"I got rid of him by promising to help out in New York," I admit, though this will really get Harper good and pissed off. "Even convinced him to ditch the truck he stole. Dominic gave him bus money, and we watched him board a Greyhound to Penn Station."

"Okay, I guess that's one way to avoid him," Aidan says carefully. "So...what's the big con?"

I start to tell Aidan, but Harp lifts a hand to shush me. She glares down at the phone as if Aidan can see her. "No," she repeats. "I don't care what this job is; she's not going to New York or anywhere to meet our family."

"How are you paying for this trip?" Aidan asks.

"Dominic got his dad to donate a scholarship trip to Holden or something." The office called me down during third period today to tell me they received my interest form for the Manhattan Arts and Culture course and had financial aid available now if I wanted to participate. Sheldon and Sharp had been stalling on giving me a decision, but the school trip to New York sealed the deal.

"Yes. A school field trip," Harper points out. "You can't just wander off to help Dad. Someone's going to start asking questions."

"Justice says supervision is pretty loose on these trips, especially for juniors and seniors."

"That makes me feel a whole lot better," Harper snaps.

I roll my eyes. She knows I can handle myself. I don't need a babysitter.

"As much as I'd love to keep arguing," Aidan says, "I have an exam on disabling explosives in five minutes."

"An exam on the first day?" I ask, shocked at this. "Are you doing any chemistry? Any material on building explosives? Or are you focusing on techniques for gathering human intel?"

Yep, I definitely overindulged in the FBI and CIA biographies during my vacation.

Harper lifts her hands in the air. "Why can't either of you just do normal things, like accounting or underwater basket weaving?"

"Wait," I say to the phone on the coffee table. "Have you talked to Miles recently? He canceled on me last night, and I don't know if they even made it back from Turkey. I'm sure they did, right? He wouldn't have missed school."

"Want me to look into it?" Aidan asks gently. "I didn't talk to any of the Becketts yesterday or today, but I'm sure everything is fine."

"It's okay," I answer quickly, not wanting to blow a cover or create an issue for the Becketts. But the worry grows in my gut. "Yeah, maybe. Carefully."

"Got it. And fax me the FBI permission slip whenever

your sister caves," he says, earning a scowl from Harper.

After we hang up, Harper won't look at me. She rushes into the tiny kitchen of our second-floor apartment and pulls out a couple of pots, setting them on the stove. Then she pulls random items from the fridge. As if she plans to cook us dinner.

Uh-oh, not good.

I reach into the pocket of my uniform skirt and pull out the fifty-dollar bill I earned from tutoring a classmate yesterday afternoon. "Let's order pizza. You've had a long day."

She glares at me, and then the anger turns to worry as the pot in her hand is neglected. "Why is this so important to you? Mom has done things to earn that jail time."

"So have I," I argue. "And a decade? I never would have agreed to help Sheldon if I knew her sentence would be that—" I swallow back the angry tears. "I have to fix this. It's my fault."

"But—" she starts.

"I'm doing it, Harper. You know this already. I know you do."

"What if you get caught and put in jail?" she drills. "What good will that do for Mom?"

"As long as I follow the undercover protocol, I have immunity. I can't be arrested for anything I help Dad and his crew accomplish."

"What if Dad finds out you're helping the FBI?"

"I don't care." I shake my head. "I don't care what he thinks. He's nothing to me. I hope he rots in jail. Are you going to be pissed off at me or be there to help when I need you?"

She stares at me for a long moment, her blond hair falling over her eyes, and then finally she sighs. "Fine." She snatches the fifty from my hand. "But we're getting olives."

Only after earning my sister's blessing do I really truly

begin to panic about seeing my dad again and getting inside this job. Maybe I do care a little bit what he thinks. I know I care what Miles thinks, and he still doesn't know. And yeah, part of me, though I'm growing more worried by the day, is relieved to have an excuse not to tell him my plans.

"When do you leave?" Harper plops onto the couch and opens her laptop, preparing to put in an online order to Pizza Hut. "How are you getting to New York? And is there an itinerary for this trip in case I need to contact you?"

"We leave Saturday at six in the morning," I tell her. "Taking a bus to DC and then a train to New York. And I'm sure there's an itinerary, but I don't have it yet. We can assume it involves museums, theater, and, knowing Holden, some college visits."

"Good," Harper says, surprising me. "I don't want Justice and Chantel stealing meetings with admissions officers from you. They've got enough opportunities already. I've been reading college chat boards, and everyone is saying how valuable face-to-face meetings are, especially with the Ivy League schools."

I'm literally speechless. I just stand there for several seconds before finally spitting out, "Who are you? And when did I become an Ivy League candidate?"

"Well, why shouldn't you be?" Harper says simply. "You're a legal person now, you've got your Social Security card, you're registered for the SAT. Pepperoni or sausage?"

"Pepperoni," I say, leaving the other topic for later discussion. Maybe Harper's just feeling bored with her big-sister role and wants to play ambitious college-pushing parent for a little while.

There's a knock at the door. I look over at Harper, my eyebrows lifted. "Did you request lightning-fast delivery?"

"I haven't even started the order."

Through the peephole, I see Dominic standing

uncomfortably, his arms swinging at his sides. "It's for me. I'll be outside."

"Put your coat on!" she calls.

I head out in just my uniform sweater despite Harper's request and close the front door behind me. On the landing, I glimpse Clyde's old apartment. He moved back to DC right after our pre-Christmas dinner, since he'd been here only to keep an eye on Miles during his semester at Holden. A wave of sadness hits. Miles was so close for what felt like so long, and now he's off the map.

Or he's decided he doesn't like me anymore. Former con girls were never his type anyway. But Miles is a gentleman; he'd tell me himself if he wanted to end things.

"So you got the message from the office?" Dominic says, interrupting my pity party. "About the scholarship?"

"Yeah, and Sheldon and Sharp gave our plan the green light." I hug myself for protection against a gust of freezing wind. God, it'll be even colder in New York. But luckily the inch of snow on the ground brightens the sky, which would normally be dark at six thirty.

"I think it's smart that you're using the school trip to do this job. Gives you a fallback plan and you're not completely under the control of the FBI."

"Yep," I agree with a nod. He probably doesn't know to what extent that statement is true. I trust Sheldon and Sharp to do what's best for the investigation, not necessarily what's best for me.

He reaches into the back pocket of his khaki uniform pants, and hands me a white envelope. I peek in and lift an eyebrow at the good-size stack of twenty-dollar bills. "Not everything is covered by the trip fee. You're gonna need some cash."

His cheeks are pink, but I'm not sure if it's from the cold or from embarrassment over knowledge of my economic situation. I'm tempted to thrust it back at him, but he's right.

I will have to pay for some things. And I'm not asking Aidan or Harper for money; they've got enough to worry about. "Whatever I don't spend, you can have back. I'm economical; I won't use this much."

"It's not a gift," he says. "I sort of sold your services."

Before my mind can wander to dark and dirty places, I remember that he likely knows about what I did for Jacob last semester. A con woman was scamming his father, ruining his marriage and Jacob's trust fund in the process, and I convinced her to take off. In my own way. I did some digging to get that done, but nothing that would interfere with my new moral code. I glance warily at the envelope and then back at Dominic. "With the FBI watching me, I can't exactly run around breaking laws. Plus, it's kind of not my thing anymore."

Dominic pulls a small sheet of paper from the envelope, where he's scribbled various things on both sides. "Pick the stuff that's within your limits, and I'll deliver the bad news and refunds for the rest."

I quickly scan the list.

Rebecca Lawless—did cousin (Jessica Lawless) have boob job?

Brice Wilson—is girlfriend (Rebecca Lawless) cheating?

Hannah Yang—needs false letter of rec for summer internship.

Lexi Jorgan—fired from Smoothie King, smoking weed at work. Erase from employee records?

"Becca and Brice are fine," I say, trying my best to use my What Would Miles Do thinking cap. "Scratch Hannah."

"Got it," Dominic says, nodding. "The Lexi Jorgan situation probably is over the line. I didn't collect from her upfront."

Lexi Jorgan is a senior in my AP German class. I know she has financial aid to attend Holden, like me. "Lexi seems pretty responsible. Why is she smoking weed at work? Pretty dumb for an AP student."

"She says she has anxiety or something." Dominic shrugs like whatever, forget that one.

But maybe Lexi is exactly who I should be helping.

"She's eighteen, right? And smoking while on a break, we can assume?" I ask, and Dominic nods. "Her boss must have forgotten about Lexi's medical condition and her card-carrying status. And if she has a medical condition, then firing her was technically—"

"Illegal," Dominic finishes. He looks thoroughly impressed but also skeptical. "Can you actually make that happen?"

"Maybe," I offer, not wanting to set myself up for failure. I've made fake IDs before and fake medical records, but this will be my first fake medical marijuana card. "I'll talk to her myself, see what really happened." And likely I won't take her money.

I scan the rest of the list. There are nearly twenty items, many similar issues—false letters, is he/she cheating, blemishes on permanent records, etc....

"All of this came up in the last two days?" I say. "And people actually paid upfront?"

"I compiled weeks of complaints and made a casual offer to each of them," he says, like that didn't take tons of time, effort, and energy—things I wouldn't ever associate with Dominic. "Some only paid half upfront. But that means you get more cash later."

He takes the envelope back, and we sort out the money for him to refund, keeping my moral conscience on track. I'm still left with a nice stack of bills.

"Cool." That ghost of a smile of his appears for a few seconds. "Guess you're all set, then."

I stare at the money, hardly believing how this has all fallen into place. If only Miles would call. That would clear my head before I have to face my dad. "Just need to pack.

And figure out what to wear."

"Oh, well, that's easy," Dominic says. "Uniforms. Holden is weird about that, like they're afraid we might be mistaken for a public school."

That could be a problem, having to swap clothes every time I meet up with my dad. I'll worry about that later. "Uniforms. Great. I've already got those."

Guess I could come up with a cover story to tell my dad, one that incorporates uniforms. A long con of some kind. It would flow nicely with any info Oscar may have given him about finding me at a fancy private school in the middle of the night.

He looks at my bare legs and the skirt that falls above my knees. "Got any tights or leggings or whatever?"

I shake my head. "This is my first full winter in the cold."

"You might want to use some of that cash for tights or leggings or something. We're doing a lot of walking around the city. You're gonna freeze."

Not many guys stare at my legs and then ask me to cover them up. But then again, Simon was more Dominic's type than I am. My teeth are chattering now, and I'm sure Dominic has something better to do, so I hold up the envelope and thank him for the help. Once inside, I make a plan to start on the long list of mostly morally clean tasks my classmates are paying big bucks for. Then in a couple of days, I can focus my attention on Dad's Big Apple con, which I know very little about because Oscar, unfortunately, isn't privy to those details.

I tuck away the envelope of cash before Harper sees it and vow to use a chunk of it to pay one of many bills lingering on the countertop.

But as I'm stuffing the wad of cash under my sweater, Dominic's efforts seem even more glaring. Why is he so deeply invested in helping me go undercover for the FBI? What does he want out of this whole deal?

CHAPTER

12

I'm struggling to shove my duffel bag beneath the charter bus when an older man skillfully adds a fancy suitcase to the luggage compartment. He sees me watching him and takes my bag, tucking it perfectly inside the compartment. Before I can thank him, he turns around to face two of my classmates—Justice and Chantel. Both girls are yawning and carting Starbucks cups.

"Is there anything else you require?" the man asks Justice, a hint of a French accent leaking through his words. "Do you have your phone? Passport? Credit cards?"

Justice pats the bag on her shoulder. "I'm all set. Thank you."

There's an air of dismissal in that *thank you*, and I'm caught off guard by it. I've heard Justice and Chantel both talk about their nannies and staff at their houses, but I've never seen any interactions like this.

After the man walks away, Chantel shakes her head. "God, is he always like that?"

"He's new," Justice says. Then she seems to notice me. "Ellie! I've hardly seen you all week."

"Yeah, I've been—"

She grips my shoulders and steers me toward the bus entrance. "Come on, let's get a good seat so we can catch up. How were finals? I think I bombed Spanish. If I get another B plus my parents will freak."

And just like that we leave Chantel standing outside in the cold, waiting for her own bags to be brought from her chauffeured car. As we're walking up the bus steps, Justice whispers under her breath, "Chantel, on the other hand, I can't seem to escape. She and Jacob have been fighting constantly. I'm so over it."

Not for the first time, I wonder why Justice continues to be friends with Chantel. I used to lump them together, but they are very different despite their similar lives.

"Thank God you got that scholarship D's dad started," she adds.

The bus is nearly half-full already. I'm scanning the seats for the best selection while Justice continues her whispered conversation. "Heard from your boy toy, Miles, lately? Oh! Should we come up with a code name, since you two clearly want to keep things low-key?"

Boy toy? Seriously? And she's taking this relationship news pretty well, considering Justice had a thing for Miles until she caught us post make out at the homecoming dance back in October.

"We talk," I tell her, though this hasn't been true for way too many days. Fear bubbles up in my gut. No news from Aidan and his search, either. But in this case, no news might be good news.

Near the middle of the bus, Mr. Lance, my favorite teacher at Holden, digs through a well-worn canvas bag and removes a clipboard. "Morning, Justice, Ellie…" He pauses to give me a nod. "I was so glad to hear of this last-minute addition to our trip. Have you spent much time in New York?"

I shake my head. "First timer."

This seems to excite both him and Justice even more. "Fantastic! You're in for the experience of a lifetime."

"What he really means to say," Justice adds, "is that there's a million things you haven't done—"

"But just you wait," Mr. Lance interrupts, singing the words.

I look between the two of them, bewildered. "What am I missing?"

Justice smacks the headrest of the seat nearby, and several dozing students are startled awake. "*Hamilton*," she says, waiting for my reaction.

"Oh, that play about Alexander Hamilton?" I say.

"Musical," Mr. Lance corrects. "And tickets are hard to come by, but Holden Prep booked seats well over a year ago at my suggestion."

"Best teacher ever," Justice adds, then she looks at me, concern on her face. "Okay, we'll need to educate you ASAP."

I'm immediately offered Mr. Lance's ancient iPod containing the musical cast album, which Justice instructs me to memorize in its entirety prior to the show. Soon I'm seated comfortably by a window, headphones on and music playing while I explore the advantages of this *Hamilton* obsession. This will likely be a great night to sneak off. If everyone is as obsessed as Justice and Mr. Lance, they'll be too excited to pay close attention to details such as my empty seat in the theater.

Before we take off, Justice is forced to abandon her spot beside me in order to provide a buffer between Jacob and Chantel. Dominic stumbles onto the bus five minutes after six, sleepy-eyed, his uniform shirt untucked, and takes the empty seat beside me. Mr. Lance is nearly done calling roll when Bret Thomas steps onto the bus looking as sleepy-eyed and disheveled as his former best friend. He quickly checks out his seating prospects, and when he glances this way, Dominic must give him the glare of all glares because he slips into the spot beside Ms. Geist, the guidance counselor and second chaperone for this trip.

I elbow my seatmate in the side. "It's not like he committed murder," I whisper. "Plus, you've gotta admit, the guy can keep a secret."

Dominic has to know that I'm referencing his current in-the-closet status, but a scowl forms on his face. "Yeah, that's the part I can't get past."

"Welcome, young friends," Mr. Lance says to the entire bus after the last name is called and doors are shut. "Welcome to Holden Prep's January Session in the greatest city in the world!"

A cheer erupts, followed by more singing. I can only guess he's quoted *Hamilton* the musical again.

"This adventure will immerse each and every one of you in culture, history, and art like you've never experienced before, even if you are a frequent Manhattan visitor." He nods toward the guidance counselor. "Ms. Geist and I are thrilled to be your tour guides for the next three weeks, and we have planned activities that allow us to journey behind the scenes and speak to experts on topics of history and art. We will also receive personalized guided tours and opportunities to sit in on classes at Columbia University and NYU, schools Ms. Geist has informed me many of you plan to apply to. We've set up meetings with department heads in your areas of interest, allowing you to form valuable connections before application season next fall."

The bus pulls away from the school's circle drive, but Mr. Lance continues his lecture as if we're all seated in the classroom. "Each of you will complete an independent project of your choice, approved by myself. A five-page proposal is due a week from today and the final project due two weeks after returning home. Study your itinerary, take note of the excursions that will be taken as a group and those that offer more freedom, and plan accordingly. Nightly curfews vary depending on activities, so please pay close attention to those times and don't make Ms. Geist or me have to play bad cop or phone home to your family. Any questions?"

No one raises a hand—probably too early in the morning—so Mr. Lance takes his seat, and soon we're on the highway leading us to the train station in DC. Beside me, Dominic pulls out a small box from his jacket pocket and pops three pieces of gum into his mouth. I'd seen him do this the other day in the motel room but hadn't seen the package or realized it was nicotine gum.

"New Year's resolution?" I prompt.

"No promises," he says in perfect unmotivated Dominic fashion. Then he quickly switches topics. "Any word from the agents?"

"Nope." I pop the earbuds back in place. "Guess I'm on my own until I've got something to offer them."

I toss my duffel bag onto the sofa bed before Justice or Chantel can claim it. Sneaking out of this hotel room will be much easier if I don't have to tiptoe past a classmate sleeping near the exit. I wave off Justice's offer to take the couch, and the two of them wheel their luggage into the bedroom portion of our room at the DoubleTree Hotel at Times Square.

I head over to the window while they debate which of the two full-size beds is better. The curtains open in one swift motion, and I immediately draw in a breath at the view. It's nearly dark out, but Times Square is lit up like every night is New Year's Eve. And for a moment, I almost wish I was just another student on this trip to a city that is proving to be as intriguing as Mr. Lance said earlier on the bus.

My purse buzzes, and I dig for my cell, then quickly read a text. It's from an unknown number and they've sent a picture of the soda machine at the end of the hall, the sign marking the eighteenth floor hung above it. Beneath the photo it says: **meet me here in 2min?**

I have no idea who this is or whether it's safe to meet them. It could be Dominic? Or possibly my dad? Or maybe, if I'm lucky, Miles.

That tiny drop of hope is enough to have me snatching the key card from the coffee table, my hand on the doorknob. Justice's voice carries from the bedroom, reminding me that I'm not alone and I can't just take off without a word. "I'm getting a soda at the vending machine. You guys want anything?"

Both girls decline my offer, and I rush out the door, punching a reply to the unknown number.

ME: K

The Pepsi machine is vacant when I reach it. I glance around, checking the hallway, and then I dig for three dollars because I can't come back empty-handed. I get one bill in and then feel fingers gripping the back of my sweater, tugging me away from the machine. My heart jumps up to my throat. I catch a glimpse of a man's black dress shoe kicking open the door to the hotel room across from the Pepsi machine.

And then before I can even think the word "self-defense," I'm on the other side of that door.

CHAPTER

13

Before I can truly freak out, I'm face-to-face with the baby-faced Agent Sharp. Disappointment washes over me, even though I hadn't really let myself believe it could be Miles who requested this meeting. Not completely.

"Thanks for that Welcome to New York City initiation," I say, forcing calm despite the near heart attack I just had.

He flashes me an all-American grin. "Just testing out our communication system."

"What system?" I scoff. "Kidnapping girls at the hotel vending machines is hardly a form of communication."

"I apologize," Sharp says, sounding sincere enough. "I meant to say that we need to create a communication system right now."

This hotel room is a more traditional room—two full beds, bathroom, TV. No separate front room with sofa bed and mini kitchen. A suitcase, clothing, laptop, and various chargers are strewn across one of the beds.

"Are you staying here?" I ask, unable to hide the disbelief from my voice. "In New York City? Down the hall from my classmates and me?"

"Yeah," he says, like this is common knowledge. "And

Agent Sheldon is staying next door—she's running surveillance right now. Did you think we'd leave you to fend for yourself?"

Yeah, actually, that's exactly what I thought. "I haven't heard from either of you in days; what was I supposed to think?"

We have a five-second-long stare off, and then Agent Sharp is the first to blink when he reaches for a clipboard on the desk nearby. "Should we get down to business, then? According to the itinerary, there's a Holden group dinner in Ballroom D in thirty minutes."

I release a breath, shake off the tension, and prepare to plan this plan. Fortunately, while uncovering a murderer together, Miles taught me quite a bit about undercover ethics and laws—of course, we ended up breaking many of those rules. But Sharp and Sheldon will need this job to be squeaky-clean and by the book so that everything is admissible in court. If I want to rid myself of the guilt that accompanies helping my own mother win a decade in prison, I'm going to have to follow the rules.

Sharp shows me a map of the hotel on his clipboard. He's labeled the two chaperones' rooms, among other details. But there's a navy duffel bag lying near his feet that distracts me from memorizing the information. A large, white tag is tied to the strap. I bend down and flip the tag over, reading it.

Hayes, Eleanor

My hand jerks back in surprise. I haven't seen or thought my previous last name for a very long time, have only said it out loud once in the past year. I stand upright again. "Where did you get that?"

"The bag?" Sharp lifts an eyebrow at the haunted look that is likely on my face right now. "Right before catching my flight to New York, I was in the evidence room and spotted this bag with your name on it. Probably got mixed up with lost and found. Happens all the time: stuff just magically walks right out of the evidence room."

"Or right into it," I say, eyeing him, then glancing at the bag again. I lower my voice in case Sheldon has returned to her room and can hear us through the joining doors. "You stole this for me? How did the FBI get it?"

He scratches the back of his head and glances nervously around the room. "It's your bag, right? And it's just clothes?"

"Right," I agree, but it's more than just clothes. The things I've borrowed from Harper for the past year are just clothes. These are *my* clothes.

"So the third-floor service elevator…see it here?" He taps a pen to the map on his clipboard, obviously uncomfortable discussing the stolen evidence.

I'm too shocked and appreciative to disrespect his wishes. "Yep, I see it."

"Took you long enough," Chantel says when I return to our room from my eighteen-minute excursion to the vending machine. "Dinner is in ten minutes."

The bathroom door opens and Justice emerges, fresh makeup on and the scent of fruity body spray trailing behind her.

"Good, you're back. I was getting worried." She glances at the bottle of Pepsi in my hand, then at the black duffel on my shoulder. "I thought you only had one bag?"

"I had two, just forgot about the second one. Luckily the taxi driver saw it in the trunk and left it at the front desk." I step into the bathroom, the bag still on my shoulder. "I'll be ready in a few minutes, but you guys can head down without me if you want."

"Okay," Chantel says quickly.

"Ballroom D," Justice calls through the door, but I barely

hear her. My fingers are already clutching the zipper of the bag. "See you in a few."

I force myself to hold still until hearing the door to the hotel room shut. Then I tug the zipper, revealing clothing tangled and piled hastily inside. We always packed up before a job, usually had to take off right after the finale. The scent of my family's camper—a mix of campfires and those cheap, gas-station air fresheners shaped like pine trees—hits me right away like it's grown stronger and more powerful in its containment. And as much as I want to hate it, the familiar warmth envelops me like an old friend. My new life is supposed to be an honest one, and there's still a great deal of pretending involved, but in that camper with my parents and Harper before she took off...it was a place where I rarely had to pretend, where I could just be.

I toss aside a pair of jeans that used to fit me perfectly, and several more articles of clothing join the jeans on the hotel bathroom floor until I'm near the bottom of the bag and feel something firmer than clothing. My fingers land on a plastic hand, and I pull until the object is free. The blond-haired American Girl doll is still wearing the blue dress my thirteen-year-old self last dressed her in. Her hair is a little frazzled, she could use a day at the doll salon, but otherwise she's perfect. I tuck her back in and lift a pair of gold heels from the bag. An image of my mother walking gracefully across the camper in these heels flashes in my mind. *"See, honey? Easy as pie. Now your turn."*

She was so beautiful—probably still is—teaching with such patience and love. No one instilled more confidence in me than my mom.

Dominic sends me a text asking where I am, so I put the ax on my trip down memory lane and collect the items strewn all over the bathroom floor. When I stand up and face myself in the mirror, I hardly recognize the brown-haired girl in the plaid pleated shirt and navy sweater bearing the Holden Academy crest on the front. The firewood and fake pine scent still lingers in the air. I close my eyes, and I can practically feel the nightly chill in the air, the crackling of burning wood, laughter in the distance from some of my family members, and my mother's voice. She would sing nearly every night.

I don't want that life again; I know I don't. But that doesn't mean I can stop myself from wishing for pieces of it.

CHAPTER
14

JUSTICE: trying on THE most perfect dress at Prada, u have to come see!!!

I scroll away from Justice's text, then pull up the address Oscar sent me and double-check. I glance up, way up, at a tall building in Midtown. The temperature is especially blistering today, and my abrupt halt in the middle of a busy sidewalk earns me a few accidental shoulder bumps. Everyone appears to be bundled up and hustling to get inside somewhere. And I'm lingering outside, attempting to pep talk myself into this building. Instead, I reply to Justice.

ME: can't right now. I'm in coffee shop typing up my project proposal for Lance

JUSTICE: overachiever. Srsly. Have u seen Dominic?

ME: no, why?

JUSTICE: he's being all stealth today. I think he's meeting a guy. I watched him install Tinder app on his phone

Huh. Well, good for him if that's true, but I can't imagine Dominic not waiting until he's alone to install a dating or hookup app. Okay, now I'm really stalling. Time to face the music. We've only got three hours free this afternoon.

Nerves flutter in my stomach, but I make myself reach for

the fancy golden handle of the building door and step inside. A security guard is seated at a desk in front of the elevators.

"Where you headed today, miss?" he asks.

"Johnson Whitman Agency," I recite. "I have an appointment at four."

He scans a paper in front of him. "Name?"

"Amelia Kennedy."

"Okay, Miss Kennedy." He hands me a visitor badge dangling from a black lanyard. "Johnson Whitman is up on twenty-two—" He starts to rise from his chair, probably to call up the elevator for me, but someone approaches from behind me, stopping him. "Where you headed today, sir?"

"Same as this lady," a familiar voice says.

I suppress a groan. Tinder my ass.

The security guard grins. "That explains the matching outfits."

I turn to offer Dominic a pointed look and see that although he isn't wearing a plaid skirt, his school tie matches my skirt. The guard doesn't even ask his name, just hands him a visitor's badge identical to mine and tells him to follow me.

Once we're alone in the elevator, I spin to face him. "What the hell are you doing?"

"I'm going to the twenty-second floor." One eyebrow lifts, and then Dominic gives a slight nod toward the ceiling where a camera sits.

"I'm doing this alone," I tell him under my breath. But it's no use. He's already punched the button for the floor, and I can't exactly knock him out with a camera pointed at us and a security guard watching like a hawk downstairs. Maybe when we get out of the elevator I can shove him into the stairwell and lock the door? From the corner of my eye I catch him popping a couple of pieces of the white nicotine gum into his mouth. Good, he's nervous. That'll help.

I count along with the bar above the elevator doors until

the number 22 lights up. I ready myself for a fight once those doors separate—I've been training while Dominic has been smoking. But instead of a hallway to pull him down, the open doors provide nothing but entry into a wide space.

And standing right in front of us, looking exactly as I remembered him, is my father.

For several seconds, I'm frozen, barely registering Dominic's index finger pressing a button to prevent the doors from closing.

"I knew it," my dad says, a huge grin spreading over his face. "The second I saw the name Amelia Kennedy on the appointment book."

Before I can do or say anything, he tugs me from the elevator and I'm wrapped in his arms. But it's over quickly, like he's not sure exactly where we stand. And for a moment, I'm not completely sure, either.

"Let me see you," he says, stepping away to look me over, and after, he moves on to Dominic. "This must be the boyfriend. But what are y'all wearing? It's like a Catholic school on steroids. Don't tell me you're stealing from nuns; I raised you better than that, Eleanor," he says with mock disappointment.

Before I can offer up an answer, Dominic says, "We swiped these from a couple of kids who left their bags unattended at Grand Central. Some ritzy prep school on a field trip. We've been following them all over the city."

Okay, I guess I'll go with his story. Dad might buy it better than the long con story I'd planned. "We've visited two museums, seen a Broadway show, and had lunch in Bobby Flay's restaurant. Courtesy of Holden Academy."

"Tomorrow we're going to Ellis Island and the Statue of Liberty," Dominic adds.

I press my foot gently to his, signaling him. *Don't push it.* Over-the-top details are always a dead giveaway. Especially to my dad.

Dad taps a beat with his foot, his gaze bouncing between Dominic and me. "Surely he's not the same boyfriend you took off with? That would be a long-ass time for you to—"

I give him my most sardonic smile and a pat on the shoulder. "Wouldn't you love to know?"

With that topic off-limits, I step around him, surveying this large open space for the first time since the elevator opened. The floor-to-ceiling windows lining an entire wall offer a nice view of Midtown and the traffic below on Sixth Avenue. Wood flooring covers the large room and white beams are placed sporadically around it. To my left, the white wall reveals three different doors. Muffled voices emerge from the middle door, and the space at the bottom of it reveals two pairs of black men's dress shoes shuffling around—an office maybe?

I stride toward the center of the room. "So tell me about this new business Oscar was going on about. Maybe I can help?"

"Running low on funds, are you?" my dad jokes. "Miss Independent needs Daddy's help. That certainly fits your costume today."

"Oh, I definitely need Daddy's help." My gaze lands on a black grand piano in the far corner of the room. "Glad we're on the same page."

"It's been months," Dad says.

Eleven months, to be precise, but who's counting? Apparently not him. "So that's a no, then?"

"How do I know where you've been? Or if anyone followed you here? And I have no idea how rusty you are right now. All I know is that you've been cruising around the city with some prep school, stealing museum admissions; where's the challenge? Skills aren't meant to be left dormant. You've got to exercise your—"

"Con muscles daily," I recite. "I was just reading about

that in *Be a Better You* magazine. Inspiring article."

Before he can answer, the office door opens and my "uncle" pokes his head out. "Thirty seconds to open calls, boss."

Another man I don't recognize steps out of the room, a stack of folders in his arms. He's probably late twenties, stylishly dressed in nice jeans, a form-fitting T-shirt, and suit jacket, his dark hair slicked back.

"An investor scam?" I guess, but no, that doesn't explain the fact that the security guard didn't blink at two teenagers booking an appointment with the agency. "Trust fund administrators?"

This fits with Oscar's concerns. Trust funds are a tough con to pull off because old-money folks seeking old banks with years of records usually open them.

Dad's mouth twitches, fighting a smile. He's got me stumped. "All right, how about we give you an audition today?"

The dude with the stack of folders laughs as if Dad's told a joke. "What about the punk over there in the stolen blazer?"

"Me?" Dominic says, pointing to his chest and looking convincingly innocent, probably because his uniform isn't stolen. "This wardrobe was a donation. Or at least it was right beside a donation bin—that counts, right?"

My dad quirks an eyebrow at me. "He's not bad. Where'd you get him?"

I roll my eyes. "Trust me, you don't want to know."

Dad walks closer to Dominic. "How's your German? Or Russian? Can you pull off Russian?"

When Dominic's eyes widen just a smidgen, Dad has his answer. "Guess not." He claps his hands. "Oh! Bruno, give me the Sydney Opera House folder."

The folder dude produces the right one and hands it off to Dad, who thumbs through it quickly before pulling out a head shot of a spikey-haired teen with a scowl worthy of Dominic DeLuca's very best efforts. Dad holds the photo beside Dominic's face. "Yep, that'll work."

He's right: the resemblance is undeniable. But who is the guy in the head shot?

"Lachlan Hudson, welcome to the agency," Dad says to Dominic, then he hands him the folder. "Memorize everything in the folder today. It's not leaving this room, got it?"

"Um, yeah, sure." Dominic nods, his nerves in plain sight. He's seconds from popping more nicotine gum. "No problem."

Dad snorts out a laugh, not sure if he's being serious, then he thumbs through the other folders and hands me one. "Emma Canterbury."

I glance at the photo of a brown-haired girl near my age. We aren't a perfect match but close enough to blame differences on Photoshop. "Okay, but what are we doing? Funding a charity theater program for abandoned puppies?"

My dad spreads his arms wide while he walks backward toward the office. "You want in, you figure it out." He turns to the folder guy. "If I cross my feet, give them the bailout forms, got it?"

He's behind the door a second later, and I'm left with a folder in my hands for God knows what, trying to process seeing my father—the man who should be in that cell instead of my mother—for the first time in nearly a year. We didn't even talk about her, not a mention. Doesn't he care?

I feel Dominic move beside me. He raises the folder and whispers, "What the hell is this?"

Standing guard near the elevator is my "uncle," a man who, despite having some top-notch conning skills, was always easy for me to manipulate. He refuses eye contact when I look his way.

"Come on, Milky," I say. "Tell me what this biz is?"

He shakes his head, lips tightly closed.

"At least give me a hint…have I done this before?" I ask.

"Doubtful," he says with a smirk. "Very doubtful."

Great. Just great.

I elbow Dominic in the side. He's just standing there like an idiot. "Read your damn folder."

"Wait, he was serious about that?" Dominic says, panicked. "What about the Australian part?"

"You really need to stop following me." I shake my head and open my own folder, quickly getting to know Emma Canterbury, a British actress who was recently in a West End production of *Fun Home*.

The elevator dings and Dominic jumps a mile. He hasn't even opened his folder. "Oh God, I can't remember my name —"

"Lachlan," I tell him sharply. "Please don't talk to anyone, and please don't follow me again."

His jaw tenses, a scowl takes over his face, but he stares at the elevator as the doors open and says nothing. There are at least a dozen people crammed in that elevator, and when the miniature mob exits, the group demographic becomes clear to both Dominic and me.

"Stage moms?" he says.

A little girl in a red dress and full stage makeup pushes past me. The heel of one of the tap shoes she's holding clips me in the arm. She flashes me a giant pageant smile. "Oops, sorry."

"Just hang back and observe," I tell Dominic. "Until we know what this is."

"I already know what this is." He raises the folder. "It's an audition."

"I know that." The pieces snap together. "Oh, like an *audition* audition."

"We've got head shots." He nods toward a mom now

seated on the floor, spreading out photos of a preschool-age child. "Maybe it's like those modeling schools. I've heard they're a scam. Charge a shit-ton of money, too."

"Maybe…" But that almost seems too easy. Why would Oscar be so worried about a modeling school scam? Seems fairly harmless, especially compared to the Dr. Ames con. With that con, we handed cash and fake IDs to countless drug-addicted teens and set them free of parents trying to help them. Kinda makes fake modeling school look heroic. As far as I know, Oscar never had any ethical concerns about the Dr. Ames con.

More moms and children of various ages with costumes and regular clothes pour out of the elevator with each *ding*. We haven't really done cons involving kids, not little kids anyway. Maybe that was Oscar's concern? Although the parents are the ones paying and getting ripped off.

I hear a kid hiss to his mom. "They're auditioning with a *School of Rock* number. I have to change my song!"

Dominic hears this, too, while he's frantically thumbing through his folder. "Actually," he whispers to me, "Lachlan Hudson is *in School of Rock*. In Australia."

"Professionals." I nod. "To add credibility."

This isn't a quick hit job. It's a long con.

I glance around the now half-full room. *What are you doing, Dad? Why is Oscar so afraid for you?*

CHAPTER
15

"You didn't see anyone collecting or offering money?" Agent Sheldon drills while pacing across the carpet in Agent Sharp's hotel room.

The room is now littered with computers and technical equipment along with half a dozen takeout containers. I don't know where he sleeps. *Unless…* My gaze roams to the open door joining their two rooms. There's an empty bed in my line of sight. Big enough for two.

"No exchange of money at all," I say from my seat at the tiny table across from the bed. "I heard that Bruno guy tell at least a dozen people that the agency doesn't charge a fee until the client books something and gets paid."

"That doesn't even make sense," Sheldon says, clearly disappointed.

"It's a long con." Sharp looks up from the laptop where he'd been taking notes. He's ignoring FBI dress code today, wearing gray sweats. "This requires establishing relationships and offering a legitimate product."

I point a finger at Sharp while keeping my attention on the still-pacing Agent Sheldon. "Exactly what he said."

"And you definitely don't recognize the man called

Bruno?" Sheldon asks, and I shake my head. "Is that normal for your family to bring in outsiders?"

"No," I admit. It's definitely not normal. "My dad doesn't even trust *me* with details of the operation because I've been an outsider for less than a year."

"I'm guessing the outsiders are providing the space in that building," Sheldon assesses while Sharp types away at his laptop, probably transcribing all this. "Even the smallest office in that building costs a fortune."

"That Bruno guy had a perfect New Jersey accent, but he seemed more like a secretary than a partner," I remind them. "My dad literally snapped his fingers and he came running."

"Maybe the accent isn't an act. Maybe he's local. And if he isn't in charge, then that means there are more," Sheldon says with a nod. Her eyes have a glint of greedy hope now. "Behind the scenes."

"Most likely," I agree. "I need more time to earn my dad's trust before I'll be able to figure out where the payoff is and who else is involved."

"Of course," Sheldon says.

I glance at my cell and then spring to my feet. "Are we done here? I have a tour of Shakespeare's Garden to get to."

After I'm dismissed, I slip inside the hotel coin-laundry room to return a missed call from Aidan.

"Hey, kiddo, I don't have much to offer," Aidan says right away, probably sensing my need for information. "I can't get ahold of Miles, and when I contacted Marshall Academy, they basically evaded giving me any real answers as to whether or not he's on campus. Maybe that's their security system, but I know the school head; we did a tour in Iraq together when I first enlisted. And we've talked about Miles before. It's weird that he wouldn't tell me anything. But then again, I couldn't exactly say why I needed the information."

"What did you tell him?" I prompt, ignoring the turmoil

of panic in my stomach.

"Just that I knew some Holden kids who knew him and wanted to get ahold of him and that it might be best if we didn't leave them to dig around," Aidan tells me. "I don't want you to worry, okay? Most of the time, no news is good news in these situations."

"That's bullshit," I say, but gently. He's trying to make me feel better. "Give me something, then. Hypotheticals… What would make him go off the map? Before last Sunday when we were supposed to meet, I assumed he was back in the country, but I never did get confirmation of that. Maybe his parents' mission in Turkey went wrong and they had to vanish, and because Miles was with them he had to vanish, too?"

"That's pretty much what I was thinking." He sighs loud enough for me to hear it through the phone. "The Becketts are phenomenal agents and will do anything to protect their son, so really, if something bad happened there is no better place for him to be than with his parents."

"Right, okay." I release a frustrated breath. I've definitely moved on from deciding whether or not my concern is justified or leftover paranoia caused by the kidnapping experience. It's definitely justified now.

"If I had access to the school's servers, I'd risk being caught to look at attendance records or something—anything to see if his person has been spotted somewhere," Aidan says, surprising me with his own growing worry.

We end the call shortly after, and I'm still clinging to his mention of school servers. I do know someone who has the skills to get inside Marshall Academy's system. A savvy DC tech store owner named Connie. She's helped me in many binds and asked for little in return. She's all about breaking the law for the purpose of finding truth. She knows Miles and she's proven to be trustworthy with sensitive information. I pull up Connie's number and take a deep breath before hitting send. I have to know, one way or the other, if he's there at school.

I have to know.

*"T*o-morrow, and to-morrow, and to-morrow, creeps in this petty pace from day to day—"

"*Macbeth*," several of my classmates shout in response to Mr. Lance standing on a huge rock and challenging us to a name-that-Shakespeare-quote competition.

"Well done, but that was an easy one," Mr. Lance says from the rock above us. His nose is red from the cold, but he doesn't seem bothered by it. He opens the bag on his shoulder and removes a hand warmer pouch. "If you get the next one, you win this."

Our tour guide informed us before leaving the hotel for Central Park that we were lucky to get such a warm day. Apparently twenty-seven degrees is well above average for January in New York City. But tell that to my frozen toes.

Beside me, Justice rubs her hands together and blows on them through her knit gloves. "I'm so winning this."

On my other side, Ms. Geist looks like she might be cold enough to challenge her students.

Mr. Lance clears his throat and takes his dramatic stance again. *"All the world's a stage and all the men and women merely players—"*

"*As You Like It*!" Justice shouts, jumping up and down.

"Yes." Mr. Lance points a finger at her, a big grin on his face before he tosses the hand warmer in our direction. "Bonus point if you can name the character speaking." Justice catches the plastic pouch with ease but comes up blank on answering the question. Mr. Lance scans our group. "Anyone?"

Slowly, I lift a hand in the air. "Jacques."

"Very good, Miss Ames," Lance says, and even though it wasn't offered upfront, he tugs another hand warmer from his bag and sends it sailing through the air to me.

Much longer arms reach out in front of me, snatching it from midair. Bret Thomas. Several shouts of protest follow, but Bret turns to me, a smile on his face, and hands over the pouch.

"Just helping out the lady," he says.

I study him for a moment while Mr. Lance pulls more items from his Mary Poppins man purse. Bret catches me staring and eventually shrugs as if to say, *Do I need a reason to do something nice?* The answer is yes, because this is Bret Thomas, the blond all-American prep-school boy who blackmails first, makes friends later. I decide to tuck the hand warmer into my coat pocket and save it for another day, especially if this temperature is above average.

Mr. Lance has a large Ziploc bag of sidewalk chalk in each hand, and he passes off one of the bags to Ms. Geist to hand out. "I would like all of you to leave your mark on this beautiful place where we honor a literary genius who has remained unmatched for centuries. Write your favorite Shakespeare quotes. From memory, no wiki quotes."

I take a piece of blue chalk from the bag and hand it off to Chantel before attempting to squat down in a skirt. At least I took Dominic's advice and bought some leggings at a store in Times Square yesterday.

"I only know *Romeo and Juliet*," Chantel complains.

I test out my chalk, drawing a large blue heart. "Then quote *Romeo and Juliet*."

"But it's cliché," she says, like I'm supposed to do something about it.

I take a note from Bret and just shrug.

I'm not going to get worked up over freakin' Chantel. I

have more self-control than that. The Miles situation has me on edge, not knowing, waiting to hear from Connie. Infiltrating my dad's con is proving more challenging than I thought it would be. I guess it was easy to allow anger at him to cloud my memory of how good he is at the family biz.

Not wanting to deal with Chantel's complaints, I get up and move somewhere else. I end up beside Dominic, who has put a fair amount of space between himself and the rest of the group. I approach him from behind and read his quote written in poor cursive with pink chalk.

Nothing will come of nothing.

I roll it around in my head but decide nothing will come of that quote, at least in its relevance to Dominic. Silently, I sit beside him and contemplate my own choice. Both my parents force-fed us Shakespeare from a young age. The works were easy to get for free and, much like foreign-language study, impressive at the right moment during a con. I'm not short of ideas for quotes, but the thought that it doesn't matter what I write, it doesn't need to follow any cover story or be graded, is a rare occurrence, and I guess that makes it more important to pick something that feels like me.

"You know, he might've been here," Dominic says quietly. "If things had gone differently, he might have gone on this trip and won those hand warmers."

Simon. That's who might have been here.

With each passing month, it's gotten easier to remember him without that familiar lump forming in my throat, but it's hard to not feel wrecked thinking about everything he'll never get to do.

"He definitely would have won the hand warmers," I say, genuinely meaning it. Simon was number three in our class before he was murdered. He knew nearly every answer to every question that a teacher could throw at him.

I reread Dominic's chosen quote with new perspective,

knowing he likely chose it while thinking of Simon. And for a moment I'm hit with crushing pain in my chest, imagining what he must feel, what I would feel if I found out that Miles wasn't just off the map, if he were—

I shake the thought from my head and refocus on the pink chalk writing.

Nothing will come of nothing.

"The job with my dad…why are you so determined to help?" I ask Dominic. "I just don't get it."

"I'm tired of doing nothing," he says, his voice low and eerie. "Simon didn't sit around contemplating shit—he acted. He sensed corruption in that secret group and he dug around."

"He got himself murdered," I remind him.

But Dominic plugs on, ignoring my comment. "And you and Miles, you didn't believe it was suicide, and you did something about it…"

"And *we* nearly got murdered," I say, but he ignores this comment, too.

"And I sat on my ass, feeling sorry for myself while holding on to some valuable information."

As much as I'd like to offer him comforting words, I can't exactly argue with his assessment of his part in the investigation of Simon's death.

"I'm sick of being the guy who doesn't do shit." He finally looks me in the eyes. "No more of that."

If he's playing me, that was an Oscar-worthy performance. And I don't think he's that talented. "You really want to help with my undercover assignment?"

He pauses a beat and then nods.

"You're gonna need some training," I tell him. "You'll have to work very hard, like *up all night studying and preparing* hard."

"Okay," he says with fervent enthusiasm. "I can do that."

"Good." I nod and then press my blue chalk to the

sidewalk, deciding on a quote that doubles as a message for my new partner.

Come not between the dragon and his wrath.

"Meet me in the laundry room on the seventh floor at midnight," I say. "Find a tutorial on Australian accents and practice."

He opens his mouth to argue, but I stop him.

"If anyone asks, tell them you're learning it to pick up girls who love accents." I roll my eyes. "It'll go with your *other* cover story."

That silences him, and after Mr. Lance compliments both of our *King Lear* quotes, our group is up and moving farther into Central Park despite the gray skies and negative wind-chill factor. I'm about to start mentally planning Dominic's lessons, but a text from Daddy Dearest, code name Hayes, interrupts me.

HAYES: need u and bf tomorrow, wear the uniforms, bring tap shoes

I show the message to Dominic and watch with some amusement when his face pales slightly at the tap shoe mention. At least there is some entertainment in all this stress and worry. I get to imagine Dominic DeLuca tap-dancing a Broadway number.

CHAPTER 16

Dad's assistant, Bruno, approaches me from behind while I'm pretending to study sheet music, and I jump a mile.

"Whoa," Bruno says, showing off his perfect Jersey dialect. "Didn't mean to startle you."

Only a few feet away, Dominic gives me a look like he's asking what's up with me. I feel the back of my neck, and sure enough there are goose bumps. On the way to the agency today, I couldn't shake the feeling that someone was following me.

"Sorry," I say in a rush. "I stayed up late last night watching a horror film. Did you need something?"

"No worries," Bruno says. "Mr. Whitman is ready to introduce you and Lachlan."

Right. Me. As in the British Broadway performer. No problem. I'm totally up for this.

The giant room full of nervous child performers and even more nervous stage moms, some dads too, returns to focus, and I work hard to regain the grip I'd had on my character. But right before leaving the hotel today, I got a text from Connie that has my mind elsewhere. And I keep reading it over and over. Even now, I glance at my phone once more, pretending to check the time.

CONNIE: no records of our guy at school. Ever.

ME: what do you mean ever???

CONNIE: I found student names but not his. Don't panic. Their security is top of the line. Maybe all the names are fake?

Maybe all the names are fake. I mean, ideally, she's right. Not only are the kids at Marshall Academy headed for top-secret careers, but they come from families already in that world. They have to be able to assure every kind of protection. But then why hadn't Miles told me this before? Or maybe when he gave me all those lectures about his school and honors program being confidential in a life-or-death way, the student security should have been common knowledge.

"You okay?" Dominic asks, appearing at my side.

I'm not too freaked out to appreciate his Australian accent. He's been practicing. A lot. But if I know my father, he's about to put Dominic—Lachlan—to the test, and I'm not sure he's prepared for whatever Dad throws at him.

"I'm fine," I lie, unable to be the bearer of bad news or worry him over what Connie revealed. "How about you? Hope you're ready for this..."

We were instructed to mingle among the crowd of auditioning families—apparently they've all been here before and this is a callback day. Dad exits the office with a smiling little boy in tights and sequins, along with his mother. The room quiets a bit when Dad stands beside us, preparing to speak.

"Hello, everyone, thank you for coming to the Johnson Whitman Agency callbacks today," he says. "Each of you showed us something special in your first audition, and no matter what happens, you should be proud to have impressed such incredible judges of talent." He turns to Dominic and me. "I'd like to introduce you to some friends of mine.

They've been covertly observing all of you today, getting to know you."

The eyes of at least a dozen children widen, fear in their eyes.

Dad offers the crowd a reassuring smile, then he points to the two of us. "Miss Emma Carrington and Lachlan Hudson. These remarkable young people have earned leading roles in Broadway productions through their hard work and dedication. Both have been in productions of *School of Rock*—Lachlan in Australia and Emma in London. They aren't here to criticize you but instead to inspire. Johnson Whitman Agency is proud to represent talent from all over the world, and we consider our clients practically family."

At that last part, my dad shoots me a warm smile. One filled with irony. He's so good at this even I'm eating up every word.

"They're also here to entertain you…" Dad's warm smile turns to a more malicious one, and cheers erupt from around the room. "They've even dressed the part."

Oh man, I guess I should have expected this. Dominic's face is completely blank. I think he's working on his poker face and this is the result. My uncle Milky heads to the piano, and my heart picks up speed. It's been a while since I've had to pull off a song-and-dance routine.

Dad turns his back to the crowd and gives us a look that clearly says, *You want in, pull this off.* "Let's hear that duet you two prepared."

"Duet?" Dominic whispers. "What duet? There's no duet on the cast album."

"Good, you've listened to the album." That's more than I can say for myself. I shove him toward the piano and raise my voice to speak to the room in my best British accent. "Actually, Lachlan fancies the spotlight more than me. He's got a solo ready for us."

I catch my father's eye, and his face is full of pride. I smile down at my shoes, knowing I've just earned his approval and trust. It's a win for the investigation but also for me, personally. Something I wish didn't still enjoy.

Dominic looks between Dad and me, and I know he knows this is it for him. He's not an idiot. He moves toward the piano, and I wait for him to make an excuse—he's coming down with a cold or required vocal rest, even licensing or copyright issues. But instead, I stand there and watch him transform. Like he picks up an invisible costume on the way to the piano, slips it on and becomes Lachlan Hudson, Broadway star. His back is straighter, his chin tilted up, his arms no longer dangling awkwardly at his sides but now swinging with purpose. And for a second I'm jealous, because I know how great it can feel to give yourself permission to become someone else. I just have to hope that I haven't created a monster.

He whispers instructions to Milky, and Dad whispers to me, "Think your boy's got the skills?"

"We're about to find out," I tell him, my eyes glued to my classmate. "But I definitely wouldn't peg him as the musical theater type."

"Yeah, I got that vibe, too," Dad says.

"And yet you turned him into an international Broadway star."

He says nothing. Doesn't need to. There is no room for the weak or incapable in any of my family's cons.

Dominic hops up onto the piano bench. "Feel free to sing along."

"The accent's not bad," Dad admits.

"But not as good as Bruno's Jersey accent," I say, hoping to get something out of him about this mysterious guy.

Dad just gives me a funny look and then turns his attention to the piano where Milky, instead of playing, is watching Dominic.

"It starts off on a dark stage. And then a beam of light," Dominic says, all dramatic, but not singing. "And you can see me and my guitar."

Everyone goes nuts, cheering. I don't know this musical very well, but I guess this is part of it. Eventually the performance does turn into song, but it's clear Dominic chose a song that isn't supposed to be sung well. I watch in awe as my very cool, very unmotivated classmate comes to life. A minute into the performance, he leaps off the piano bench and works the crowd, gaining some screaming fans.

I scan the crowd, keeping track of Dominic, but I'm quickly distracted by something. The mom who had been in the office with Dad minutes ago places a folder on the floor behind her so she can clap and cheer along with everyone else. She hadn't gone into the office with that folder. It was given to her.

"I'm gonna work the crowd," I tell Dad.

Weaving my way toward that folder, I clap and dance along with several of the kids, even offering catcalls to Dominic when he strips off his blazer and tosses it up into the crowd. I press my foot on top of the folder and slide it carefully toward me. I bend down, pretending to adjust my shoelace and open the cover of the folder, scanning the first page briefly.

And just like that, the entire con, my dad's big New York City operation, unravels into a plan that finally makes sense.

CHAPTER
17

"The payoff," I blurt out after Agent Sharp answers the phone. "I figured it out."

"You okay? You sound like you've been running."

That's because I just sprinted up four flights of stairs to make sure no one at the "agency" could hear me. Plus I'd been sitting on this information for two hours, dying for an excuse to sneak away and report to Sheldon and Sharp. "I'm fine."

"Good," he says, as if he'd been worried. "Now, what did you find out?"

"My original assessment was right: the agency definitely isn't collecting money or charging fees themselves—" I glance around the empty stairwell and then pause to listen. After deciding it's all clear, I continue. "But the information packets they're handing out recommend all these services—photographers for head shots, voice teachers, acting teachers, nutritionists, dance teachers…"

"And you think that if we looked into these places—"

"It'd be one big happy family reunion." I mean, it was kind of weird that the team for this con would include only my dad and Milky. I had a feeling the rest of them were somewhere in the wings.

"I don't know," Agent Sheldon says in the background. I must be on speakerphone. "That's a big leap to take with no guarantee these clients will call upon any of the recommended services. The agency doesn't require professional head shots or voice lessons?"

"If they required it, there would be no clients. Those people would see right through that kind of scam." I release a frustrated breath. Why does the FBI put agents in charge who clearly have no understanding of the art of human manipulation?

"I'm not sold on this theory," Sheldon says.

"Look, you want my dad because he's stolen tons from innocent people, right? But you're forgetting the most important part of his crimes."

"What's that?" Sheldon and Sharp ask together.

"Most of his income was earned by convincing innocent people to put the money right into his hand. Happily. It isn't black and white; there's skill and chance that weigh heavily on the outcome." Even straitlaced Miles wouldn't have needed me to spell this out for him.

"I'm still not convinced we're gonna get any payoff from this op," Sheldon says with a sigh. She's disappointed. She's also an idiot. "If we pull you now, we might still be able to use you again on the inside of the next job."

The next job? This is a long con. Could be a month, maybe even two, before there's anything worthy of an FBI investigation. And by then it might be too late for Mom's appeal or momentum might be lost. Besides, I'm right. I draw in a slow, deep breath, counting to five. *You will convince them, Ellie. You will find evidence.*

"The heart of the con lies in these outsourced services; you gotta trust me. You gave me this investigation because I'm the one who knows how my family operates." The hair on my arm stands up again, like it had earlier when I was so sure someone was following me, along with the goose bumps on my neck. "I gotta go. I'll text you the list from the packets and you can do some digging."

I tuck the phone away and try to slow my racing heart. No one is here. No one followed me. But despite the pep talk, I still don't want to take a chance, and instead of heading back down the stairwell, I open the door labeled FLOOR 26. I walk about twenty feet and hear the click of the door. I spin around like a paranoid idiot, but the hall is completely empty. I shake my head and return to walking down the hall in search of an elevator or another stairwell. I'm completely on edge, so when I hear the slightest shuffle of feet behind me and then feel the brush of fingertips on my shoulder, instincts kick in—well, instincts and a handful of self-defense lessons.

My phone falls to the ground with a *thunk* when I reach up to grip the arm of my assailant. I use momentum and the attacker's weight to send them sailing over me and onto the tile floor of the vacant hallway. I know I'm supposed to run now. A couple of months ago, when I'd finally performed this move for the first time, sending Miles flying over me onto the school wrestling mats, I'd leaned over him and asked, "What now? Stomp on his nuts? Assuming it's a male."

"Run," Miles had croaked, still fighting to get air into his lungs. When he'd sat up and could breathe normally, he explained in more detail. "Run and don't look back to see if you're being followed. That head start will save your life."

Clearly I have a death wish, because here I am hanging back long enough to see that same face looking up at me.

CHAPTER
18

For one tiny second I have the urge to press a heeled boot right into his gut for freaking me out like that, but I'm swimming in conflicting emotions and can't seem to pick one long enough to take any action. Or to move at all.

But then Miles opens his eyes and looks up at me, and I'm so relieved to see his perfect face that I drop down on the floor beside him. "Are you okay? I'm sorry, I didn't know—"

He nods, the wind still knocked out of him, and I stop rambling and just stare, blinking several times to make sure I'm not imagining things. I open my mouth to ask him what he's doing in New York City, but he recovers quickly, springs to his feet, and brings me with him. He scans both ends of the hallway and then tugs me into a dark alcove that serves as an entryway for a law office that apparently is closed on Sundays.

Out of harm's way and watchful eyes, and with both of us upright, I look him over, unable to turn off my investigator mode. First thing I notice is that the sling is gone. His hair is longer than the last time I saw him, hanging slightly over his ears, and brushing his collar in the back—a clear violation of the Marshall Academy dress code. He's wearing dark jeans, a dark-gray shirt, and a navy ski jacket. The hair definitely lacks the military schoolboy vibe, and the outfit screams guy-who-might-be-hiding-a-black-ski-mask-in-one-of-those-pockets.

But Miles moves one step closer to me, and all I can see is blue. Light blue surrounding dark pupils. His hands land on my arms, and my insides warm. I shake my head, refocusing. "You were following me earlier, weren't you?"

Miles nods, takes another step closer. "I can't believe you did that move so well. I don't know whether to be offended or proud."

"You'll be offended tomorrow when the bruises show up." My heart is still climbing back down from my throat, my brain still attempting to process the fact that a minute or two ago I was on the phone with Sharp and Sheldon, with no idea if Miles was even alive, and now... As much as I want to play it cool, I can't. One second, I'm looking at those blue eyes that have been absent from my life since our December tenth Christmas dinner, and then I'm throwing my arms around his neck and squeezing way too tight to be cool and casual.

"You're okay," I say stupidly, and then I press my face into his T-shirt collar, inhaling. He even smells like Miles. Like the sweatshirt I'd borrowed from him a while back and never returned. I jerk back suddenly, just enough to see his face. "You are okay, right? No one is after you or—"

He lays a hand on my cheek, his thumb gliding over my skin. "I forgot how pretty you are. Forgot how much I love the sound of your voice."

I'm not too far gone to notice his lack of answer. "What are you doing here?"

"Looking for you," he says simply, like I should have known this. "I know my parents called you last week. I didn't show up last Sunday like we'd planned. Then I heard Aidan called my school. Dominic's been texting nonstop. I figured you must be..."

With his face only a couple of inches from mine, Miles

seems to forget his words, and soon his mouth is on mine. And we're kissing like two starving people unable to articulate why or even how our previously hot-and-cold relationship had grown warmer and heavier despite the long break. His arms envelop me, and my hands slip inside his jacket, tugging him closer. And for a moment—just a short moment of weakness—I want to be done with this. Done spying on my dad, done worrying about my mom, done feeling guilty. I just want to be a girl making out with her boyfriend. If I could have that, I might even consider Miles's offer from a month ago of running away with him to military school.

But then I remember that Miles is clearly not at military school and we are clearly not a regular teenage couple.

With great effort, I release my hold on him and gently nudge some space between us. "I have to go. I left my—"

"What are you doing here?" he asks, his face displaying both disappointment and concern, which tells me he knows this is more than a school field trip for me. "That was supposed to be my first question, but then I"—he clears his throat—"got sidetracked."

There's no reason I can't trust him with this information, and keeping details about my family nearly split us apart for good. But I did tell him about my past and he still wanted to be with me. After I promised him I was done with that life. I keep my gaze focused on his chest, unable to look right at him. "You know how my mom is in prison?"

Miles's jaw tightens, but he nods. "I remember."

I give him the forty-five-second version of how I tangled myself into this undercover operation, and he listens without interruption until I'm finished. "Ellie, you're putting yourself in the worst position possible. You can't trust these FBI agents. They only care about catching the bad guys. You sure as hell can't trust your dad. It's a lose-lose situation."

The nerves, the fear that bubbles up in me upon hearing Miles's assessment, is a testament to how much I must value his opinion. That scares me even more than his warning. "My family is up to something bad, really bad. Clearly the FBI is too incompetent to figure it out, so I have to get to the bottom of this. I can't just walk away knowing what I know."

I'm prepared for him to argue, to toss more logic at me, but something I said changed the game. He stares at me, silent for a long moment, and then says, "Okay."

My forehead wrinkles. "Okay?"

"I get it." His kind eyes fill with warmth. "I'll do whatever I can to help you."

Before I can ask how or why he gets it after telling me I was in the middle of a losing game, Miles pats the vibrating phone in his pocket and attempts to hide the panicked look that has just taken over his face. "I have to go."

"That was my line." I hear footsteps in the distance, from the stairwell by the sound of it, and I look at Miles and raise my eyebrows. Did he know someone was coming? "How did you—"

He interrupts me by pressing a kiss to my lips, and I'm immediately reminded of him kissing me like this after we'd been locked in that dungeon in the woods and Jack and his gang of assassins gone wrong had just decided it was okay to kill us. He pulls away and whispers, "Be careful, Ellie. Promise?"

What happened to "call me if you need anything"? Does that mean I won't be able to call him? But I don't get to ask because Miles jams a key into the door of the law office, slips inside, and seconds later, he's on a ledge outside more than two dozen stories above a very busy street. *Don't go out there. Don't even look out there.*

Miles is clearly running from something—or someone— otherwise he would have used the stairs and the front doors like a sane person. If I go after him, I could ruin his hiding efforts. And I've worked hard to not be that girl who wouldn't take his word and had to dig up everything for herself. I'd put Miles and his parents at risk with some of the stunts I pulled, and I won't do that again. I've watched Miles Spider-Man climb his way up to our apartment balcony in mere seconds; he knows what he's doing.

I step out into the hall just as the door to the stairwell opens. Bruno is moving quickly like a man on a mission but stops when he sees me.

"Hey, Ellie…" He glances over my shoulder then back at my face. "There you are. I was looking everywhere. The boss needs you downstairs."

He may have been looking everywhere, but clearly it wasn't me he wanted to find. "Sorry, I've been trying to find a drinking fountain, but no luck. At least not on floors twenty-three through twenty-six. And now I really need a drink—all those stairs."

Bruno points a thumb back at the stairwell. "Twenty-seven has a soda machine."

"See? Vigilance does pay off." I flash him a grin. "I was almost there."

"Sure does," he says. "I'm gonna visit the little boys' room. I'll see you back at the agency in a few."

We part ways, and I walk as quietly as possible so I can study his pace. Either Bruno really needs to relieve himself or he's trying to catch up to someone who clearly wants to get away. Maybe someone who climbed out a window and walked onto a ledge twenty-six stories up just to get away.

Someone like Miles Beckett.

CHAPTER
19

"**W**hat if the teenage FBI program has MB out doing fieldwork again?" Dominic says.

I nearly drop the plate in my hands. A woman across from us in the hotel breakfast buffet line gives us both a strange look. I busy myself piling eggs onto the plate. "What program? And MB? No idea who you're talking about."

Dominic looks like he's dying to roll his eyes but doesn't. I told him about seeing Miles. I had to tell someone, and he'd been so worried. I also told him Miles was acting strange, but we've never talked about why "MB" was at Holden last semester outside of hunting Simon's killer.

"I know about the honors program at Marshall Academy." Dominic reaches around me for a doughnut, putting us closer, our heads nearly touching, and he lowers his voice. "And I know about his secret spy parents."

"Secret spy is redundant." I shuffle farther down the buffet line and scoop some fruit onto my plate. I have no idea where he got this information from, but I know I can't confirm it. I won't be the one to do that. "All I know is that the Becketts have government jobs. Like DMV workers do or the IRS."

"That night after the cabin in the woods…?" Dominic

prompts, and I nod him on. "I went to see MB at the hospital. I was pissed off because I thought he was a cop or a Fed. I told him shit. Personal shit. You know?"

"Yeah, I know." But really, for Miles and me it was the reverse. It was me who had been let into Miles's life, offering little in return until only recently.

"So he told me why he was at Holden." Dominic points to an empty table with two chairs, and we head that way. "Around three in the morning that same night, MB's dad showed up in my room, freaked me the fuck out, and gave me the talk about being in the circle. Did you get that talk, too? I got the feeling it was a regular thing for them."

"Uh...yeah." My talk was more like a weekend vacation full of home-cooked meals and unconditional kindness, but I guess it had its freaky moments.

Dominic slides into the seat across from mine and unrolls his silverware. "What do you think? Could he be on an assignment?"

"I don't know what he's doing, but I do know one important thing."

"What's that?"

I sigh before saying, "If he needs us to know what he's doing, he'll tell us. Otherwise try to put it out of your head. Digging could get him hurt, especially if he's undercover."

Dominic gives me a bewildered look. "That is so not an Ellie Ames move. Or are you and MB playing me?"

"In the future I plan to avoid letting anyone else earn my trust. The ethical dilemmas are a nightmare."

I'm about to take a bite of my eggs, but Harper just texted me a picture, and I set my fork down so I can open it.

"Report cards are in," I tell Dominic, and then I lean down to scrutinize my grades in true honor-student fashion with butterflies in my stomach and all my second-guessing during final exams replaying.

```
AMERICAN LIT A+
GERMAN, AP A+
US HISTORY A+
PHYSICS, HONORS A
PHYSICS LAB A+
ALGEBRA 2 A-
PHYSICAL EDUC PASS
UNWEIGHTED GPA 4.61
JUNIOR CLASS RANK 7/132
```

"Oh my God," I practically scream, and then I ignore Dominic's efforts to hush me. "Oh my freakin' God. How did I pull off an A minus in algebra? That final was impossible, and I had a B plus going into it."

It becomes clear how loud I'm being when people nearby halt their conversation to look over at us. I drop my phone onto my lap and look up at Dominic. "So how about you? Did you do okay? I know finals week was crazy, and we missed the first review day, but—"

Dominic has suddenly become very interested in his breakfast. His eyes are focused downward, onto his plate, and he shoves in bite after bite of pancakes.

I knew Dominic wasn't a stellar student, but he looks like someone who bombed finals. "Hey," I say, getting his attention. "You did good yesterday. With my dad and with the Australian accent, and your performance."

He looks up. "Yeah?"

I nod. "Definitely."

"Tell anyone about that performance and..." He points a bite of pancake at me threateningly.

"Right." I roll my eyes. "Because that would be easy to explain."

Justice approaches our table with Chantel and Jacob trailing behind her. "Ellie, we need your help."

"Letters of recommendation? Embellished résumé? Compromising photos of your ex?" I guess because Dominic's panhandling of my skills to get me on this trip has led to even more classmates asking me to do their dirty work, much of which I have to turn down for ethical reasons. "I'm not writing anyone's Ellis Island Ancestry paper. I had a hard enough time with mine. And you guys...if your ancestors are from Virginia...well, we know how they paid for labor in the eighteenth and nineteenth centuries. Even I can't find an honorable spin on *that* history."

Justice points an accusing finger at me. "Someone's been listening to *Hamilton*."

"Most of my ancestors were persecuted for being Jewish," Jacob says.

I pause to look him over. "Okay, I'll write *your* paper. Or better yet, you write it and I'll read it and probably learn something new."

"Some of my ancestors were Cherokee Indians," Chantel declares.

I lift an eyebrow. "You know that for sure? Might want to look into it before you go public. Hate to see you in an Elizabeth Warren situation."

Chantel opens her mouth to argue, but Justice cuts in. "We don't need anything like that. Just report card gossip. Mary Henley bombed fall semester apparently and fell from number six to fifteen. I'm still number nine. We know one through six, but we're missing seven and eight."

"And someone said we should ask you," Jacob adds.

"Oh yeah?" I look at them and realize my reaction to report card time was nothing compared to my classmates. I guess eleven or twelve years of high-achieving prep-school brainwashing will do that. "Who told you to ask me?"

"Ms. Geist," Jacob says.

Justice adds, "And Lance."

"But seriously, can they even rank you?" Chantel asks all snooty. "You haven't been here very long. You only have two semesters—"

"Two semesters is the minimum required to be ranked at Holden," Jacob tells her, and she sends a glare that has him snapping his mouth shut.

"Oh please, that's bullshit," Justice says to Chantel. "Both of us would be ranked much worse if we only counted this semester's grades. Junior year is hard."

Finally the arguments have quieted, and now three pairs of eyes stare at me, waiting. All the report card talk must have gotten to Dominic, because he snatches the phone from my lap—the screen is still on—glances at the picture, and then hands it back to me.

"She's number seven." He pushes his chair back and stands. "Planning to be late for the college reception?"

Justice looks at her cell. "Oh shit, we only have one minute."

While she tugs me from my chair by the uniform sweater, I glance longingly at my plate of breakfast. I've only taken two bites. She follows my gaze and then, with a sigh, snatches the muffin from Dominic's plate and sets it in my hand. The other three are ahead of us, making their way through the hotel lobby and toward one of the ballrooms. I spot Agent Sharp leaning against the front desk, an opened newspaper concealing his face.

I turn away from Sharp and peel the wrapper off my muffin. All these roles I'm playing have majorly cut into my meal times, and I woke up starving this morning and really looking forward to trying out the all-you-can-eat feature of the hotel buffet.

"Who are you going to talk to first?" Justice asks. "I'm thinking Brown and then maybe Columbia…"

I tune her out when I get a look at the ballroom. The

center of the room is clear this morning, and instead of round tables, rectangular ones line the room. The tables are decorated with trifold display boards and brochures.

We walk past a booth for Duke University, and Justice wrinkles her nose. "Gross. Ivy League wannabes."

I guess, when I studied today's itinerary, I hadn't thought about what "Reception with Universities" might mean.

"Ellie!" Mr. Lance says, appearing out of nowhere. "I have someone I want you to meet."

Something that looks a lot like envy crosses Justice's face, but she conceals it quickly. "I'll see you in a bit. I'm gonna find Columbia. My dad knows the rep here, and I promised him I'd introduce myself."

"Yeah, sure," I tell her, but a stab of guilt hits me. I don't deserve to be Mr. Lance's favorite student. I don't even know how I got this part. I mean, yeah, I'm good at sucking up, but so are most of the students at Holden. In fact I've picked up a few ideas from my classmates.

Mr. Lance leads me to the Brown University booth. The man seated behind the table straightens in his chair and holds out a hand. "Eleanor Ames, correct?" *Ames. Correct.* I shake his hand, feeling like a major poser. "I work in admissions at Brown. Your teacher and I go way back. I heard you might have an interest in our summer enrichment program?"

"Did you?" I glance at my English teacher, who is trying his best to look innocent. "Enriching summers are always a goal of mine."

"Actually," Mr. Lance says, "I was hoping you could sell her on the program. Ellie is a rare Holden student without an educational consultant to force-feed her program information."

The admissions guy lifts an eyebrow, a hint of interest on his face. "Scholarship student?"

"Financial aid," I clarify, not sure if there's a difference. I glance around at my classmates, and I'm suddenly aware of how much I blend in today. All of us are always in uniform, but today, Chantel, Justice, and I emerged from our hotel room accidentally having chosen the same white oxford button-down and navy sweater-vest combo. I can't imagine being in this guy's job in admissions and having to choose from a pool of seemingly identical students.

"Your grades are good?" the guy asks me.

"She's ranked seventh at Holden," Mr. Lance says. "Great practice SAT score. But you know me, I only recommend students who are a great fit for Brown."

"Thirty-two students recommended by your English teacher," the guy says. "You know how many were admitted?"

I shake my head.

"All of them." The guy smiles and points to the empty chair in front of the table, and I sit like an obedient honor student. "So…what do you know about Brown?"

I glance up at the symbol on the display above his head. "It's part of the Ivy League."

"True," he says. "But we're also the only Ivy League school with a completely open curriculum. No required courses, you choose what you want to study, you can even choose whether or not you want to be graded on your work."

"Well that doesn't sound like my mental picture of college at all," I blurt out, then add, truthfully, "It sounds better."

"Yes, if you're the right type of student. Independent learners are what we seek. Not all students can handle the freedom Brown offers."

I think about this for a moment. "Independent learning has definitely been a large part of my education." It'd have to be, because lock picking and pickpocketing aren't exactly part of the Common Core Standards, certainly not a part of Holden curriculum.

"Ellie," I hear whispered from somewhere to my right.

I glance sideways for a brief moment and draw in a quick breath when I see Oscar carefully peering through a staff door off the side of the ballroom.

Oh damn, I had a feeling he'd pop up somewhere.

"Ellie," he hisses again.

This time Lance notices and gives me an expectant look. "Friend of yours?"

I laugh, hiding the nerves. "He's from the Belton Academy. Did you know they're on a field trip here, too? Justice and I met some of them in the workout room yesterday." I pull something out of my skirt pocket. "I promised to loan him my laminated map of the subways. He's taking his girlfriend to lunch today during their free time."

Lance's forehead wrinkles, probably due to my thousand-words-a-minute speech. "Belton Academy? Not sure I've heard of them."

"It's in Russia," I say quickly. I turn to the admissions guy. "Excuse me for a minute."

On my way to the door Oscar's hiding behind, I bump into Dominic. I yank the sleeve of his blazer and lead him out of the ballroom.

"I just saw Oscar," I whisper to him. But there's no need to tell Dominic. Oscar's right outside the door. Probably with Agent Sharp following his every move.

"Dude, why do you keep blowing our covers?" Dominic asks him before I get a chance.

Oscar is wide-eyed and worried, his blond hair sticking up in every direction. His clothes are dirty. "Your dad told me to keep an eye on you—"

"Did he?" So much for family trust. Whatever. It's not like I trust *him*. Why should I expect trust in return? "And how long have you been keeping an eye on me, Oscar?"

"Just since you got here. He booked me a room on your floor."

"You've been here for a week?" Dominic says.

"Forget that, okay?" Oscar releases a frustrated groan. "I'm not the one you should be worried about. Someone else is following both of you." He raises his arm, and I realize he's holding a jacket. The jacket Miles was wearing yesterday. "I finally got him and now I don't know what to do with—"

Got him? My family doesn't do violence, but for a moment I imagine Miles's body lying somewhere and—

"Where is he?" I say before my imagination gets carried away.

"Locked him in my room," Oscar tells me, looking even more panicked.

I look at Dominic, trying to send him a message telepathically. *It's MB*. I'm not sure if he gets the message or not, but he points to the elevator. "Show us."

CHAPTER
20

Oscar, who doesn't usually handle confrontations well, looks frazzled, but he nods immediately, agreeing to Dominic's request. Inside the elevator, I take Dominic's hand, holding it like a proper girlfriend. When Oscar turns to push the button, I trace the letters MB inside Dominic's palm. His eyes widen just a smidgen, and then he offers the smallest nod. Message delivered.

But when we step inside Oscar's room and he moves the furniture he'd used to block the bedroom and bathroom doors, there's no one tied up on the bed as I'd imagined Miles would be. My gaze shifts to the window, and sure enough it's open a crack. I guess I'm not surprised that window escapes have become Miles's signature move.

"Oh no, oh no." Oscar spins in a circle, his hands resting on his head. "He's gone. Oh shit, this is bad—"

"Maybe if we knew what he looked like we could keep an eye out for him," Dominic says. "Did you get a picture?"

"No, goddammit!" Oscar tugs a hand through his hair, practically yanking it out. "I swear that guy is after Ellie, and if he's one of Bruno's thugs—"

"What thugs?" Dominic asks. He rests a hand on Oscar's

shoulder. "Sit down, man. Relax. Let's figure this out together."

"Bruno? The guy who's working for my dad?" I ask.

Oscar looks up at me, desperation in his eyes. "He's bad news, Ellie. I tried to tell you."

I'm listening to this bit of news about the mysterious Bruno, I really am, but my immediate concern is with the guy who clearly just climbed out the window of this room. Dominic proves to be a mind reader because he says, "Give Ellie that jacket. She can take it down to the desk and see if the hotel staff know of any guests wearing that coat."

"Great idea," I say, grabbing the jacket from Oscar.

When I'm exiting the room, I hear Dominic say in a pacifying voice, "Start at the beginning, and tell me everything about this guy."

I race down the hall and swipe the key card to my room. I can't believe Oscar's been here a freakin' week and I didn't notice. The guy's got invisibility skills, that's for sure. Or I'm slipping. Our room and a few beside us all have balconies, so I head straight for the sliding door and nearly have a heart attack when I spot Miles standing on the balcony two rooms down. I poke my head outside and wave to him. Seconds later he's standing on the carpet right in front of my duffel bag. I quickly close the door, shivering from only seconds of exposure to the January wind chill. Having lost his jacket wrestling Oscar, Miles is wearing only a T-shirt and jeans. His nose is red and his hands are redder, dry, the skin cracking.

"How long were you out there?"

He does his best to look completely fine. "An hour, maybe more."

"Jesus," I mutter, then reach for the blanket I left lying on the couch. I toss it over his shoulders and pull the edges together in front of him. I take his freezing hands and try to cover them with my warmer ones.

Miles slides his hands from mine, opens the blanket, and wraps it around both of us. He lays his cold cheek against mine. "You know this would work even better with all our clothes off."

Despite all the panic of the last few minutes, I laugh. Then his cold hand touches my cheek, and I get right back to business. "Come on, you gotta put your hands in warm water before you get frostbite. I'll make some hot tea."

After a few minutes underwater, his hands look better but still chapped and showing early signs of blisters. I force him onto the couch, hand him a cup of tea, and then I dig through Justice's and Chantel's bathroom supplies until I find a bottle of lotion. Miles wrinkles his nose at it. "It smells like flowers."

"It's the best I could do." I take one of his hands and work gobs of pink lotion into it.

He sits perfectly still, watching me. "So the blond guy who locked me up? He's family?"

"Sort of," I say, moving onto his other hand. "My parents have always called him my cousin."

"Does your family usually marry cousins?"

I give him a bewildered look and release his hand. "Um, no."

"He told me you and he were supposed to get married."

The lotion slips through my hand and falls to the floor. "What?"

"Then your mom went to jail and everything was ruined." Miles reaches for the cup of tea now that his hands are good and slippery. "He was pacing the room and kept saying everything was ruined and he couldn't protect you and your dad was gonna get us all in trouble. I felt sorry for the guy. He's great at tailing a suspect but definitely no interrogator."

"He said we were getting married?" I ask again. I mean what the hell? "Seriously?"

"He used the word 'betrothed.'" Miles takes a sip of his

tea, hiding behind the paper cup, but I still catch that hint of amusement on his face. "He seems like quite a catch."

"He's delusional," I conclude. "A complete nutcase."

"He did say he had planned on waiting until you turned eighteen to propose," Miles adds. "Seems logical to me, hardly the words of an insane man."

I suppress a shudder and then force my thoughts away from this appalling bit of news. "You can't keep roaming around this hotel. The FBI agents are on patrol, plus Holden students will recognize you, and obviously Oscar will."

"You're right." He touches a finger to my lips, quieting me. "But I'm here now."

Slowly I move his finger from my mouth and lean in to kiss him. No one is better at distracting me with kisses than Miles. I'm lost in it, loving the way his hands feel on my skin, his lips on my neck, but somewhere in the back of my head a voice keeps asking, *What is this? What are we doing? Is this what it means to be in a relationship with Miles? Stolen kisses at random times with no warning or idea of when we'll see each other again?* After a lifetime of indefinites, I'm kind of over that thrill.

The questions get to me and I pull away, putting space between us.

"What's wrong?" He reaches a hand out to touch my face, but I slide back. "Ellie?"

"Why are we meeting like this? With you hanging out a window nearly freezing to death." I shake my head, hoping to remove those images from my memory. "Why can't you just call me? Or tell me where you're staying and I'll come there during my free time. It's gotta be safer than you showing up here or at the building where my dad's operation—"

"I can't do that," he says, painfully, truthfully.

"What if there's an emergency? What if I need your help? You said to call you if I needed anything, but you've been off the grid. After what happened with Jack and Rider back in November, I get a little freaked out when you're nowhere to be found." *Dial it back, Ellie. You're one step away from holding him captive in your hotel room.* "And I'm not the only one worried. Dominic has been a mess; he's stuck on the fact that he didn't help me look for you at the party after Jack had taken you."

"Did you tell him you saw me yesterday?" Miles asks in a tone that is very different from the one he used to suggest we get naked for warmth. I recognize this voice from last semester when he and I were still on the fence about trusting each other.

"Yeah, I told him, and he also knows Oscar found you today."

"Then everything is fine," Miles states, like he's just solved a problem.

"It's not fine. Nothing is fine." I stand up, needing to move. "The truth about Simon's death being a murder and not suicide is out in the open now. Aidan's name was cleared. Jack is dead, the St Felicity's people took care of the other dudes who helped kidnap us."

Miles shoves the blanket off his legs. "What's your point, Ellie?"

"My point is"—I spin to face him—"who the hell are you running from?"

"Besides your cousin?"

I cross my arms over my chest. "Why did your parents ask me to erase you from Holden's school records?"

"You already know the honors program is top secret." His tone is no longer defensive. It's full of exasperation.

"Oh, I see. It's normal procedure. So Marshall Academy takes no responsibility for protecting its students? They expect all the parents to have access codes to hack into a system and make sure their kid is lifted from the records?"

"My parents are extra cautious. Understandable considering their jobs," he says.

"Who are you running from, Miles?" I ask again, knowing this may put us at a standstill.

We stare at each other for several long moments, and I know that he's not going to tell me. And I'm not going to offer an ultimatum, but we both know I'm also not going to let things continue like this. "Just tell me if I should be worried, if you're running from someone involved in Simon's death. If I'm in danger."

He stands and steps out in front of the coffee table. "If you stay away from your dad, then there's no danger."

"That doesn't even make sense!" I lift my hands, frustrated. "My dad is a lot of crappy things, but dangerous isn't one of them. I've never even heard him so much as utter a threat, let alone—"

Someone knocks softly on the door, stopping me. I glance at Miles and then rush over to the peephole. If it's housekeeping, they'll barge right in if no one says anything. That happened to me yesterday. Dominic is standing outside the door, his head shifting left and right, checking for watchful eyes. And he's alone. No Oscar. I open the door just enough for him to slip through and then I lock it again and put the chain on.

"Okay, Oscar is gone for a while. He went to look for your dad—" Dominic spots Miles and a grin spreads across his face. "Dude, where the hell have you been?"

I give Miles a pointed look. "Great question."

"Oh, you know, around," Miles says with an air of dismissal.

It's probably my fault Dominic is fine with this answer; I'm the one who gave the lecture at breakfast stating that Miles will tell us what he's up to if he needs us to know and otherwise to stay out of it.

"Oscar was seriously going batshit over the so-called thugs Bruno is in with," Dominic tells me. "I thought he was just confused or paranoid, but then he mentioned the Zanettis. He doesn't mean Zanetti as in Loredo Zanetti, right?"

Dominic waits for me to answer, but I shrug. "Who is Loredo Zanetti?"

"Seriously?" Dominic asks, like he doesn't believe me. He glances over at Miles.

"He's a mobster." Miles's expression is completely blank when he says this, which I've learned is what he looks like when he's just been dropped a giant bomb. He turns to Dominic. "Are you sure he said Zanetti? And not Nanzetti or Zenniti? Jacob Nanzetti is listed in the FBI database as a suspect in an ongoing investigation of several mortgage recovery scams."

"It was definitely Zanetti," Dominic says firmly. "He even went on about them being Jersey scum. The Zanettis own restaurants in Jersey, right?"

Okay, so maybe Bruno's Jersey dialect is real.

Miles nods slowly. He looks like he's far away from here, putting something together inside his head. "I still have some FBI database privileges. Let me look into it."

"Thanks, man." Dominic gives his shoulder a squeeze like they're old buddies, like Miles is working with us not running from us. "As much as I'd love to hang out, you should probably take advantage of Ellie's crazy cousin being out and escape while you can."

"Yeah, good idea." Miles moves toward the door, and it takes everything in me to not call him back. He turns to look at me for a beat before opening the door. He holds my gaze. "If you need me, text me, okay?"

My heart swells even though it's just a tiny olive branch. It's something. But I can tell he means if I need him, like *kidnapped and held captive* kind of need. Not the *I miss hearing your voice* need. I don't know if that's the hero complex speaking, especially now that mobsters were dropped into the conversation, or the guy who is supposed to be my boyfriend.

"Hey," Dominic says, lifting the jacket from the floor. "Don't forget this. It's fucking frigid outside."

"Yeah, I know," Miles says, rubbing his raw hands together. "But I'll get a new one. I don't want that to be an identifier."

This time he exits out the door like a regular person, and I can almost fool myself into thinking he can come back this way anytime. But I know he won't. Today was too close of a call, and I left him with mixed signals.

"So he's really okay." Dominic plops down onto the couch. "What are we going to do about these Zanettis?"

"It doesn't even make sense," I argue, even though my head is still stuck thinking about Miles. "My dad is stealing money from the stage moms peddling their kids via tap-dancing skills—where exactly do mobsters fit into this?"

"Beats me," Dominic says. "But I think you gotta ask the boss man."

"Yeah, maybe." I pick up my phone from the coffee table and see that I have a missed text. "Speak of the devil."

HAYES: Lunch? On me

I show the message to Dominic and he nods. "Go. I'll cover for you with Lance and Geist."

We both quiet at the sound of a key card being swiped on the other side of the door. Seconds later Justice walks in, a huge stack of brochures in her arms. "Why did I just see Miles Beckett in this hotel?"

"Uh…" Dominic starts.

"And why did he smell like my lotion?" Justice shakes her head. "Actually, don't answer that second question. Ignorance is bliss."

"He may have arranged a visit to NYU that coordinates with the Holden trip," I say.

She gives me a bewildered look. "Why didn't you just tell me? I could have helped you sneak away earlier or made sure you had some time alone."

"I don't know, I mean, he skipped the school tour to come here, so…" I don't know what else to say to save this. "You could cover for me this afternoon? So I can meet him for lunch."

"Done." She walks toward the bedroom. "I need a power nap. College talk is exhausting. Wake me up in thirty?"

When the door to the bedroom she and Chantel are sharing closes, Dominic leans his head back and sighs. "God, how do you do this shit all the time? I'm on the verge of a dozen nervous breakdowns."

I laugh, mostly because he looks fine, not ready to crack at all. "You just sit there in your stressed-out state, and I'll go ask my dad if he's made friends with any mobsters lately."

"Have fun with that."

I leave Dominic in my room and head back down to the ballroom so I can make an appearance before taking off to meet my dad. He and I definitely have a few things to talk about.

CHAPTER
21

Dad hands me a waffle cone filled with vanilla soft serve topped with rainbow sprinkles. "Hope this is still your favorite."

"It'll do." I snatch a spoon from the counter of a taco stand near one of the entrances at Chelsea Market. At least he paid for the ice cream. I turned down lunch in a sit-down restaurant for fear of Dad's famous dine-and-ditch move. Old classics hold a special place in his heart, so he says. "I ran into Oscar today."

"Really? Where?" Dad asks, playing dumb. He turns his back on the doors leading outside. "Let's walk through and look at everything. I'm not keen on eating ice cream outside today."

I glance at his cone—chocolate and vanilla swirl with chocolate sprinkles. "Mom's favorite," I say, and he nods but adds nothing else. "I saw Oscar at the DoubleTree at Times Square. I'm staying there with some friends. Apparently he is, too."

"Huh."

I jab my elbow into his side. "Come on, I know you sent him there."

"I figured you knew, considering Oscar told me you knew." He snatches napkins from *The Fat Witch Bakery* and hands me one. "I'm just surprised that you caught him. Oscar doesn't get caught."

"He was trying to get my attention and honestly seemed really freaked out. He's convinced you're working with a family of New Jersey mobsters."

Dad stares straight ahead, continues to stroll through the center of a long strip of inside shops and eateries. His expression is blank, reminding me so much of Miles when he has lots to talk about but won't. "You've been hanging around for a few days now; what do you think about Oscar's claim?"

"What do I think?" *I think you look too comfortable for someone whose wife is locked in prison for the next decade. I think I want to know how you make it look so easy to forget her.* "It doesn't make sense—mobsters and child talent agencies? Not exactly a swirl-together pair."

My dad raises his waffle cone. "Nice metaphor. Are you keeping up with your literature quota?"

Literature quota. That's my family's code for read just enough of the important books to have some insight to spit back at the right moment. I think that's why I like Mr. Lance so much. He lets us read the whole book.

"Thumbed through Plato's *Republic* last night, a little Voltaire this morning. I'm debating between Dickens and Poe for this evening's reading," I say, unable to keep the bite from my tone. "But first I'm gonna spend some time analyzing why you won't answer my question about working with mobsters."

"Personally, I'd go with Poe," Dad says. "But stick with the short stories. His poetry sucks."

My stomach twists. He's dodging the question. Maybe he really is working with the mafia? And maybe my dad isn't the only one in over his head. Feeling a little sick, I toss my waffle cone into a garbage can.

Dad stops me, rests a hand on my shoulder, and for a moment he's that guy in the car promising his eight-year-old daughter that yes, he tricks people for a living, but she is the exception to this rule. "Look, Ellie, it's not what you think."

"Boss man! There you are," a deep voice says from behind me.

A grin spreads over Dad's face, and when I turn to see who it is, I'm grinning, too, despite trying to fight it. The old man standing in front of me has the same mischievous face, wild gray hair, and slight limp to his walk as he approaches us. "Grandpa Barney!"

Okay, so I don't hate *everyone* in my family.

Dad hugs the man who has always been like a father to him. "I thought you got lost in Jersey or one of the Carolinas."

"This place is definitely not my speed," Grandpa Barney says, then he turns to me and does this dramatic blinking move. "Wait a minute…this isn't…it couldn't be *our* Eleanor?"

"She just popped up in the city a few days ago," Dad tells him. "Shocked the hell out of me, too."

"I'm too old to have hell shocked out of me, unfortunately," Barney says.

I roll my eyes. "You're not old." I glance behind him, looking for more family members. "Where's Sally?"

Dad's careful front wavers a bit. He glances at Barney, who shakes his head ever so slightly. Sally is Barney's second or third wife, I'm not sure which. Doesn't matter, because she's the best of all of them. She took care of Harper and me when we were younger, whenever both our parents were off working a longer con.

"Sally's not feeling her best right now. Long trip will do that. She's resting back at the hotel," Barney says. "Now, come here and let me get a good look at you."

I want to ask more, but it's obvious that I'm not supposed to. When I'm standing much closer to Grandpa Barney, it's also obvious this past year has aged him. More lines crease his already wrinkled face, and his shoulders seem to be hunched farther forward. He rests his hands on my biceps and gives them a squeeze, and I'm relieved that his strong grip is still intact. "I had a feeling your pops would lure you back to us. Eleven months of planning this con, surely he'd thought up a part for his little girl."

"Oh, he definitely has a part for me," I say, forcing a smile. But I don't elaborate, because *eleven months* rolls around in my head, taking up space. Eleven months. Right around the time the FBI hauled my mom away to prison. She was gone, and he just went right back to planning the next big job for my family? What kind of person does that?

I turn my back on Dad and face Barney. "I take it he has a part for you, too?"

"You know me, always the star of the show." Barney taps a fist to his chest. "At least until the day this heart stops ticking."

If I was feeling sick before, it's nothing compared to right now. And faking calm just isn't gonna happen. An escape plan is my only option. I glance at my phone. "I have to go."

Barney looks disappointed, even opens his mouth to argue or stop me, but I give his shoulder a squeeze and say, "It was good to see you. Tell Sally I said hello," before walking away and hunting down the nearest exit.

I can't shake the image of Barney and his frail old body limping around in the presence of Bruno and these Zanetti mafia creeps. Why would Dad make him come all this way, especially if Sally is sick, to help with a con that potentially involves dangerous mobsters? He's a selfish freakin' asshole, that's why.

I'm fuming and walking so fast that I barely notice the cold outside. But before I can get on the subway, a hand grips my shoulder, stopping me. I spin around and face my dad, who is still good-looking and fit but who seems a little winded from chasing after me.

"What was that about?" he demands. "You've got Barney all worried now."

"I've got Barney worried?" I repeat. "I'm not the one in business with the mafia. What the hell are you thinking, putting an old man in danger for a con? Or do you even care? No wonder Oscar came to find me. You're way too far in junkie mode to see the shit-hole you've dug for yourself and everyone else on your team."

Dad glances around, his face tense, his hands balled up. "Sally's in the hospital. Cancer. Bruno's family is helping her get treatment here for free."

The news hits like a punch to the gut, but I can't dismiss the fact that my dad has again ignored my questions. "I see," I tell him, nodding. "That's why you're deviating from the way our family always does things? No weapons, no violence, no confrontation—isn't that what you've told me a million times?"

"What weapons? Have you seen any weapons?"

"News flash, Dad. Mobsters carry weapons. It's what they do," I snap. "So that's what this con is all about? Helping Sally. She's been sick for eleven months, I assume? You're taking all these risks for her and Barney?"

"Not exactly," he admits. "The Sally part was an added bonus."

"Yeah, I figured." The cold wind whips against my heated face. I tilt my head upward, at the clouded gray sky. Maybe I can't do this. Maybe leaving really was the best thing I've ever done. But what about Mom... "What about Mom?" I say out loud. "Have you even thought about her? Your head is so far up your ass with this con it's like she doesn't even exist."

"At least I stuck around!" Dad thunders, getting a few short glances from New Yorkers walking briskly past us. "You couldn't deal with what happened, I get that, but you haven't been here with our family. You didn't see what it was like after—you took off like you were the only one broken up over what happened."

He definitely knows how to hit where it hurts the most. Right in my guilty gut. I raise a hand to stop him. "I don't owe you an explanation."

"What about tomorrow?" Dad asks, some of the anger falling from his voice. "Are you out? If you are, tell me now, no more of that *vanish in the middle of the night* bullshit."

"I wouldn't miss it for the world," I say, before turning my back on him again.

My feet hustle toward the subway, my mind still back there on that sidewalk hearing myself say, *I don't owe you an explanation.* Tears prick the corners of my eyes. I don't owe *him* anything, but I do owe *someone* an explanation.

I'm still overflowing with way too many feelings to even see straight. But twenty minutes after leaving my father on that sidewalk, I bang on Agent Sharp's door.

The door opens slowly, and I don't hesitate before putting my demand out there. "I want to talk to my mother."

CHAPTER

22

The room behind Agent Sharp is dark. He leans into the door, holding it open, rubs his eyes with one hand, and attempts to flatten his wild bedhead with the other hand. He's also not wearing a shirt. Just gym shorts.

"Good, you're up." I push past him and wedge my way into his room. I feel around for a light switch and flip it on.

"Why aren't you at NYU, sitting in on a class?" He snatches a T-shirt from his suitcase and pulls it over his head. He knocks softly one time on the adjoining doors between his and Sheldon's room. "You up?"

I wait while Sharp is in the bathroom, probably wetting his hair, because he returns with it combed, a toothbrush in his mouth. Sheldon appears a couple of minutes later. Unlike Sharp, she's dressed in her standard FBI outfit of black pants and a white dress shirt, her hair in that stiff bun like always.

"I want to talk to my mother," I repeat, before Sharp tries to translate. After that fight with my dad today, I can't—I won't—offer him something in order to repent my guilt for what happened to Mom. He's a free man, when he should be in prison. He's already gotten something out of this deal. So have I. Mom is the one who drew the short stick.

"We can't take that risk," Sheldon says. "We don't know who she's in communication with. Prisons have their systems often outside the law. She's a master manipulator; she'll have no problem earning sympathy with a guard or two, someone willing to get messages to the outside or put her on the phone with your family under the cloak of a lawyer call. If she told anyone why you're here, our operation is done. Ruined."

"I'm not going to tell her anything about New York City," I say firmly. "And I'm not doing anything else until I talk to her."

We're at a stalemate, as we seem to be nearly every time I ask the FBI for something. Agent Sheldon turns to Sharp, who's now drying his face with a towel. Silent conversation seems to flow between them, until finally Sheldon says, "All right. But you'll talk to her right here, under recording, understood?"

I swallow back a lump of apprehension. Not exactly the audience I'd wanted to rid my guilt in front of. "Fine."

The process of getting a prisoner on the phone turns out to be quite lengthy. I sit in the desk chair in Agent Sharp's hotel room for forty-five minutes. Every possible movement I consider making is too much like fidgeting, like nerves, and I'm not one to show nerves openly.

I draw in a breath and force my hand to remain steady when Sheldon holds out her cell and I reach up to take it. Despite the demand that this conversation take place in front of them, both agents walk into Sheldon's room, at least offering me the appearance of privacy. The door is still open between the two rooms.

A voice I haven't heard in what feels like a lifetime, a voice I thought I'd forgotten, offers me a confused hello, and I nearly hang up right then. What am I doing? Why did I think this would be a good idea?

"Hello?" she repeats.

I jerk the phone from my ear, my finger hovers over the End Call button, but then I remember that I have to face Dad and this job again tomorrow, and how am I supposed to gather evidence against him if I'm still overflowing with guilt over the last family job we did together?

"Mom?" It comes out in barely a whisper. I clear my throat and try again. "Mom, it's me…Ellie."

The long beat of silence lasts an eternity. "Are you okay?"

The warmth in her voice envelops me. I pull my knees to my chest, rest my forehead against them, and close my eyes so I can pretend there aren't two FBI agents within earshot. "I'm okay. What about you— Is it— I mean, what's it like?"

"Well, it's not exactly a Gatlinburg vacation, but I get along just fine."

I hear mostly truth in her voice, but this is my mother. Not only is she a gifted liar, but she's also bound by maternal instinct to ease any of her children's worries.

Silence fills the miles between us again. I glance at the stopwatch Agent Sharp left on the table counting the ten minutes we have to talk. "I heard about the sentencing," I say, forcing the words out. It's surprisingly freeing. More words bubble up toward my throat with ease. "Mom, you have to appeal. If you tell a judge about—"

"Honey, stop right there." She cuts me off. "This isn't a conversation I can have right now, and besides, it's pointless. Tell me what you've been up to. It's been so long. I know you didn't call just to ask a question you already know the answer to."

True. I did know that she'd never turn in my dad or anyone else, even if it's obvious a job like the Dr. Ames one could never be a single-person con. Nearly five minutes have passed, and I haven't said what I called to say. "It's my fault you're there… I did something—" I stop before "FBI" gets dropped between us. That's on the list of forbidden topics. "I wasn't like you. I couldn't just keep quiet and let myself get caught." *Come on, Ellie, pull yourself together.* "I wanted to see Harper, and all I had to do was hand over information about what we were doing at the bank in Charleston. So I did. I'm sorry, Mom. I'm really sorry. If I knew it would be ten years—"

"Okay," she says. "It's okay. You don't have to tell me anything else. I'm sure you did the best you could."

No, not really. The corners of my eyes are wet. I hadn't even realized I was crying. I swipe them with my sleeve, pull myself upright. "I'm going to fix this. You're not staying there ten years. I swear to God I will—"

"No, Ellie, don't do anything," she warns. "You'll just get yourself in trouble."

The stopwatch hits ten minutes, giving me an excuse to go before I'm asked to promise her anything. "My time's up; I'll be in touch."

Without any hesitation, I hang up.

Sheldon and Sharp reenter the room right away, clearly having heard every word of that call. I hand Agent Sheldon—the woman who pounced on my mother, cuffed her, and read her her rights—her cell phone and, wanting to avoid any chat about my emotional state, I shift topics. "My dad's coworker Bruno is a member of the Zanetti family. Apparently my family is collaborating with the mafia."

I fill them in on the details. It's a great distraction from that phone call. Agent Sheldon grows wearier and wearier by the second. Sharp has his fingers linked behind his head; he looks more shocked than his partner. When I finish talking, Sheldon immediately heads for her room.

"I have to call this in." She points a finger at me. "Don't leave this hotel, understood?"

The door between rooms swings shut, and I shift my attention to Agent Sharp. He's tense, his jaw flexing like maybe he's grinding his teeth. In one quick motion he swipes the key card from the table in front of me and heads for the door. "Come on."

I stand and follow him out into the hall.

"Go change," Sharp says, sounding pissed off. "Meet me in the gym in five minutes."

The gym?

CHAPTER

23

"Who taught you how to block a punch?" Sharp says, disappointment in his voice.

"My sister's boyfriend," I lie. Aidan taught me a lot of things, but self-defense wasn't one of them.

Sharp nods like this makes sense. "Secret Service. They've got a less efficient style. I'm not a fan."

"Well, they hate your methods of information sharing," I tell him.

"Less talk, more workout," Sharp says.

The hotel's fitness room has a large, blue mat spread across one side, and the other side has cardio machines and a multifunction weight bench. The door to the fitness room is glass from top to bottom and I keep glancing at it, making sure none of my classmates are walking by. Not sure how I would explain this.

"Disarming," Sharp says. He makes his hand into the shape of a gun and points it at my chest. "One hand wraps around the barrel of the gun; the other smacks the forearm of their gun hand."

"Wait…" I shake my head, trying to keep up. "Whose gun hand? Why are we doing this?"

"Sheldon's by the book," he says.

"Is that what she is?"

"I mean she'll want to pull you from the operation," Sharp explains.

"Because of what I told my mom?"

"Because of the Zanettis. It's one thing to toss you back into an environment you spent most of your life in, but con artists and mobsters are definitely not one and the same. You'll have to prove to Sheldon that you can handle it." He drops his arm and takes a step back. "Unless you want out? If you do, just say the word."

After the fight I had with my dad today, I definitely want out, but where would that leave Mom? I doubt I'm allowed to take the prize money home if I don't finish the race. "So you didn't know about the Zanettis? Not even in a working theory?"

"No, not in any scenario," Sharp says. "And it's not just you who might be out. The FBI will likely need another team here. Sheldon doesn't have experience in organized crime."

I lift an eyebrow. "And you do?"

"Not in this country," he admits. "I served in the air force for twelve years, and eight of those were spent chasing down drug lords and criminal families in South America."

"Well that explains the crew cut." Through the fitness room door I spot Mr. Lance turning the corner. I step around Agent Sharp and hop onto the elliptical machine. Sharp drops to the mat and starts a series of push-ups, giving the impression of two strangers politely sharing the small space.

Mr. Lance spots me right away and pokes his head inside the room. "Hey, Ellie. Did you enjoy your NYU class? Which did you sit in on again?"

"Economics." Thank God I studied the itinerary, especially considering the fact that I'm missing half the activities. "It was a little over my head. But I do have the sudden urge to visit Wall Street; is this normal?"

He laughs, prepares to leave me in peace, but instead pokes his head back in. "Where is your buddy? No wandering alone. It's the number one rule of Holden Does New York."

I really hate that nickname. "Justice is on her way down. I'll wait for her next time, I promise, even though she's an elliptical hog."

The moment he's out of sight, I stop my unnecessary exercising. I can't believe people use this thing on purpose. I turn to Sharp, needing to get down to business. "Do you really think a thirty-minute lesson in punching and disarming will make Agent Sheldon believe I'm ready to handle mobsters? I mean, I haven't even seen any of them besides Bruno. It's possible I might not see any of them at all."

"True," he reasons. "That's very possible. Confrontation, especially of the violent nature, is still a last resort, even with crime families. Though their idea of last resort often holds a different meaning."

Dominic sends me a text to meet him in his room, and Sharp gets official word from his partner regarding the future of our operation moments later.

"Sheldon has an update for me—we'll be in touch soon," he says, his hand already on the door handle. "Get the DeLuca kid to practice a couple of those moves with you and do some light research on organized crime families in America. You might find it helpful."

"So you think we're still a go?" I ask.

"The Zanettis are a game changer, but the tone of Sheldon's text suggests a green light." He pauses at the door, turning to fully face me. "Most important thing to remember with mafia families is that they're sworn in for life and above all, including God, family, and love. Whatever they've set out to do in this con, that's what they're going to do. There's no swaying or manipulating a different outcome. If your dad and crew have any of those ideas in the plans, then they're in a world of danger."

I swallow back an image of Dad, Oscar, and Grandpa Barney stuffed in a speedboat, cement blocks tied to their ankles. I'm still hanging on to Agent Sharp's warning when I knock on Dominic's door a few minutes later.

"You were right," Dominic says as soon as I'm inside the room and the door is closed. "About the information packets."

My mind has been so focused on mobsters today I had forgotten about the actual con. "I didn't know you doubted that theory."

"Well, no," he says, "but I knew we needed evidence."

My forehead wrinkles. "And you have evidence? How?"

"Yes, I have evidence of monetary exchange." He exhales. "But I'm not sure if we can give all of it to the FBI."

"Explain." I wave an impatient hand, encouraging him to get to the point. "Please."

"I knew we couldn't check out the contracted services, because your family might recognize you or might have heard about me," he says, raking a hand through his hair. "So I sort of hired someone to go through the open audition yesterday, get the information packet, and then check out a few of the contracted services. I gave her money to pay for head shots or whatever."

My mouth falls open, but it takes a while before I can speak. "Wait…what? You hired someone? Like who?"

Dominic shrugs. "Just called up an escort service. Turns out they're pretty flexible about what customers need them for."

"Oh I'm sure." I shake my head. "But seriously? That was pretty stupid. You could blow our cover or the FBI's."

His jaw tenses, but he doesn't seem too surprised by my reaction. "I didn't see her, paid for everything online. Got the evidence from her via an anonymous email account that

I just opened. I told her my little sister wanted to audition, but I needed to see if the agency was a scam first."

Okay, that's a bit better. "What did she find out? And how old is this escort? It's a child talent agency."

"Children and young adults," Dominic reminds me, probably reciting the speech he's heard my dad give during open auditions several times now. He snatches his already opened laptop from the bed and places it on a small table beside the dresser for me to see. The first picture was taken inside what looks like a small music studio; there's a piano and some technical equipment. A woman with long brown hair, and gray streaks throughout, is seated at the piano.

Even without seeing her face, I recognize her. "Candy."

"You know her?" Dominic asks.

"She's Oscar's mom."

He flips through several more images, and I am able to identify three more members of my family—two at a photo studio and another at a dance studio.

"The escort had dance and voice lessons, plus head shots all in one day? How much did you pay her?"

"She made appointments at all three, paid in advance," he says. "But she did participate in the personal training session."

He tenses before flipping to the next photo, as if anticipating my reaction. "Recognize her personal trainer?"

"Oh shit." I lean in closer and blink just to be sure I'm seeing this right. Miles? "How— Why?"

I tug my phone from my pocket and punch in a text to Miles, my fingers banging against the screen of my phone with more force than needed.

ME: we need to talk. Now.

Dominic sees my text and seems to remember something. He produces a tiny slip of pink paper from his back pocket. "Your future husband told me he got a tracker on MB. I swiped the package from his dresser while he was freaking out this morning. He hadn't even turned it on yet, so I registered it myself, checked up on MB, and then shut it off. But not before writing this down."

"That little shit. I can't believe he got a tracker on Miles." I stare at the address on the pink paper, committing it to memory, then I snatch it from Dominic, take it into the bathroom, and flush it. "Hang onto that evidence for now."

I punch another text to Miles.

ME: never mind. I know where u r. On my way

CHAPTER
24

Okay, so maybe storming off to find Miles without much preplanning wasn't my best idea ever. Geographically, Brooklyn seemed close enough to Times Square. But now I'm circling an apartment building for the third time, in the dark, trying to locate the entrance. The street isn't even well lit, I'm starving because I skipped dinner, and the bottom half of my sweatpants are soaking wet because a bus sped past and sprayed a bunch of icy slush at me. Maybe this whole *Miles, why the hell are you working with my family* chat could have waited until morning.

I'm about to call it quits when an Exit Only door near the end of the building opens, revealing a woman struggling to look at her phone and keep control of a small brown dog tucked under one arm.

"Let me get the door for you," I offer, reaching for the handle and flashing the woman my most innocent smile.

She looks grateful when she steps outside. "Thanks."

I pause for a second, waiting while she places the dog on the salted sidewalk. It heads right to a patch of old snow to sniff around. I'm inside the building and down the hall before the woman questions what just happened. She might not even think twice about it. I find apartment 16A, but instead of knocking I stand there like an idiot worrying about, of all things, the state of my hair, the fact that I'm in sweatpants, and I can't remember which underwear I'm wearing.

God, Ellie. You came here to question him, not to hook up.

Right. I came to question him.

The door to apartment 16B opens and a guy walks out, but he stops when he sees me. I pretend not to notice and finally give a light knock on the door.

"I did not know you guys delivered here," the neighbor says.

I glance at him and realize he's pointing at the huge brown paper bag I'm carting—a half-assed, last-second cover story for my presence here. The logo of a popular Manhattan deli is on it.

"Oh yeah," I say, nodding. "We do. For an extra charge."

"Man, I love that place." He leans closer, trying to peek in the bag. "What have you got there, anything good?"

I grip the opening of the bag, holding it shut—it's full of trash I snatched from the hotel recycling bin. "Sorry, orders are subject to our privacy policy. Deli-customer confidentiality. We'll do the same for you, guaranteed."

"Oh, okay." He gives me a bewildered look and shakes his head. "Have a good night."

Finally the apartment door opens. One glimpse of Miles and for a second, I forget why I'm here. He peeks around me, watches the retreating neighbor. "I just need to grab my wallet. Mind setting that stuff on the counter?"

I step inside what appears to be a very tiny studio apartment. The bed that sits in the center of the room occupies nearly half the apartment. To the left is a tiny kitchen with a single countertop. To the right is a door that if opened would likely reveal a bathroom. The whole place is maybe three hundred square feet.

"Did anyone follow you?" Miles asks.

"Just a couple of people. I told them to wait outside."

"Funny, real funny. Want to know where your cousin planted that tracker?"

He doesn't wait for me to answer. He hands me a blue stainless steel water bottle with a narrow neck. I recognize it because he used it all the time last semester.

I unscrew the cap and attempt to angle the bottle at the light. "Did he stick it to the bottom?"

That would definitely be tough to spot because of the narrow opening.

"Nope," Miles say. "He just dropped it in when I wasn't looking and let me drink it."

"Seriously?" I'm momentarily stunned by Oscar's brilliance. "How do you know?"

"Process of elimination." Miles shrugs. "I've got a device that detects trackers. I couldn't find it in an exterior location despite setting off the alarm in my midsection. I'd guess it's something between my small and large intestine."

"Process of elimination indeed." Shaking my head, I hand the bottle back to Miles. "It might be my fault. I basically called him predictable and told him he needed to up his game."

"Does he know—"

"Where you're staying?" I finish. "No, he doesn't. Dominic hijacked the mission, turned the tracker on himself. He got the address, then shut down the chip, destroyed the evidence."

"Remind me to thank Dominic," Miles says, releasing a breath.

He looks so tense that I almost step forward to rest a hand on his arm, touch him in some comforting way, but then I spot neon-orange and blue tennis shoes lying on the floor by the door—the same shoes he was wearing in the photo Dominic showed me—and I'm back to business.

"What are you doing with my dad, Miles?" I blurt out. "Why? And when? Did you... I mean do you—"

Lines of worry crease his face. He steps closer, but I retreat until my back touches the counter. "I didn't know it was your dad until I saw you with him this week. And then I couldn't talk to you about it because I thought that..." His face flushes, and he doesn't finish.

But it's clear what he thought. That I'd lied to him. That I was still loyal to the people I promised him I wouldn't be loyal to. It hurts, but it's not like I expected him to forget all the details of my past, to never doubt my intentions. That would be asking a lot. But it still hurts.

"Okay, so what are you doing here? How did you get inside this job? Are you working for the FBI again?"

"Not *again*, exactly," he says. "More like *still*."

"Yeah, that doesn't really answer my question." I'm up to my ears in evasive answers today, and I'm getting pretty sick of it. "You didn't even know about my family until I told you, and then less than two months later you're inside one of their biggest, most dangerous cons. Tell me what I'm supposed to think about that, Miles, because I'm pretty fucking confused right now."

My voice elevates with each word, and Miles looks even more concerned. Then I curse myself for even showing him that I care. I thought he needed to see my cards for us to keep being us, but now it feels like we're playing a different game and I haven't been given the instructions yet.

"I'm going to answer your questions, I promise." When he steps toward me this time, I have no more space to back up. He lifts a hand as if to touch me but pulls it back at the last second. "You must be going crazy right now. Being four different people at once—even for you that's... I can't imagine. And seeing your dad again, working with Agent Sheldon, the woman who put your mom in prison."

"What are you doing?" I lean back, afraid of letting his warmth hit me. "How did you find out that I wasn't here out of loyalty to my family?" The answer forms right after I've finished asking the question. "You heard my phone call to Agent Sheldon?"

Someone had been following me the other day when I called from the stairwell to report about the agency information packets. And Miles had revealed himself shortly after.

"I did hear the phone call, but I knew before that. At the open auditions, I was watching the footage. That's part of my job." He gets brave and this time follows through with his attempt to touch me. Though his fingertips rest so lightly on my cheek. "I saw you and Dominic talking, watched your body language, and I knew things weren't as they seemed. But I didn't know if you were there on your own agenda or someone else's. Didn't know where Dominic fell into your plans."

There's heat and tenderness behind his words, but I'm not ready to give in yet. "So you and my dad work together? You've talked to him?"

"He has no idea you and I have any connection or history. Neither do my handlers. Sharp and Sheldon don't know, right?"

"Right," I concede after pausing a second to try and recall when I mentioned Agent Sharp by name. "And since you're erased from Holden's records now, they aren't likely to put anything together."

I remove his hand from my cheek. I'm still stuck on this image of Miles and my dad working together. For weeks, after Miles moved out of the apartment beside mine, I imagined him in his trademark gray and navy sweats, climbing a rope with a drill sergeant whistling at him from the ground. I'd pictured him seated in a classroom, wearing his military school uniform, back straight, hair trimmed to regulation. It's like that Miles vanished when I hit the delete button on his records the night I broke into Holden.

Concern and hurt flicker across his face when I lower his hand back to his side. "Tell me what you're thinking."

"I'm thinking…" Frustration builds as I work to form an answer. I step around Miles and move farther away, closer to the door. "For the first time ever, I've told you everything. No secrets. I'm not sure I like this feeling. Not sure I'm made for this kind of thing."

Now there's no doubt I've hurt him, and he leaves the evidence there on his face for the length of several heartbeats. Then the blank Miles look appears and he nods. "I see."

We stare at each other from opposite sides of the room. This should be my exit, but I'm rooted to the spot. The Miles in front of me is identical to the boy who sat with me in front of the fireplace in his parents' guesthouse and admitted that he hadn't been that close to any girl before. That he liked the real me better than the confident, sure-of-herself version.

I cross the room in two seconds flat as if under a curse, but again I hesitate. He just stands there watching me with those beautiful blue eyes, saying nothing, but I can hear the words inside his head: *It's your move.* The force controlling me is magnetic. I lean my forehead against his chest and just stay like that.

Probably worried about scaring me off, it takes a bit for Miles to lift a hand and attempt to touch me again. His fingers land lightly on the back of my neck, and it's like that night at the homecoming dance. The smallest touch feels like a dozen Miles Beckett hands all over me.

His lips brush against my temple. "I didn't expect this, either, Ellie."

"Expect what?" I whisper, thinking he means the assignment with my family.

"Feeling this…" He takes my hand, pulls it to his heart. "This weight, like a physical ache whenever I think about you or see you. I mean, I knew that there was something here, I just didn't know it was this much."

His words float over me and I'm right there with him, my chest heavy, my stomach in knots from fear and excitement. Miles's mouth finds mine, his kiss hungry and intense. Hands roam through my hair, down my arms, under my jacket. I drag him backward. We both fall onto the bed. I lean over Miles, and he tugs off my jacket, tosses it to the floor. His T-shirt follows my coat. I'm so busy enjoying the taste of his mouth, the warmth of him stretched out beneath me, that I barely notice Miles lifting my shirt halfway then releasing the material. His hands land on my face and when I tug my mouth from his, he holds me at a distance.

"I'm sorry," he says, so dead serious I'm wishing for a joke to follow. "About not talking to you. If it were the other way around, I would have been crazy worried."

I dip my head down and kiss his neck. "You're definitely gifted at apologies."

"Anything else I'm good at?" He works my shirt over my head and then kisses me again. "I wouldn't hate an itemized list."

"Everything," I say against his mouth. "Just everything."

The dinner I skipped; the cold, damp sweatpants I'm wearing; the urgency I had getting over here and probably should have getting back all vanishes for a little while. The more he gives, the more I want.

A while later I'm stretched out on top of Miles, his careful fingers in my hair and gliding over my back, and it suddenly seems so easy to take things further, so very possible.

"Do you have any con—"

"No," Miles says before I even finish, like he'd been thinking about it, too.

"What happened to the Boy Scout who's always prepared for anything?" I joke, but my face still heats up. I wish I hadn't asked the question, not before he brought it up anyway.

"Preparedness usually comes from being in a bind," he says.

"So next time…" I prompt, enjoying the blush on his cheeks. It's darker than mine, I'm sure.

"I'll be a perfect Boy Scout." He grips my waist and flips me over. "But I do think we have plenty of ground to cover before going there."

His lips drift down my neck, down my chest and stomach. I close my eyes and sink into the soft mattress. His fingers are toying with the waistband of my panties when a loud knock echoes from the door.

Both of us jolt upright, nearly banging heads. Miles looks at me and holds a finger to his lips.

"Delivery from Number One Wok," a voice says from the hall outside the door.

My heart falls back down from my throat. "It's Dominic."

The relief on Miles's face is almost more concerning than the knock on the door had been. Who did he think had come calling for him? The Zanettis? But instead of asking, I scramble to get my clothes back on. Miles pulls his T-shirt over his head while also straightening the comforter covering the bed. By the time he ushers Dominic inside, everything is in perfect order.

"Next time, let's skip the ninety-second wait in the hall." Dominic assesses the place, then his gaze bounces between Miles and me. "Like I can't already figure out what the two of you might do when you're alone."

Miles sighs. "What's up?"

It must be something if he hauled it all the way out to Brooklyn behind our chaperones' backs.

Dominic holds out his phone, giving us a view of the

screen. "My first tracker. Planted it on Bruno. The guy left his watch lying on the bathroom sink, then walked away to answer a phone call. It was almost too easy."

"Brilliant," Miles tells him, clapping his shoulder.

Dominic grins, clearly proud of himself. "So…who wants to spy on some Zanetti mobsters?"

Miles and I look at each other, and then he turns to Dominic. "I'm in."

I snatch my coat from the floor. "Me, too."

CHAPTER
25

The door to the conference room opens and Dominic enters. I look up from the stack of folders I'd been placing at each spot in preparation for the agency parent meeting later tonight. Dominic offers me the smallest of nods, and I celebrate internally, keeping the excitement off my face—the room is loaded with cameras, probably so someone like Miles can study the footage later and help pick the most vulnerable and maybe the wealthiest parents, and I'd rather not have to explain my plans for tonight to anyone in my family. Definitely not anyone in Bruno's family.

After three hours of surveillance last night at the bar where Bruno met a few other men for drinks, literally zero intel was gathered. Dominic just confirmed Miles's success in scoring a car, so we can hopefully follow Bruno via the tracker and then, assuming the location where he lands provides us the ability to sneak in, we'll plant a listening device so we can hear this time, instead of just watch from a distance.

"I heard Bruno tell Milky that he can't work tonight because his brothers want to have dinner," I whisper to Dominic.

"Yeah, I heard that, too." Dominic grabs half of the folders and follows closely beside me as I move around the room. "So how does it work?" he whispers. "There must be a limited range, right?"

"Assuming we get something inside, we'll have to be close. Probably half a mile, maybe less."

We finish up in the conference room and return to the big audition room. My uncle Milky is at the piano, accompanying a little girl while she belts out a song from the musical *Wicked*.

"Thank you, Emily." My dad lifts a hand, cutting her off. Then he looks to me and asks, "What are your thoughts on Emily's song?"

I hesitate, creating a dramatic pause while I mentally prepare my British accent. "Have you had any voice lessons?"

Both mom and daughter look dejected. The mother answers first. "A few. Her strength is tap. She only performed a song because it was required. Emily, do your solo," the mom commands.

The child, who is likely no older than ten, begins tapping, and all of us stand there mesmerized until she hits her final pose.

"That's brilliant," I tell her truthfully, then I exchange a glance with Dad, who gives me the nod to go for the big punch. "But how many non-singing child tappers have you seen on Broadway? How many child tappers have you seen doing anything that makes money or has commercial appeal?" The smiles fall from the little girl's and her mom's faces. "Her singing has potential. Especially after hearing she's not been trained. A good vocal teacher won't overwhelm her with corrections. He or she will work to evolve the singer already in her."

"So you really think she's got a shot?" the mom asks.

"Definitely," I say with a nod. And yeah, I feel guilty as hell, but whatever. I can hardly worry about giving a child false Broadway hope when there are mobsters to stop. "Especially with the work ethic Emily obviously has for tap, apply that to vocal training and she's limitless."

The smiles return. The mom opens her folder and glances over the information. "What about this Bertha Reynolds, is she any good?"

"She's the best," Dominic says, nailing that Australian accent. He's getting better every day. "She's been my voice teacher for years."

I nearly elbow him in the side to stop him—Lachlan is from Australia, so how can he have a New York City voice teacher? Beginner's mistake.

"Bertha was the dialect and voice teacher for the original production of *Matilda* that opened in Sydney," Dad says to cover Dominic's mistake. "Give her a call and let her know you're with the agency. She won't charge a penny over industry standard."

Dad walks them to the elevator, and I can't help but think that Emily is the twelfth or thirteenth kid today who will be booking a lesson with "Bertha" (aka Oscar's mom). Don't know how she's going to fit in all of those lessons. The elevator dings, and we all watch as the last of the kids auditioning disappear behind the closing doors.

"Jesus Christ, if I have to play 'Defying Gravity' one more time I'm gonna shoot myself," Milky says. He stands and tosses the piano a disgusted look. "Don't know how I got this job. I asked for the personal trainer."

I offer Milky a sympathetic pat on the shoulder, but it's half-assed considering I sat in on nearly all of those "Defying Gravity" solos. I glance at Dominic. "I think that's our cue to leave."

Dad stops us on the way out. He points a finger at Dominic. "Be careful about dropping back story...can't get loosey-goosey with that stuff. Bertha's gonna have a fit about changing her character mid-con."

"Right, sorry," Dominic mumbles, staring at his feet. "Won't happen again."

Even though I lectured him about exactly this sort of thing right from the start, I still feel a pang of sympathy for Dominic.

My dad turns to me. "You did good today, honey. Your mom would be proud."

Though my anger is more under control today, I'm still pissed at him for whatever mess he's gotten himself into. It certainly doesn't help when he drops my mom into the conversation. But like a good liar, I force a grin. "I learned from the best."

We say a quick goodbye to Bruno, who's on his laptop in the office. I watch him for signs of distrust—like if he found the bug Dominic planted—but he's his usual agreeable self when he offers us a friendly wave.

Today is the coldest day in New York thus far. Instead of walking the ten blocks back to the hotel, Dominic and I hop on a bus. Both of us scroll through our phones to catch up on missed texts.

MILES: 2 out of 3 of Bruno's drinking buddies from last night are in the FBI database as suspected mafia members

I show the message to Dominic. His forehead wrinkles. "The third guy maybe just hasn't been caught yet."

We sit on that for a minute, and then Dominic switches topics. "So did Miles explain things last night? How he got on your dad's team or why he didn't know about the Zanettis?"

"Well, he offered to explain," I admit, diverting my eyes from Dominic's. "But then we got distracted and then you showed up dangling mobster whereabouts in front of us and that plan got lost."

"Later, then," Dominic states firmly. "I need the whole story."

"Uh-oh," I say, still looking through my phone, specifically at several texts from Justice beginning about thirty minutes ago.

JUSTICE: need u at hotel asap
JUSTICE: WHERE R U????
JUSTICE: HURRY!!!

I show Dominic, and he immediately rises from his seat as the bus slows at a stop still five blocks from our hotel. I follow him off the bus but struggle to keep up with his quick pace and long legs.

"I thought you were a smoker," I say, reaching for his shirt to slow him down so I can hit send on my reply to Justice.

ME: brt

"I quit, remember?" He looks over his shoulder at me. Right. The gum. "Besides, I was only a casual smoker. Think Lance or Geist noticed we weren't at the museum today?"

"I don't know." A burst of adrenaline hits me along with dread that comes with the possibility of disappointing my favorite teacher. "It must be something like that. What else could it be?"

In the hotel, the wait for the elevator is too long. Dominic and I tackle the stairs, taking them two at a time for about three floors and then stopping to catch our breath at the landing. We're both panting by the time I swipe the key card into my door.

"Did she say to meet her in your room?" Dominic asks.

But there's no need to answer him. When we step inside, the door swinging shut behind us, Justice and Chantel are pacing the front room.

And in a chair near the windows, tied up like a prisoner, mouth taped shut, is Agent Sharp.

CHAPTER

26

Chantel has a bottle of pepper spray aimed at the hostage, and by the looks of how red his eyes are and the tears tracking down his face, she must have used it already. The tape on his mouth is preventing him from saying anything, but Agent Sharp's eyes are wide and uncertain, probably because he's not used to teenage girls holding him hostage.

Well, welcome to my world.

"Fuuuck," Dominic mutters from behind me.

I glance at Justice and then Chantel. "What is this?"

"This guy"—Justice snaps, pointing a finger at Sharp—"has been following you."

"Stalker." Chantel shakes her head. "Bet he's got nude pics, too."

Justice lifts an eyebrow. "Should we check his phone?"

Okay, Ellie, think. Need a cover story. One that doesn't involve the FBI. I cross my arms and throw a glare at Sharp. "I know he has nude pics. I also know he wasn't supposed to follow me to New York, because I told him not to. We broke up months ago."

For a moment, while I'm watching both girls' faces

change as they process this made-up backstory, I freak out, realizing that Sharp might be too old to pass as an angry ex. *Twenty-five*, I tell myself. He can pass for twenty-five. Seventeen and twenty-five? It's doable. In a bind.

Chantel gives him a knowing look. "A stalker ex. I knew it."

"Untape him," Dominic demands, playing along. "Let's hear what the asshole has to say for himself."

Justice rips the duct tape off like a Band-Aid on a skinned knee, earning a yell of pain from Agent Sharp.

"Why are you following our friend? Explain yourself," Justice demands.

Despite the complicated situation, I feel a pang of warmth spread over me, hearing Justice call me her friend, seeing both these girls glaring at a man they thought had been trying to hurt me. Would I do the same for them? I will now that I know they've got my back. After I free the federal agent from my two very fierce friends.

Agent Sharp looks at me, his face a bit red. I mean seriously, how did this even happen? A federal agent versus two teen girls who have barely had to lift a finger to do anything physical their entire lives.

"I'm...I'm sorry," he says, spitting out the words and almost sounding like he means it. He stares harder at me, as if hoping I'll telepathically offer him the right words to say. *Come on, Sharp, you've been trained in creating covers, right?* "I just wanted to talk to you and..."

I give him the slightest nod of encouragement. *Keep going. You got this.*

"And you wouldn't return my calls," he finishes. "Then I freaked out about teachers—"

"Because you're so old?" Chantel interrupts. "Thought we didn't notice that, huh?"

"Old and a stalker." Justice shoots another glare at him.

"Maybe we should search him. Any evidence we gather could come in handy later on."

Before she can get a hand in his pockets and likely remove an FBI badge, I stop her. "No, we can't do that. If the roles were reversed and we were guys feeling around in a girl's pockets…" I pause while Justice offers a disappointed nod of agreement. "Come on, Benji, let's have a little chat out in the hall. Alone."

She opens her mouth to protest, but I add, "It's fine, I swear."

After the girls get Sharp untied, Chantel thrusts the bottle of pepper spray at me. "Keep this aimed at him just in case."

I cradle it carefully, like an egg I'm trying hard not to crack. "Uh, yeah, will do."

"Don't worry, I'll keep an eye out," Dominic tells them, and then he follows us out the door. "I'll keep an eye out."

By the time we're alone in the hallway, my heart has calmed down from its fight to get out of my chest. No teachers have caught me skipping out on field-trip activities. Justice and Chantel bought the bogus ex-boyfriend story. Everything is okay. At least for now. And suddenly the FBI agent standing in front of me, teary-eyed and looking both violated and humiliated, is about the funniest thing I've seen in a while.

I'm laughing so hard I hand the pepper spray over to Dominic and rest my hands on my knees to catch my breath.

Sharp lifts the bottom of his T-shirt to his face and rubs his eyes with it. "Glad you're having a good laugh at my expense."

"Sorry." I pull myself together and look him over again. "How did that even happen?"

"Well, for starters I was trying to remain undercover," he says, clearly annoyed. "And that usually involves not looking like an FBI agent or anything similar. Plus, the blonde is way faster and stronger than she looks."

This time I do a better job being sympathetic and keep my laughs inside. "You could have used backup to protect you from those bad girls. Where was your partner?"

He rolls his eyes. "She was tailing you."

The laughter dies in the back of my throat. "Why?"

"You aren't a trained agent, you're an informant," he says, lowering his voice to barely above a whisper.

"Oh." My face heats up. "She doesn't trust me."

All the covers I've been wearing lately, all the arguments with Miles and my dad, the constant fear of getting caught, it finally gets to me, and I turn my back on both of them and stride down the hall.

"Ellie!" Sharp calls after me.

I hear the door to our room open and assume Justice has told him to get lost, because when I glance over my shoulder, he's heading the other way.

Dominic jogs to catch up with me. "Forget Sheldon. She's got a stick up her ass."

"It's fine, forget it." I don't want or need Dominic, of all people, attempting to reassure me that I'm a trustworthy person. "If I were Sheldon, I wouldn't trust me, either."

This is true. Unfortunately. And I don't know if it will ever be *not true*. Starting over is bullshit. It's something people much dumber than me tell themselves to alleviate guilt. Good for them if they can buy that lie, but I can't. Sheldon feeling the need to tail me everywhere is more proof of that.

"Hey—" Dominic starts.

I lift a hand to stop him. "I said it's fine."

He nods, glances down at his shoes. "Are we still on for tonight?"

"Why wouldn't we be?" I snap, and then take a deep, calming breath before speaking again. "I mean yes, we're still on. Offer to trade seats at intermission and then—"

"I know the plan."

"Good." I push open the stairwell door at the end of the hall and give him one last look. "Don't follow me. Go do something else besides…this. You need a break."

And so do I. Actually, I need to talk to the person who probably understands how I'm feeling better than anyone. I head down the steps without a destination in mind and pull my phone out to make a call.

Harper answers on the first ring, and I immediately take a seat on the stairs and start telling her everything.

CHAPTER
27

Dominic smacks the headrest of my seat. "Here he comes!"

I spot a figure dressed in dark clothing making his way from the back door of a bar toward where we're parked across the street. I reach over the driver's seat of the car Miles got a hold of tonight and fling the door open. Seconds later he plops into the seat, silently shuts the door, and soon we're cruising down the block, parking in a much more conspicuous location.

Once he shifts the car into park, Miles leans his head against the seat, closes his eyes and allows his breath to return to normal. Dominic and I sit silent waiting for the verdict.

"It's done," Miles says and when both Dominic and I let out a yelp of excitement he offers me a tiny grin. "Luckily only a few mice in the crawl space." I shudder, earning an even bigger smile from Miles. "I planted the bug against the wall behind them. I could hear Bruno from below even before turning anything on so it should work."

"You really are a spy-in-training," Dominic says, sounding pretty impressed with our team leader.

"You got the tracker," Miles reminds him. "Got us started on this job. That's no small feat."

"Yeah, yeah. You're both superstars, now can we listen to the mobsters? I'm missing act two of *Hamilton* for this." I open Miles's laptop and help him get things started up. Soon voices that don't belong to the three of us fill the car.

"What happens if none of these rug rats wants to pay for that extra shit Hayes and his crew are peddling?"

Goose bumps form all over my arms and neck hearing my dad's—my family's—name dropped into the conversation.

"I think that's Faustino Zanetti," Miles says. He types something into the FBI database he's just pulled up, probably to confirm this theory. "Goes by Faust or Fausti. Served nine months for assault. He's still on probation."

"What do you think happens?" Bruno says, his Jersey accent now familiar to me. *"We bail. Like always. But it's a pointless question 'cause the money is fucking rollin' in like a tidal wave."*

About thirty feet in front of us, the sign outside Zanetti's Fine Italian Cuisine flickers and then turns off, leaving us even more in the dark, just the mobsters' voices to keep us company.

"No shit," another guys says. *"It's working out, then?"*

"Do you know that guy?" Dominic asks Miles.

Miles shakes his head. "I have a few guesses."

"Hayes is a fucking genius," Bruno says. *"If he knew how to use a pistol I'd be scared shitless of him."*

Laughter erupts. The sound of clinking glasses follows shortly after.

Tonight, for the first time, I'm seeing Bruno's chameleon skills. Working with him, he's humble, open-minded, and very aware of norms in the world of Broadway kids and stage moms. Here he's all short answers, simplified logic, swearing every other word.

"Okay, then," the presumed Faust says. *"If Hayes and his crew are that good, why the fuck do they need your dumb ass?"*

"First off, I go where Bossman tells me to go. You know the drill," Bruno says. *"Second, they need us because we're legit."* He laughs a cruel sort of laugh. *"Those of us who haven't served time, anyway. Hayes and his crew don't exist, not like us. No real identity. They can only deal in cash."*

"And those pageant moms are all about the credit," the unidentified man says.

"Exactly," Bruno says. *"We route the credit card payments through the restaurant accounts. Plus we got dirt on Jojo. He owes us a favor."*

"That's how you're getting all them Manhattan offices," Faust says. *"Let me guess, Hayes and his crew dug up the dirt and you—"*

"Held the gun to Jojo's head while we blackmailed him," Bruno says, earning laughter from his family members.

"They're coming outside," Dominic tells us, but his gaze is glued to his phone.

"How do you know?" Miles and I ask at the same time.

"Bruno," he says simply, and then he smacks the back of the driver's seat, causing Miles to jump. "Go! We gotta get out of here."

Without further question, Miles passes off his laptop to me, puts the car in reverse, and then turns it around, avoiding driving in front of the restaurant. Once we're a good distance away, Miles repeats the question. "How do you know they're leaving?"

"Bruno sent me a text," Dominic says. "Said he was done with dinner and heading back to the city."

I tug my seat belt around me and fasten it before glancing in the back seat to get a good look at Dominic. "Why would he tell you that? And how did he get your number?"

He scratches the back of his head, and even in the dark

I can see his cheeks flush. "We, uh…we sort of hung out the other night."

My mouth falls open. "You hung out with a mobster?"

"I thought it might help," Dominic argues. "He's a huge Knicks fan. My family gets box seats every season. Not that we go much."

"Wait," I say, trying to catch up. How much has he been doing on his own? "When did you go to a basketball game? How did I not notice?"

"Two nights ago," he says. "You were doing that assignment with Justice or something."

"Were you planning to meet up with him tonight?" Miles asks, sounding as stunned as I am. "Is that why he told you he's heading back to the city? You didn't think that was worth mentioning before now?"

"I wasn't sure," Dominic answers back. "Plus I knew both of you would be all, 'you're not experienced enough for this, you're too stupid for this.' But yeah, I *am* planning on meeting up with him now. I just confirmed."

"No way," Miles says firmly before I can tell Dominic he's crazy. "It's too dangerous."

I'm still reeling over the fact that they have things in common. I mean the Knicks? That can't be enough to warrant more this instant friendship. "What are you not telling us? I feel like we're missing part of this story."

Dominic can't make eye contact with me when he says, "Well, my family's Italian, so…"

"No," I gasp, putting that together. "You can't audition for the mob!"

"I agree." Miles shakes his head. "Like I said, it's too dangerous."

"Whatever," Dominic says. The dark car doesn't hide his glare. "It's not like I signed a contract or anything. Neither of us has even dropped the word 'mobster' into any conversation. Besides, do I bite your head off every time you tell me something you've done? And give me some fucking credit. I might be flunking out of Holden, but I'm not an idiot. I can handle Bruno Zanetti just fine."

I stare at my classmate, barely recognizing him. "But what if he finds out we're conning the con man? Your head will be on a mobster platter."

"And yours won't?" he snaps.

Miles winces at that but says nothing. He's focused on speeding along the highway to get from Newark back to the city.

"He's not gonna find out anything," Dominic adds. "As far as he knows, you're clueless about my mobster career goals."

"We'll deal with Dominic's new BFF later," Miles says, ending that argument. "Stay focused on the intel we just scored. When we get back to my place, we'll start piecing it together. And I'll tell you what I know on my end."

Dominic flops back against his seat. "About time."

***

Miles opens the door to his apartment before I even have the chance to knock. He ushers me inside and I can already feel the inquisition coming even though I'd only been gone twenty minutes to buy dinner. "Anyone tailing you? Or did you see—"

"No," I say firmly, my tone giving him no reason to question me further.

Dominic takes the pizza and two liter of soda from my hands and heads toward the kitchen. Miles unzips my jacket, slips it off me, and then holds my hands between his, warming them. "Thanks for getting dinner. We'll all think better if we're not starving."

I lean into him for a second, resting my cold cheek against his much warmer one. Then Dominic coughs loudly, and Miles drops my hands and steps back. I dig through my pocket and hand Dominic his credit card. "Thanks for buying dinner."

He folds a slice of pizza, stuffs a giant bite into his mouth, and shrugs.

Soon we've all got paper plates of pizza. Miles doesn't have a couch, so I'm seated on the perfectly made bed, leaning against the wall, and both guys are sitting on the floor. Miles has a notebook in front of him, a pencil in one hand, another behind his ear, and two more neatly placed beside the notebook. I smile down at my plate of pizza, remembering a few times when I'd made fun of his pencils. He likes them sharp but doesn't like to sharpen.

"The only thing I'm left wondering about after listening in on Bruno," I say, jumping right into discussing the intel from tonight, "is the identity of this Jojo person Bruno said they blackmailed."

"He's someone who has the power and means to offer up office space for free," Miles adds, his pencil already moving across the page.

Dominic stands and heads over to the kitchen counter to refill his glass of soda. "And someone who is vulnerable to blackmail."

"Everyone is vulnerable to blackmail if you can find their weakness." I pick a mushroom off my slice of pizza and place it onto the plate before taking a bite. "And no one knows how to uncover a weakness better than my dad."

My phone buzzes, and when I read the text, I laugh a little too loudly, startling both Miles and Dominic.

JUSTICE: how could u leave in the middle of Hamilton??? For what? A few minutes of fun with Miles? I don't even know u anymore

"What?" Dominic asks.

I wipe my hands so I can reply. "Justice. She hates me now."

"For not watching Act Two?" Dominic asks, and I nod. "Yeah, she hates me, too. But it was the perfect place to sneak out. I didn't hate the first half, though. Thought I would fall asleep but it was pretty good."

ME: Act 1 was crazy good. I hate myself right now too. Are we past the midnight check-in?

JUSTICE: yep. It's all good. See u in morning?

ME: I owe u one

I owe her about a hundred, actually. For nearly my entire life I was a taker not a giver. But now I'm constantly fighting this need to keep everything even. Surely there is something that I can help Justice with in the near future. I'll have to look into that. After we stop the mobsters and the con men.

"Okay," Dominic says, and the way he sets his plate on the counter and then leans back against it, arms crossed, it's clear he wants answers from Miles. "How did this happen? You in New York with Ellie's family?"

"Well, it's kind of—" Miles starts, but Dominic interrupts.

"I mean, you didn't know about the Zanettis' involvement, so obviously you're not undercover working for them," he assesses. "And I'm not an expert, but Ellie's family doesn't seem like the type to just open up their arms to a new guy with no other attachments. They all watch me like a hawk."

Miles has abandoned his pizza now, too. He looks right at Dominic, avoiding my gaze. "Clyde."

"Your uncle?" Dominic says.

"Clyde," I repeat, sinking back onto the headboard. Now it's beginning to make sense. Why hadn't I thought of that? Like me, Miles's uncle is a reformed criminal, given immunity by the FBI to turn over his boss. He also contracts for the FBI and CIA quite a bit, mostly dealing with check fraud. "If Clyde already had a good rep with my dad, why wouldn't the FBI put him undercover? Why use his nephew?"

"Clyde's work with the FBI isn't a secret." Miles takes a

drink of his soda, and I take note of the fact that he doesn't look me in the eyes. "Your dad knows his history, thinks it's a shame that he's benched. Clyde mentioned that his nephew might be able to help."

I hear only truth in his voice, but still I narrow my eyes at him. "And that was enough? Just a, 'Hey, my nephew needs a job and he's cool with ditching military school and becoming a con man'? My dad actually bought that?"

Especially knowing that Clyde got most of his paychecks from the FBI—the same organization that put my mom in prison.

"Exactly what I thought, too," Miles says. "It seemed too easy. But now I think I understand. Your dad wanted some heat on his side. Someone who could help out in a jam."

In a mobster jam. Yeah, I'm not too thrilled about Miles's purpose on this team. I turn my attention from him to Dominic. He's standing there staring, processing. Finally he just shakes his head, bewildered. "Damn, that's messed up. And super weird."

He bought it. All of it.

They quickly shift to hypothesizing about the third Zanetti family member with Bruno tonight—the one we hadn't seen—but I tune them out and fake interest in my pizza. Miles seemed like he was telling the truth, but there's a piece missing, I know there is. It's all too smooth, too easy. There's a seed at the beginning of all of this plotting and planning that brought Miles here to New York City. Before this trip, when I saw him last, he had every intention of heading back to school after his winter vacation in Europe. What changed? He says he didn't even know it was my family he'd be working for. He didn't know about the Zanettis' involvement. What did he know?

"I'll be back in a couple of hours," Dominic says.

I glance up from my pizza, and he's already headed for

the door. I must have missed something when I zoned out.

"I'll go with you," Miles says, getting to his feet.

"And how exactly did we meet?" Dominic rolls his eyes. "How do I explain that?"

"What he really means," I say, "is that you can't go because you're not Italian. They won't let you join."

Once I've finished my mobster joke, I turn to Dominic, dead serious now. "Seriously, Dominic? You're an idiot. And you have a death wish."

"You know what?" He turns to me, a half-hearted glare aimed in my direction. "I'm fucking tired of being the idiot."

He snatches his coat from the floor and swings the door open before stepping out into the hall.

"Wait." I slide my plate off my lap and spring to my feet. "Dominic!" I call after him.

"Let him go," Miles says, stepping in front of the door. He's got his phone out and he's punching the keypad swiftly. "I've got someone keeping an eye on him."

I swing my arms back and forth awkwardly. I feel like an asshole. My hand lifts, gesturing at the door. "I didn't mean to call him an idiot."

"I know." Miles stuffs his phone into his pocket and lifts his eyes to meet mine. "What should we do while he's out?"

My stomach flutters with nerves, though I don't know why. Maybe because last time we were alone in this apartment I told Miles to be a Boy Scout and prepare for next time. My cheeks heat just thinking about that. Any of that.

I divert my gaze over Miles's shoulder at the bed. "We should probably get these plates picked up. I've heard horror stories about cockroaches in Brooklyn apartments."

Miles looks like he wants to argue for a second, but then he allows me to step right around him and jumps in to help, gathering glasses and washing them in the sink. But instead of the busywork adding to anticipation of later activities, my thoughts drift back to what Miles told Dominic, about his role in my family's con, how he's here to take necessary measures if the mobsters get out of hand. And soon I'm anxious for completely different reasons.

I dry my hands with a dishcloth and turn to Miles, who is standing at the sink only inches from me. My eyes sweep over him, from his dark hair to his fitted long-sleeve shirt, showing off some amazing abs, to the jeans that hug him just right, and then his bare feet sprinkled with drops of water from the faucet.

He catches me staring and one brow arches up. "Now that we've prevented infestations, what do you—"

"Do you have a gun?" I blurt out. "Because I need you to teach me how to take it from you."

CHAPTER

28

Miles blinks once. Shakes his head. "You mean disarm?"

"Yes." I nod. "That."

"Not exactly what I had in mind," he says, looking disappointed. "But okay."

"Sharp tried to teach me for, like, five seconds and then…" My voice trails off when Miles procures a gun from the back of his pants. "You had that with you all night?"

"We were parked in a high-crime neighborhood, less than a hundred feet from a group of known mafia members." The exasperated look he gives me would be cute if there weren't a firearm resting between us.

Guess I asked for this. I wave a hand at the weapon. "You're gonna take out the bullets, right?"

Instead of answering, he separates the bottom part of the gun from the rest, holds it up for me to see, sets it on the counter, and then he takes my hand, leading me into the open space in front of the bed.

He holds the gun out for me to take. "Point it at me."

"Okay," I say slowly, and I'm surprised by the tremble in my hands as I train the weapon on him. "Are you sure it won't go off?"

"I'm sure," he says gently. Then in one swift motion, the gun is transferred from my hand to his.

I blink, quickly rewinding the last few milliseconds, trying to figure out how that happened. "Yeah, I can't do that."

"It's easier than you think." Miles flashes me a dimple-filled grin before turning the gun on me. He wraps one of my hands around the barrel and then places the other hand at his wrist. "Grab the end, hit my wrist, and at the same time allow the gun to rotate around your hand."

I try it several times and get somewhere, but nowhere near as quick as it needs to be. Every time we switch places and Miles shows me again, it looks like a magic trick. "There's no room to hesitate," I assess.

Miles nods, a weary expression on his face. "You hesitate, you take a bullet."

Fear bubbles up in my stomach, pushing me to concentrate harder. After about thirty minutes, I succeed in at least preventing Miles from retaking the weapon. His face breaks into a grin. "All right. That's not half bad."

"Where did you learn this?" I ask.

"Krav Maga training," he says, then probably in response to my blank look, he lowers the gun. "Summer before last, the honors program took a field trip to Israel. We trained alongside the IDF for eight weeks."

"IDF?"

"Israeli Defense Forces."

"The summer before last," I repeat. "A bunch of fifteen-year-olds trained with the Israeli army? For a field trip?"

This tiny window into Miles's past only serves as reminder that something isn't right. I'm torn between moving closer to him and running far away.

Worry creases his forehead. He sets the gun on the bed and moves closer to me. "Don't do this again."

"Do what?" I ask, stalling.

"You're conflicted, I can see it in your eyes." He's right in front of me now, his warmth drifting my way, stirring up all kinds of feelings. But unlike the other night when he approached cautiously, waiting for me to make a move, tonight he borrows some of those Krav Maga moves and swiftly hooks an arm around my waist, picks me up, and then sets me down on the kitchen counter.

The power of hovering a few inches above him is too much to resist. I tug him closer, my legs hooking around his back, and then I bring his mouth to mine. In an instant the world becomes as small as this apartment, and Miles's hands and lips become the only thing I can think about. I yank his shirt over his head, tossing it to the floor. He's much smoother, gentler, bringing my sweater above my head. His warm fingers glide up and down my back, his lips teasing mine until they part, and he deepens the kiss. My heart fights to get out of my chest. And then we're pressed together again, my legs hooked around his waist, my hands in his hair, his bare skin against my skin and I don't know which heartbeat is mine anymore.

My fingers grapple for the button of his jeans, and he leans into me for a moment, making the task easier, and then his mouth pauses in its journey down my neck.

"Dominic might be back soon," Miles says, sounding a little breathless.

I tug hard on the waistband of his jeans, drawing him even closer. "He can wait in the hall."

Miles laughs, then pulls back to look at my face. "I would want more time if we were going to…"

"Of course." I roll my eyes, but the action is false. Inside I'm warm all over. "Always have to be the best at everything, huh?"

His gaze roams from my face to my nearly bare chest, and then his mouth is on mine again. He whispers against my lips,

"Didn't realize it was a competition."

"Everything is a competition." I hop down from the counter, hook my index fingers into his belt loops, and drag him toward the bed. "But you're right. We can wait until we have more time."

Yeah, the possibility of sex with Miles is appealing, but the idea of Dominic interrupting is far less appealing. Plus it is kind of a big deal, considering we haven't done that before, not together anyway. For Miles, not ever, assuming what he told me back in November was true. I know some guys lie about being virgins, but he really didn't have any reason to lie.

"What are you thinking about?" Miles asks, bringing me back to the here and now.

I nudge him until he falls back onto the bed. "How your mom called you shy, and how I still think that's a load of crap."

"First off…" He brings me down on the bed beside him and leans on one elbow, looking at me. "Mentioning my mother in a situation like this is kind of a buzzkill. Second, maybe 'shy' wasn't the right word."

"Then what?" I lift my hand to his cheek, feeling the little bit of stubble. "Undercover as shy? Passionate about sharp pencils but pretending to be shy? Trying too hard to make window escapes a signature move?"

"Is that what you really think of me?" He quirks an eyebrow. One finger glides from my neck down to the tiny bow centered on the front of my bra. "I was going to say selective. I keep only the best company."

"Stuff like that kind of ruins the fun in making fun of you," I admit. "How long do you think we have?"

"In New York? In life? On this earth?" he rattles off, and then laughs when I pinch his shoulder. "Maybe an hour."

"An hour to live…" I prop myself up, facing Miles. My free hand lands on his shoulder and then slides all the way down his chest. The smile on his face dies and the heated look from earlier returns. He rolls onto his back, freeing both hands to cup my face, and pulls my mouth to his. My hand still rests at his hip, my body half on top of him. With my fingers busy exploring, the waistband of both his jeans and boxers slide south. From the corner of my eye, I catch a flash of something dark or shadowed on his skin. While Miles's lips explore my collarbone, I glance downward, my eyes narrowing to focus on his left upper thigh, just below his hip bone.

"Do you—" I start, and then become momentarily distracted by the feel of his fingertips running over the satin material of my bra. I draw in a breath and refocus. I slide down, out of reach of Miles's lips, and tug one side of his jeans and boxers lower again. I look up at him, shock probably all over my face. "You have a tattoo? Since when?"

Technically I hadn't looked at this part of his body without clothing before. My hands have been there, but my eyes had been focused elsewhere.

"Since Christmas break," he says, and when I slide even farther down to get a good look, his breath catches, heart pounding against his chest where one of my hands now rests. "Best tattoo shops are in Europe."

I'm too busy studying the symbol to analyze his answer for truth. "It's Chinese, right?"

Miles nods. I know this only because I hear the movement of his head against the pillow. I haven't looked away from the dark ink below his left hip. Something is so familiar about this, but Chinese is not a language I've learned. Unlike Miles, who was born in China, lived there for several years, and then brought his Chinese nanny, Mr. Lee, all over the world with him until he went to boarding school.

My other hand now rests on his stomach. I tilt my head, viewing it from a new angle. Upon closer examination, it's clear the symbol is actually several symbols. Possibly a series of words or a phrase. "What does it mean?"

"It means"—one of his hands tangles in my hair, the other reaching for me—"that you're making me crazy."

I'm suddenly aware of where my head is and the region I'm so very close to. My face heats and I quickly slide up until I'm eye level with Miles. "Sorry."

"Not complaining," he says, capturing my mouth with his. "But it's only fair if I check you for ink, right?"

"Right," I say, smiling and turning flat on my back like he'd been. His fingers head straight for the elastic waist of my leggings, but his mouth slowly, patiently makes its way down my chest, my stomach, below my belly button, until I can't even remember my own name let alone think about why that tattoo might be familiar to me.

But amid the haze brought on by warm lips that are now brushing over each of my hips, a voice in the back of my head urges me to stop and think about what I just saw. And then a name pops into the front of my mind.

Aidan.

Oh shit. This is messed up. I can't think about my sister's boyfriend while Miles is—

The awkwardness of this moment triggers another very awkward moment. Something that happened when I first moved in with Harper and Aidan. The haze begins to clear, nearly showing me a full picture, but then Miles's voice bursts through my thoughts.

"Is this okay?" he asks so gently, hypnotically, that I nearly blurt out *yes* without even knowing what I'm agreeing to.

I glance down and see him preparing to slip my black leggings off, but his blue eyes lock with mine, waiting for permission. My stomach flutters with both nerves and excitement. "Yeah—I mean yes. It's okay."

Soon my pants join the other clothes scattered around the studio apartment. Miles kisses below my hip, my inner thigh, the outside of my underwear, and I know exactly what he meant minutes ago when he said I was making him crazy. And then without warning, the haze vanishes again and a clear graphic image of Simon Gilbert bursts into my mind. His body stretched out on the medical examiner's table during the autopsy. A sheet covering his head. And below his left hip—

I gasp, sitting up suddenly, startling Miles. My chest rises and falls so rapidly I can barely speak. The heat between us cools. Cold dread knots the pit of my stomach and icy beads of sweat form all over my skin. There it is. That missing piece. The seed that started it all. Dammit. Why did I have to go looking for it?

Concern fills Miles's beautiful blue eyes. He sits up, shifting close enough to touch my cheeks. "What's wrong?"

"You…" I say, but words get lodged in my throat. My gaze drifts to where the ink is now hidden and then back to his face. "Aidan…Simon. The tattoo."

Comprehension forms on his face. He draws his hand back, eyes wide.

I finally spit out the words I'd been trying to form. "St. Felicity's."

CHAPTER
29

My eyes squeeze shut as I try to recall that awkward second day of living with my sister and Aidan. I'd humiliated myself, stumbling half-asleep into an occupied bathroom where Aidan, coming off a night shift for the Secret Service, had just stepped out of the shower. He'd been so quiet, kept the lights off, using only the early dawn light, probably not wanting to wake Harper, and I walked right in. Got a full-frontal view of my future brother-in-law.

I scoot back, placing a couple of feet of empty space between Miles and me. "That's their mark, isn't it?"

Aidan had handled my intrusion with polite professionalism, but my sister thought it was hilarious. Once the ice was broken, I'd asked her about his tattoo. He wouldn't tell her what it meant, so she'd tried to figure it out on her own.

"One of the symbols might mean light," she had called to me from behind her laptop. I'd been trying to forget the whole ordeal, so I'd avoided aiding her in research. "Or fire. The other I think is pet. Fire pet? That doesn't make sense."

"Ellie…" Miles starts but trails off, silently confirming that I'm right.

"Light or fire?" I say aloud to myself, wanting to untangle

every last bit. "Life?"

Miles's eyes widen a smidgen, giving the answer away.

"Life," I repeat. "Life and pet…what am I missing—" Miles's explanation of St. Felicity's comes back to me.

Invitations happen practically from birth, but you don't accept until you're old enough to make a pledge of loyalty for life.

"Pets are loyal," I say, ignoring his efforts to interrupt. We just stare at each other for several long heartbeats until I finally whisper the answer my sister had almost landed on nearly a year ago. "Loyalty for life."

I knew about Simon. I knew he had been a junior member of the league of assassins. But I didn't know about Aidan— God, I can't even think about… Harper doesn't know. I'm sure she doesn't.

And Miles.

I lift my eyes to meet his. "Why? After they tried to kill us? How could you join—"

"They didn't try to kill us; Jack's rogue group did," he says firmly.

The story he told Dominic about how he ended up here, it was missing a piece. A third group to account for Miles. "Did St. Felicity's send you here to kill someone? The Zanettis? Are they that dangerous?"

"Nobody sent me here," Miles states. "I volunteered. I was following a lead."

My whole body turns to ice. "Were you ever going to tell me?" I wait a beat and then find the answer on my own. "That's what you meant when you said you hadn't expected us to be so—"

The look he gives me—intense, rich with pain, dripping with so much—causes my voice to catch. I stop before too much pours out of me. I've already given away enough. And now I feel naked—figuratively and literally. I spring to my feet and scoop up my leggings and sweater.

"Aidan," I mutter under my breath while shoving a leg into my pants. "I never thought— I have to tell Harper."

Miles is on his feet again, too. His hands land on my arms, holding me firmly in place. "You can't tell Harper anything."

I shake out of his grip and pull my sweater on hastily. "What do you mean I can't tell her? Of course I have to tell her."

"Ellie, look at me." Miles forces my chin up so our eyes meet. "You can't tell her anything. Not ever. And I've never meant that more than I do right now."

Fear bubbles up in my chest. "But you do realize that Aidan was arrested by the FBI barely two months ago for being paid to murder Simon Gilbert. As a hit man, assassin— whichever word you want to use. And it turns out they were right; he is a freakin' assassin!"

"Shhh," Miles says, looking panicked. "Just because he pledged doesn't mean he's been called to duty. He may never be."

"Called to duty?" I shake my head. It's too much. A new thought ignites. "I know you volunteered, but what do they want you to do here? Do you have to—" I'm not sure I can say it but I take another stab at it. "Kill someone?"

The color drains from Miles's face, and his body turns to stone right in front of me. The memory of Miles pointing that gun at Jack after he came so close to ending us, I can still see his finger tremble over the trigger, can still hear Clyde's voice urging him to put the gun down, saying he wasn't ready to take someone's life.

"What did they do to you, Miles?" I ask, even though I'm afraid of the answer. "I thought your family wasn't part of St. Felicity's. Jack said your dad turned it down."

"I thought that, too." His eyes close briefly and he exhales, seeming to refocus. "I have been given a job already, but I haven't had to... I mean I haven't..."

Killed someone. That's what he can't say.

"How did this happen? You're seventeen. How could anyone ask you to do this?"

"Only one person could ask me to do this," Miles says, fierceness in his voice now. "Or better yet, only one person could convince me to do this."

"Your father?" I guess, completely clueless. "The president?"

"Simon." The name falls from his lips with such genuine respect and value.

"Simon's dead," I remind him. "When exactly did you get that tattoo?"

"A month ago." He studies my face as if waiting for me to say something, but I can see it's him who's deliberating, him who is reminding me of the boy who offered me so little information about himself when we first met, made me work and dig for every tiny thread. He must have made his choice, because seconds later, he shoves the bed aside, revealing a small, barely visible door. "Come on, I have some stuff to show you."

"I take back my comment about window escapes being your go-to," I mutter. "Clearly secret rooms are now top of the list."

He seems too flustered by the sharp turn of events to offer any retort. I'm too flustered *not* to joke about this, any of this. Just to keep myself sane and calm. Before opening the door, he grabs a battery-operated camp lantern from under the bed. I follow him through the door, both of us needing to duck our way in. The door clicks shut, leaving us in complete darkness. Then the light from the lantern fills the small space the size of a large walk-in closet. I glance around, not surprised to see the black felt covering the walls. When Miles was my neighbor, he'd had a secret room just like this one. Complete with photos of my classmates and me pinned to the walls. This room has no photos and instead holds only words scribbled on torn pieces of paper and pinned to the walls. Like with the photos in the other secret room, many of the words are connected by pieces of string.

On the wall adjacent to the small door, six words catch my eye. They're pinned and lined up in a perfect row.

SQUIRREL (102)
KING (875)
RAMONA (45)
RIVER (429)
WICK (20)

"Code names." Miles notices me reading a paper on the far right, out of line with the others, the word TOOTH written on it. "Except this one is just a nickname that I haven't deciphered yet."

"And the numbers?" I prompt.

"Correlate with employment or associated organizations," he says. "CIA, FBI, United Nations…"

I give him a look that I hope is scathing. "These are your brothers, right? Brothers for life."

"St. Felicity's isn't an all-male organization."

"Great," I say. "Equal-opportunity assassins."

He sighs. "These names represent remaining members of Jack's rogue for-profit group. Alleged members, anyway."

That puts the ax on my sarcastic remarks. "Seriously? How did you figure out—"

"Simon," he says simply. "Remember that envelope I showed you before Jack hauled us away?"

"I remember," I answer, cutting him short.

The day Miles showed me an envelope Simon had sent him days before he was murdered was the same day a SWAT team showed up at our apartment to take Aidan in on murder charges. I was so confused and took one look at the photos in the envelope—several were of my sister in her former job as a stripper—and the judgment on Miles's face as I confessed everything about my family. Then I knocked him out using a self-defense move he'd taught me and ran off with the envelope.

"There were numbers written on the back of one of the photos," he explains. "Took me forever to decipher them. One I'm still working on."

"And?" I prompt.

"The numbers correlated with a bank in Turkey." He eyes me warily, waiting for my reaction. Clearly he went to Turkey with more purpose than a simple holiday getaway or even for his parents' jobs. He went to investigate something Simon left him.

I divert my eyes from his and focus on the wall. "You should have told me."

"There was nothing to tell," he argues. "It was a whim. A ridiculous tangent that only someone like me, a student with freedom to explore every ounce of curiosity and a month's vacation between semesters, could pursue."

I lift a hand, gesturing around the room at all the puzzle pieces spread over the walls. "Clearly not a whim."

"Got lucky." He shrugs. "A real agent wouldn't have been able to jet across the world to look into a number left on the back of a picture."

"So you said," I respond drily, because I'm beginning to wonder what exactly is left to separate Miles from a so-called real agent. "And what did this Turkish bank reveal?"

"A safe deposit box. In my name." Miles's voice catches, and I can only assume the idea of Simon taking these great lengths, showing how much he trusts his old boarding school roommate, isn't easy to swallow now that he's gone. "He left me a list of names. Which I burned immediately after memorizing them."

"That's it?" I say, not hiding my frustration. Do these military schoolboys ever take a direct approach? Everything is always ten steps when it could be one. Always circling a perimeter but rarely striding through it. "He couldn't have written the names on the back of the photos? You had to go all the way to Turkey just to get a list of names?"

"Names of very dangerous individuals who happen to have a great deal of power and resources," he says, as if I need a reminder how dangerous Jack and his band of brothers were. "And he also left this note."

His index finger points at the wall behind me. I turn slowly and walk toward a small slip of paper with handwriting I recognize from all the biology lab reports we did together and from that envelope of pictures.

The only way to catch them is from the inside. I'm sorry. -S

Even though I'd already discovered and deciphered the tattoo, this note is what actually makes me believe the truth.

And my heart is already breaking.

CHAPTER

30

Simon and I were friends for only a few months, and obviously there was a lot I hadn't known about the California senator's son, but seeing his handwriting again, I can't help the haunted feeling that creeps up in my belly. I imagine for Miles, who knew Simon much longer, that feeling is magnified, especially because this note is to him. And if I'm understanding things correctly, following this wild agent-to-be chase, this note is to Miles in the event that Simon was unable to do whatever it is Miles is supposed to do.

"The inside," I say slowly, reading the words from the note for the fifth time. "As in inside St. Felicity's?"

A long silence sits between us until Miles finally says, "Yes."

I keep staring at the note, unable to look at Miles as his confirmation sinks in. And suddenly I hear even more in that confession, in that one yes he just uttered. I turn sharply to face him. "Inside St. Felicity's but also inside Jack's group."

My feet instinctively move backward, away from him. "That night he kidnapped us, Jack offered you a spot on his team. And since Jack and others there that night aren't around to offer the real story, you could easily slide that offer back onto the table to the remaining members of the group. That whole time we were held there, for hours, you were listening to those assholes talk. They said something or gave away a security code, something that would get you in without question."

Miles steps closer, reaches a hand out to smooth down my probably wild make-out hair. "You really are good at this. It's mind-blowing."

"If I were good at this, I would've figured it out a week ago," I snap, and then I shove his arm away. "Why are you doing this? Why can't you just hand over the list of names to the godfather of St. Felicity's and let them handle it?"

Why couldn't Simon have done that? He might still be alive if he had.

"Right." Miles lifts his hands, exasperated. "Because every group must have a leader? If they do, I've yet to meet him or her. And as for the members I *have* met? How am I supposed to know they aren't part of Jack's group, too? Hell, I don't even know if it's *Jack's* group! He may have been calling the shots to the handful of guys with him, but that doesn't mean he was calling *all* the shots. We don't know who is involved outside of those names he left. There's a reason Simon didn't tell anyone."

"Yeah, and look how that turned out for him," I remind him.

Hurt flickers across Miles's face. "He left me this job; am I just supposed to ignore it?"

Yes! I want to scream. Instead I lean against the wall and scrub a hand over my face. "Simon was murdered trying to play undercover hero. Am I supposed to be happy that you've decided to pick up where he left off?"

He opens his mouth to argue but stops, seeming to rethink his answer. "I...I don't know."

And for a moment he's the same Miles who took me to

the fort he built in the woods near his house, the same guy whose hands roamed over my body with boyish curiosity after he admitted his inexperience with girls. But if I dig deep into my memories, study them more closely, I'll be able to see that he was never completely mine. Some part of him has always been devoted to a lifetime of service—as a spy, as an agent of some kind, as a hero to someone else...or something along those lines.

"So Jack's group, the bad assassins, is involved in my dad's con somehow?" I assess, shifting back to business.

He offers only a swift nod.

"And sometime between the last time I saw you, the night of the pre-Christmas dinner, and when you showed up in New York, you managed to pledge a lifetime allegiance to an organization of noble assassins, then found some of the bad assassins and convinced them to let you in on their money-making schemes?"

He looks like he wants to deny it but seems to know better. "Simply put. But yes."

"If St. Felicity's is such a secret organization, how did you join so suddenly?" I ask. "I can't imagine they have a 1-800 number that prospective members can just dial whenever they're ready—" The answer lands right in front of me. "Your dad. He's a member, too, isn't he? And he revealed this when you revealed why you wanted to go to Turkey. He probably has a phone number."

Miles nods. "There's a home base in Bucharest. I went through a ten-day initiation program."

There's a hint of something deeper, darker when he says *initiation*, but I'm not sure I want to know. And ten days? I think that coordinates pretty well with the length of his radio silence. I can assume he wasn't allowed cell phone privileges while in Bucharest. At least now I know he wasn't just blowing me off. As if the truth is any comfort.

"What happens if I make good on my promise to the FBI? If I turn in my dad," I say. "How much danger are you going to be in with the Feds busting up the fun? I doubt you want them getting their hands into your investigation."

"I'll be okay," he says.

Miles has succeeded in lying to me before but this time I hear it hovering in the space between his words and him looking at me..

I look at him, desperate for someone to send me in the right direction. If such a thing exists. "What do you want me to do? Back out? I will if it means you'll be okay. I can use the Zanettis as my excuse."

The words are out before I can stop. Damn those clingy girlfriend responses. I need to figure out how to bury them.

"And what about your mom?" Miles asks.

"I don't know." I shake my head. "Maybe there's another way."

He closes the gap between us, gets his arms around me before I can protest. "I'm sorry. I should have told you."

Anger bubbles up in me. I tug out of his grip and shove him back. "This isn't something you can apologize for, Miles."

"Not even for someone who's gifted at apologies?" He grins, flashing me those dimples.

His teasing only infuriates me more. "I already know how this will play out. We'll sneak around until something happens that puts me in danger. Again. And then you'll vanish. For my sake. Because you're Miles who follows rules, uses logic, and has enough willpower to stay away for the right reasons. If it comes to choosing them or *something else*…we both know where your loyalty lies." I point to his left hip where the tattoo is covered by his jeans. "It's almost like you were born to be a noble assassin."

With that, I turn my back on him and make my way out of the tiny secret room. The apartment is lit only by a small lamp, but after the dark room it feels as bright as Times Square. I squint while slipping on my shoes and coat, waiting for my eyes to adjust.

Miles is taller and takes more time getting out of the small room, then shoves the bed back into place.

"Ellie—" he starts when he sees me preparing to leave.

"What?" I tug the zipper on my jacket and then rest a hand on the door before finally offering eye contact. Part of me is afraid he'll be able to say the right words, ones that make me forget he isn't going to choose me in the end. And ending this is easier on my terms.

He tugs a hand through his hair, looking more nervous than I've ever seen him. "You aren't—I mean you can't tell anyone. I need your word."

Definitely not the right words. Justice was right. I should have ditched tonight's escapades and stayed for the whole show. I squeeze my eyes shut, wishing myself back to that theater and out of this nightmare where my boyfriend turns out to be an assassin. "I'm not an idiot."

Guess you'll just have to trust me, Miles.

I'm almost out the door, but warm fingers catch my wrist, holding me in place. Miles has that same smoldering look in his eyes. "I'm here if you need me. Always."

I let him hold onto me for a few seconds, savor it, even. Then I free myself and step into the hall. "I've heard that line before. But that guy didn't answer his phone when I called."

He looks like I just slapped him but offers no argument. So I just leave him in the hallway like that. I don't know if it's for good or not. All I know is that things are very different now.

CHAPTER
31

If I thought I was conflicted before about this undercover operation, that was nothing compared to now. With Miles playing 007 with the league of both good and bad assassins, plus Dominic trying out for a spot in the Zanetti family, my mission to turn this con upside down suddenly holds a lot more consequences.

This makes me a bit jumpy at my next open audition, which of course my dad quickly notices.

"What's with you today?" he asks moments after I chewed out Uncle Milky for tapping my shoulder to get my attention. "Is it your boyfriend?" Dad's gaze wanders to Dominic, who's standing across the big agency audition room, chatting with Bruno. "I didn't want to be the one to tell you this, but I'm pretty sure those two are hooking up."

I bite down on my lower lip and say nothing.

Dad shifts his attention back to me, studying my face. His eyes narrow. "But you knew that already, didn't you?"

"How could I not know?" I shrug, playing it cool. "Like you said, it's pretty obvious. Plus, it's not like we were ever serious."

"Serious enough to leave your family and run away with,"

Dad reminds me.

Right. Forgot about that part.

"I didn't run away to be with him." *I did it to be with my sister, and you ruined everything.*

My father gives me a long look, all amusement and deception gone from his face. "I know that."

Then he walks away, leaving me in the wake of that cryptic message. I gape at his back, relieved he can't see my face. What's that supposed to mean? Why does he think I left? And why is this just coming out now? He's the one who's brought up the *ran away with a guy* scenario so many times when discussing my long absence. For a moment I panic that maybe he knows about the FBI, more specifically my involvement with them. But if he knew or even suspected any of that, he would have never let me near this con.

Needing some company and a distraction, I move across the room toward Dominic, hoping to strike up a conversation. But he sees me approaching, shoots a hard glare in my direction, and crosses his arms, ending his conversation with Bruno abruptly.

Okay, so he's still pissed at me for last night. For calling him an idiot.

In the wake of everything else that happened with Miles after Dominic left, I'd forgotten about this fight, and since we'd arrived here separately, well, this is my first reminder. I turn and head out the door to the stairwell. Parents and their triple-threat darlings will be arriving soon for more open auditions, but my head's not in this game today. I just need to walk, to think. I shoot my dad a text so he won't get suspicious.

ME: grabbing some food a few blocks away. U want anything?

HAYES: sure. Pick me out something.

I thunder down two flights of stairs to floor twenty-one, open the door, and stride down the hall with enough confidence that no one in any of these offices will ask me who I am or where I'm headed. As if on autopilot or mechanical mode, I walk the entire floor and head straight for the stairwell opposite to the one I used to get here. My pace quickens as I trot down the next flight of stairs, my feet creating a soothing rhythm. I think my body was secretly missing all the cardio training I'd been forced to do as part of my self-defense program in the weeks prior to coming to New York. I hadn't realized the calming effect such a mundane, repetitive task provided.

Of course thoughts of self-defense quickly lead to thoughts of Miles…of our fight last night, of everything he revealed. I'd woken abruptly at five this morning, sweaty and panicked, having had a nightmare where Connie, my friend who owns the tech shop in DC, handed me a stack of photos. Each picture had been identical. Miles lying in a pool of blood, the tattoo etched to his left hip exposed for everyone to see. St. Felicity's mark. What did it really mean to be part of that group? How could he have just dived right in without thinking about it, without planning or considering the consequences?

Without asking me.

But it's not like I could have really stopped him. Our relationship was new, fragile. Built first on lies and then on some pretty shocking truths. Still, Miles was supposed to be the careful one, the planner. I'm the impulsive one. Except I'm not so sure that's true anymore. Because all I want to do is restore what little I had before Miles took off on his vacation to Turkey and spent ten days in Romania's capital doing God knows what.

"Excuse me, young lady," a voice calls out from inside a large office. A familiar voice.

I stop and take in my surroundings, realizing my little

impromptu workout has led me all the way down to the fifth floor. I backtrack and read the sign on the office door: ARTHUR ACADEMY OF CLASSICAL THEATRICAL STUDIES.

I lean against the doorframe of the office and smile at the old man behind the desk. "Classical theatrical studies? Is that even a thing?"

Grandpa Barney returns the smile, then drops his feet from the desk and stands. "Let me guess. The Johnson Whitman Agency sent you? They have a real eye for talent."

"So I hear." I step inside the office and stand beside a chair that rests across from the desk. To my left is a door, half-glass, that leads to a small classroom. The desks have all been pushed to one side, and a bright-blue rug covers much of the generic tile floor.

After Barney walks around the desk, I'm able to fully see a sign resting against the wall that reads: S&S SCHOOL OF DRIVING. He catches me looking at it and shakes his head. "Shame how they got caught up in that scandal, offering fake driver's licenses to noncitizens."

More like someone got this driving school caught up in the scandal. Maybe the unidentified Jojo the Zanettis claimed they and my dad blackmailed. This means Jojo must be someone who can either create fake accusations toward a small business or bring to light legitimate accusations. Regardless, it has to be a person with a lot of eyes and ears around this city. Maybe a prominent lawyer or a district attorney. Or someone in local politics or government.

"I thought you said you were the star of the show?" I ask, eyeing Barney skeptically. No one is even here for acting class or whatever this scam is.

Barney spreads his arms wide. "That's right. Star of the show, front and center. And if you work as hard as I have, you can be in the spotlight just like I was in my time."

Oh, I see. We're in character now. Not sure who we're in

character for—no one around here—but whatever, I'll play along. Workout those con muscles.

"I'd love to hear about the lessons your studio offers." And so would the FBI. "You came highly recommended by Johnson Whitman Agency."

"Because I am the best," Barney says simply. He gestures toward the chair for me to sit and returns to his spot behind the desk.

After we're seated, he slides a fancy brochure in front of me. I scan it quickly, committing the outrageously priced classes and one-on-one sessions to memory. Though the cost might be market price for Manhattan—a city filled with parents willing to pay forty thousand a year for kindergarten.

"This looks great," I tell him, staying in character. "I'm especially interested in the Monologues for Medical TV Dramas workshop."

Barney smiles. "You've definitely got a face for television."

We both laugh at that, and then a comfortable silence falls on us. I sit for several seconds, content to not do or be anything specific. But then I watch Barney's face change from enthusiastic and theatrical to lined and worried.

"How is Sally doing?" I ask, then add, "My dad told me about the hospital. And the cancer."

"She's…" His shoulders sag a bit. "She's feeling pretty lousy. But chemotherapy will do that to ya."

My insides twist with concern and guilt, but guilt over what? Being healthy? Not being around my family when this illness hit? What am I really guilty of?

"I can't imagine." I clear the lump from my throat. "I'm just so used to Sally's relentless energy and enthusiasm, it's hard to think of her any other way."

"Then don't," Barney says firmly. "Keep her exactly that way in your heart." He studies me for several seconds and then says, "What about you? You look like someone who just found out the world is a giant circle. What's on your mind?"

Scary how close that is to the truth. I trace a line on the desk with my thumbnail, stalling, debating. "Do you—I mean hypothetically—have you ever wanted to go legit? Be a regular guy who goes to work every day, gets paychecks twice a month, spends thirty years paying a mortgage?"

"Well technically I've been that guy many times," Barney jokes.

I roll my eyes. "I mean for real, not an identity created for a con."

He lifts an eyebrow. "Like your sister?"

"Maybe." I shrug, not wanting the conversation or his thoughts to drift too close to Harper, since no one in my family knows that I live with her. "That's what she wanted, right? She told me that once when I was little."

"If that's what she truly wanted, then I hope to God she got it," Barney says, completely serious. "But for me, this life is what I know. I'm not a kindred spirit who needs to roam free. I hate change and new ways."

Funny, I've always thought of my family's ways as free-spirited, the constant moving, the high of a new con. But at the same time, it is a restrictive life, allowing only so much mobility, and many of our cons are the same thing over and over, just with different colors and other interchangeable elements.

I tell Barney that I've been gone too long already and need to get back, but before I go, he leaves me with some pretty surprising parting words.

"I'm not too old or close-minded to know that our way of life isn't the only way," Barney says. "Your mom and dad live their life following their heart, and if you do that, they'll be proud of you no matter what path you choose."

But that's the thing. Do I even want my parents to be proud of me? Or would I rather have Harper and Aidan proud of me? Or Miles?

Miles and Aidan. A couple of noble assassins. Maybe I don't need their pride.

But those words don't exactly feel right. Especially not where Aidan is concerned. I mean, I know him. The way he loves my sister unconditionally, the way he takes care of both of us. It isn't like any of that can be dismissed. And before he worked for the Secret Service, Aidan was a marine. A soldier. Someone who took an oath to die for his country if need be. From the little he's told me about his time in the Marines, I know he was part of a special ops unit. A group that could potentially be sent in to rescue hostages or take out a guy like Osama bin Laden. How is that different from what St. Felicity's does? And why am I more willing to accept Aidan's loyalty to that organization than Miles's?

Because Aidan likely made the choice to join before he knew my sister or me, a voice inside my head says. *Miles left you. He picked them.*

The truth hits like a brick to my stomach. He picked them. And he will continue to choose them over me, to choose finishing the job Simon began in the past over moving forward with me. And I'm not about to toss my heart out there only to be shattered into pieces. A good con always has to know when to bail, when the risk is too high to be worth it. I might have a million different flaws, but I'm a damn good con, and I definitely know when to bail.

Miles has definitely become a risk too high to be worth it.

CHAPTER

32

"Washington, DC, might represent the face of American government and politics globally and in the eyes of most of our country's citizens, but the true birth of our nation, its roots and fundamental building blocks, began not in DC or Philadelphia but right here in Manhattan."

I set my phone back on the table—I'd been using it to read my paper aloud—and I'm met with scattered applause from my classmates seated around the hotel conference room for tonight's lesson.

"What did we like about Ellie's paper?" Ms. Geist prompts. "Remember active listening is part of your grade."

Several hands shoot up in the air. I wait for Mr. Lance to jump in and choose someone, but he's sitting quietly at the far end of the table, his gaze trained on me rather than the hands in the air.

Geist calls on Jacob, who glances down at his notebook in front of him. "I really liked Ellie's points about our country being built by immigrants—"

"Yeah, immigrants who stole the land from Natives," Howie, another junior who I don't know very well, says.

"No interrupting," Geist reminds him.

Jacob finishes his comment, clearly reciting back what I'd read from my paper simply to prove he listened and receive the points for doing so. Three more classmates follow Jacob, offering identical responses. That is until Bret speaks up. With all the tension between him and Dominic and all the time I've spent around Dominic during this trip, I've hardly spoken to the guy at all since we got to New York. Probably for the better if I'm being honest.

"I think it's clear from her paper," Bret says, eyeing me, a hint of amusement in his voice, "that Ellie is a liberal."

I roll my eyes. "What's your point?"

"My point is that our junior class is filled with spawns of corporate America, most of who are not liberals, and it took balls for Ellie to hate on their political views."

Several arguments break out, many of them stating something along the lines of "my parents' views aren't mine," but Geist holds a hand up to quiet everyone.

"We aren't here to debate politics or current events. Tonight's discussion is on the American Revolution. Let's stay on topic." She gives Bret a pointed look and then turns to me. "I was most impressed with Ellie's grasp of key elements of the argumentative essay. This form is something all of you will be asked to write many times over in college." She turns in her seat to view the far end of the oval table. "Mr. Lance, do you agree?"

He shifts in his seat, placing an awkward pause between Geist's question and his answer, but finally says, "I agree that she has an adequate understanding of the structure of an argumentative essay."

Everyone waits for him to say more, and when he doesn't, heat creeps up my neck into my cheeks. It's the most evasive answer I've ever heard Lance give, and I have no clue what I've done to earn this type of attitude. I duck my head and glance down at the agenda for tomorrow, pretending to study it.

Geist waits a beat longer and then calls on Chantel to read her paper. I sit there for nearly an hour, obsessing over Lance's comment and all the possible scenarios that might end with his ambiguous disapproval. When everyone is filing out of the conference room, heading back to their own rooms for the night, I can't take the guessing anymore. Instead of walking out the door, I drop into the seat beside him and state bluntly, "You didn't like my paper."

He shrugs. "It was perfectly written."

"Okaaay…" I say slowly. "But?"

"By perfect, I mean perfection on twelve different levels," Lance states, and finally some emotion is present in his voice, though it seems to have more of a negative charge to it than a positive one.

I sink back in my chair. "You think I cheated?"

"You're too smart to cheat."

"Then what?" I release an exasperated sigh. This was supposed to be the easiest part of my day. I'd enjoyed writing the paper, hadn't had any trouble getting it done, took less than five minutes to read aloud, and then I got to relax for the rest of the hour. Except I'd spent it worrying about what he thought. "If it's perfectly written, meets all the requirements, and you believe it's my own work, why do you look so disappointed?"

With Dominic still pissed at me, the FBI agents begging for evidence every five minutes, and Justice's hang-up over my leaving that show early, I'm so tired of disappointing people.

"Your paper featured ideals regarding immigration and politics that represent my opinions perfectly," Lance says. "But you managed to use language that was slightly different, to create parallel arguments meant to tap into my ego, my need to convert others to my belief."

Still very confused, I feel my forehead scrunch up. "So I'm a good listener and I remember what you tell us in class. How are those bad things?"

"They're not." He sighs. "It's what I expect from most of my students at Holden. They're driven by motivation to get the best grade possible, as many letters of recommendation as possible. But you? I thought you were driven by a love of learning, by curiosity. Instead of you playing the A game, I would have loved to see you research first, form opinions later. Instead you spent your research time studying me and my opinions, analyzing what you thought I wanted to hear, and then you found the sources to back it up." He studies my probably mortified look and then adds, "Is that how you've always done things? Have I enjoyed having my ego inflated so much that I didn't notice until now?"

When he asks that last question, there's a hint of hurt in his voice. How could I hurt an English teacher's feelings with a perfect paper? But it doesn't take long for me to understand.

He thinks I've conned him. He's gone out of his way to support me with college admissions directors, like the guy from Brown, put his own reputation on the line for me. Now he's wondering if our relationship is based strictly on my desire for personal academic gains or simply to manipulate someone in a position of power. And the thing is? I don't even know for sure if his theory holds true. Is it ingrained in my DNA to always use what I know about a person for personal gain? Have I been forced down this path ever since the night I sat with my dad in the car and he made me understand why we take such care in learning about those we plan to con?

"So this is a personal thing?" I ask. "Not academic."

"'Act in such a way that you treat humanity, whether in

your own person or in the person of any other, never merely as a means to an end but always at the same time as an end,'" he recites.

I look down at my hands. "That's Kant, right?"

"Yes." He leans on one elbow, looking me over carefully. "I thought this was a two-way street, that we were learning from each other, that I knew who you were. But figuring out that I might be nothing but a mere means for you…you can imagine how disappointing that might be for someone."

I almost want to say, *Yes, I can imagine it. Yes, I feel bad. I'm sorry.* But only two of those things are true. "You're simplifying a very complex argument. No one in my life is either a mere means or a rational autonomous being, to quote Kant. Everyone is both." Okay, maybe Agent Sheldon is just a mere means. But that's only because she has the same view of me. I stare at my teacher again and take a deep breath before plunging into the deep end. "You were right about something. You don't know me. You couldn't. Because most of the truths about my life are hidden even from Holden's records."

"Then tell me," he says, like it's that simple.

"You wouldn't believe me even if I did tell you." I push my chair back and stand. "But I never asked you for anything. I never asked you to help me apply to college or introduce me to Brown's admissions director. If I've subconsciously tried to inflate your ego through my academic work, it's only because I want you to like me. Because you're a great teacher. And yes, I know how to manipulate the hell out of people; you have no idea—" I shake my head, biting back incriminating details. "But I'm trying not to be like that. In fact, it's the only thing I'm completely sure that I want to achieve."

I don't wait for his reaction or any response on his end. I'm too afraid to hear it. Too afraid to admit how hurt I am by this person I didn't even know I valued so highly. Maybe my feelings have nothing to do with Lance and more to do with my constant fear that I won't ever shake the person I used to be. Miles got over it, but just when one person joins Team Ellie, another one is leaving.

As I'm headed down the hall, I glance out the windows displaying Times Square. The lights are practically blinding, but even with that, I spot a man crossing the street, heading toward a bench. A man who is probably gifted at concealing himself in plain sight, but still I see him clear as anything. I turn abruptly and head toward the stairwell.

Agent Beckett and I need to have a little chat about his son.

CHAPTER
33

I seat myself on an icy bench and feign interest in my phone. About a minute later, I hear the shuffle of another person taking the spot at the opposite end of the bench. I know better than to look at him. Instead I continue my fake obsession with Snapchat and wait for him to speak first.

"How's New York City treating you?" Agent Beckett says.

I shrug and chance a sideways glance at him. Lines of worry crease his face. My heart picks up speed. "Did something happen to—"

"He's fine," Agent Beckett says, referring to Miles. "I've worried about you."

"Why?" I ask. "It's not like I've acquired tattoos recently or joined any shady organizations."

"Right," he says, and I hear the tension in his voice, the words he can't speak here, out in the open.

Despite the fact that I've always respected both of Miles's parents, I can't help the anger that ignites inside me. No longer caring about being covert, I turn to face him. "Why would you let him…" My voice trails off. He can fill in the blanks. "He's your son. He's only seventeen. I don't get it."

"I let him because he told me he was doing it no matter

what I said," Agent Beckett says. "And because he's right. There *is* work left for him to do, and it isn't the kind of job that can be passed off to someone else. But he isn't alone, Ellie. I'm right here with him. Always."

"So do it for him," I plead. "Uncover the dirty agents for him."

"I wish I could." He looks over at me, and he really does seem gutted over this. "But my reputation in government work and the investigations I've done, they make it too difficult to play the dirty-agent-undercover role. I'd never get anyone to open up the way Miles has—"

"Wait," I interrupt, my heart pounding even faster. "You mean he's already made connections? Earned the trust of…" Guys like Jack, but I won't dare say that aloud. Guys who aren't above kidnapping seventeen-year-old kids and murdering a US senator's teenage son.

Regret is all over his face. "Just remember, Ellie. My son is brilliant. He knows what he's doing. He's better trained than many agents twice his age."

Hearing Agent Beckett—a very experienced CIA operative—say those things about Miles does offer me at least an ounce of hope for his safety. It isn't like I can hate Miles for being honorable and loyal to his best friend.

I sink back onto the bench, putting one more piece of this puzzle together. "So this new mission was the reason that you wanted me to do what I did at Holden that one night?" The night I deleted Miles Beckett from the school records.

"Couldn't have your family connecting you and him together through Holden's records," he explains. "Unlikely but still too risky."

We sit in silence for a bit, both of us watching the traffic and people out for the evening. Then I stand, preparing to leave. "Glad we had this chat," I say, though he probably doesn't fully deserve my sarcasm or attitude.

"Ellie," he calls out, stopping me. "It isn't easy what you're doing. Take it from someone with experience turning in a family member."

It takes me a second to realize what he's saying, and when I do, it isn't easy for me to hide the surprise from my face. I take a few steps closer and glance around before whispering, "Clyde?"

Miles's uncle. Agent Beckett's brother. He used to be a criminal. Like me, the FBI used him as an informant, offered him immunity in return for valuable information. I never would have guessed that his own brother turned him in.

Agent Beckett nods. "You can't take it back once it's done. But right now, you can still back out. Walk away without any consequences."

"But don't you get it?" I tell him. "That's exactly what I'm doing. Taking it back."

"At what cost?"

The question floats in the air behind me as I turn to walk away, putting more and more distance between myself and another Beckett. My confidence in the job I'm doing fades with each step I take toward the hotel, and by the time I'm back in the heated building, I'm now absorbed in worry over what will happen to the rest of my family if I provide evidence to Sharp and Sheldon. What about Barney and Oscar? Will all of them be taken in?

On the way back to my room, in the hall, I bump into Dominic. "Hey," I say, pausing for that long, awkward beat where our last conversation fills the silence. The one where I called him an idiot and he stormed off.

"Hey." He makes eye contact with me only briefly and then stares over my shoulder. "Sheldon and Sharp are looking for you."

My stomach knots. They want evidence. They want out of New York City.

"What's wrong?" Dominic asks immediately.

I shake my head. "Are they down the hall?"

"Yeah, I think so." He reaches for my sleeve before I can walk away. "Are you having second thoughts?"

I release a breath and turn to face him. "About turning in mobsters? No. But Barney and Oscar and Milky…"

"What are you…" He shifts from one foot to the other, clearly uncomfortable. "Are you going to?"

Agent Beckett said it wasn't too late to back out.

I lift an eyebrow at Dominic's concerned face. "Worried about your new BFF?"

Dominic's face contorts, and for a second I think he might hit me or punch a wall or something, but instead he glances around the hotel hallway and says in the lowest voice possible, "Last night Bruno invited me over for poker night… some of his friends, too. And, well, I got some evidence. From Bruno's place."

My eyes widen. "What, like a dead body?"

"No! Jesus Christ, Ellie." He looks a little panicked now and leans in closer. "Like bank deposit slips. Some unopened mail that might be bank statements."

"Could be something to build a case," I say slowly, thinking. "But money alone doesn't mean fraud. We need to prove that the agency has no intention of seeking out work for those kids."

"You know that's probably more than half the talent and modeling agencies in the city," Dominic says.

I look up at him, complete shock washing over me. "You're right. You're so right."

This isn't the Dr. Ames con where we had no actual rehab or boot camp facility, no professional addiction counselors. All the things my family took payment for should have existed in the case of an honest business. But show business isn't like that.

"I need to find Sheldon and Sharp," I say after several seconds of mulling over this new discovery.

"Okay...?" Dominic prompts. "What about the evidence I have?"

"Sit on it," I tell him firmly. "Bruno will know where it came from and, well, you know what that means..." I make a motion of slicing my throat. Color drains from Dominic's face, but he nods. Before heading down the hall, I turn to Dominic. "Thanks for taking that risk. Don't know what I'd do without you."

The look of both shock and pride on his face is worth the swallowing of pride it took on my end to utter those words.

***

"This is not how the FBI works," Sheldon snaps at me. "You don't get to keep dictating the terms of this operation."

"You asked me to follow the money," I argue. "It isn't my fault that you didn't specify which direction I had to go in."

"You're working right under the nose of a highly skilled crook, and now you want me to chase some hypothetical third party?" Sheldon says. "And let your entire family — of criminals — off the hook in the process. Just stick to the plan and find me a crime in this agency."

"There is none," I tell her for the third time in the last fifteen minutes. "They are legitimately offering what is advertised, at least to the extent of similar businesses that have been in operation for years."

"Oh, so you're telling me those outsourced services are run by individuals with credentials to legally work in this country?" Sheldon counters.

I fold my arms across my chest. "Are you really gonna go back home and tell your FBI peers that you set up this big operation in New York City all to catch a handful of undocumented workers?"

Her head looks ready to explode all over this hotel room.

I glance around. "Where is Sharp?" I ask.

He's good at being the middleman. The voice of reason.

"He's in the workout room," she says, still fuming.

My gaze lands on a newspaper lying on one of the double beds. The headline says: *Jojo Offers Foster Kids a Chance to Speak at City Council Meeting.*

Another paper sits about a foot away, flipped open to the Arts & Life section featuring a column titled: *Jojo Takes Family to See Hamilton on Broadway.*

Agent Sheldon looks beside herself when I turn my back on her to get a closer look at one of the papers. "Who is this Jojo person?"

"He's a city council member we're investigating," Sheldon answers mechanically, before switching gears. "I think we just need to retrace all the details thus far, create a storyboard and see if something comes out of the current evidence."

"It won't," I say, not taking my eyes off the paper. It can't be a coincidence, can it? Finally I spin back to face her. "Is it possible this city council member, Jojo, might be involved with the Zanettis?"

Sheldon looks genuinely confused for a second but quickly crosses the room and takes the paper from my hands, studying it. "That's a great big leap with no evidence to back it, but he's definitely up to something."

I'm not ready to tell her about the surveillance that Miles, Dominic, and I did involving the Zanettis, so I come up with an alternative on the spot. "Dominic heard Bruno talking about Jojo."

Sheldon waves a hand toward the newspapers, pointing out others lying on the table that I hadn't seen. "The man's a media favorite; I'm sure lots of people are talking about him."

"Bruno said"—I close my eyes, recalling the exact words; Sheldon will want exact—"that Jojo owed them a favor, that they had dirt on him."

I open my eyes again and see that Sheldon has ditched the indifferent look she wore moments ago. "Bruno said that my dad dug up the dirt and he and his family held a gun to Jojo's head."

"Why am I only now hearing all of this?" Sheldon starts pacing. "You can't just pick and choose which information you share."

I ignore her lecture and dig for one more bit of info. "City council...that's not, like, a big deal or anything, right?"

As someone who went to school with a senator's son among other kids of politicians who have offices in DC, city council member hardly seems like a power position.

"In New York City?" Sheldon heads for her laptop on the table. "It's definitely a big deal."

Now it's my turn to pace. "So the Zanettis blackmailed Jojo with something my family found..." I nod to myself. "That fits. We've been known to excel at blackmail."

I stare at the good-looking man in the newspaper photo. His charming smile reaches all the way to his eyes as he sits behind a long table, admiring a kid standing in front of the microphone, probably speaking to the city council about life in the foster care system. Caption beneath the photo reads: *City councilman Joey Joplin, affectionately called Jojo, was moved to tears by young Byron Campbell's story at Tuesday night's city council meeting.*

"The Zanettis forced Jojo to offer up some fancy building space," I continue, more to myself than to Sheldon, who is now busy pounding away at her laptop. "Probably fast-tracked all their business credentials. The Zanettis needed my family to sell the product, because who would put their kids in the hands of those New Jersey thugs?"

"Every party in this scam is interdependent," Sheldon adds. "I wouldn't be surprised if the Zanettis put a good bit of cash into Jojo's campaign fund."

Her hands hover over the keyboard, suddenly still. The look on her face is one of pure discomfort, and it doesn't take long for me to realize she hadn't meant to jump on my train, to be my partner like she is Sharp's.

And I really wish my face wouldn't heat up after figuring this all out. Who cares what Sheldon thinks of me? Screw her.

She's too one-dimensional. In one swift movement she snaps her laptop shut and returns to standing. "Stick to the plan. Get your dad alone and push for the confession, with or without the mention of this hypothetical third party."

I release an angry breath. "I'll get his confession but no one else's. I didn't agree to convicting everyone in my family."

She busies herself stacking papers on top of the table. "You were right earlier. I'm not interested in catching small fish."

Even though she doesn't tell me to get out, the dismissal is clear in her tone. Being on the same train of thought as me, the idea of really working together, it was too much for straitlaced Agent Sheldon.

I give her ten more seconds to redeem herself, and then I storm out of the room, letting the door slam shut behind me. I thought Miles was infuriating when I first met him—his high moral conscience, his hot-and-cold feelings toward me—but that was nothing compared to the way Sheldon treats me. She could definitely use a lesson from Mr. Lance's friend, Immanuel Kant.

The long hotel hallway provides a good runway for my pent-up frustration. I make it nearly to the end, but someone grasps my arm, stopping me.

"What happened to you?" Agent Sharp says, concern on his face.

I tug my arm free but stay in my spot. "Sheldon. That's what. But whatever. It'll be over soon."

"Is that what she told you?" He lowers his voice, leaning

in like he's afraid she's listening.

Both of us glance around at the same time, checking the hallway—all clear.

"That's what I told myself." The storm in my gut calms enough to be curious. "Why?"

Sharp looks around again then nods toward the stairwell. I follow him down several flights to a lower level that appears to be only for staff. He pushes open a random door, and soon we're walking down what appears to be an underground tunnel.

My gaze roams around the cement walls and the low lights hanging near the ceiling every couple of feet. "What is this? A secret FBI lair? Or is it your special place where you come to contemplate your feelings?"

Sharp laughs. "That last one, definitely. Sometimes I recite poetry to myself."

Now that's an image I can't quite swallow. "Seriously, where are you taking me? I'm starting to see shades of all those serial-killer plots."

"Just service tunnels." He points left, down a new tunnel. "Leads you to Penn Station if you walk a bit. Supposedly Washington's spies used these tunnels to get around the city and pass information during the Revolutionary War."

"Guess they weren't afraid of catching the plague from all the rats that were likely running around down here in the eighteenth century."

"Brave men," Sharp muses. "True loyalty pushes past self-preservation."

Yeah, I'm aware. In fact I'd like to go back to being unaware of that fact. I stop, preparing to turn back. "Thanks for the tour. I've seen enough already."

Sharp leans against the wall, facing me. "This isn't a tour. I just didn't want to chance any listening ears."

Doesn't he inspect his room for bugs daily? I know I do.

Especially with Oscar running around, getting a little better at things he used to suck at. I tap my foot impatiently. If he's planning on giving me another self-defense lecture, I'm not in the mood.

"It's Sheldon," he says.

"If you're about to tell me that you *like her* like her, I might throw up," I say.

"What I mean is," he adds, looking nervous now, "she hasn't been completely honest with you."

"Probably because she doesn't trust me," I respond. Where is he going with this?

"Look, Ellie, if anyone found out I told you this…" His face pinches with worry. "I'll lose my job. But it isn't right what she's doing."

I shift from one foot to the other, catching some of Sharp's nerves. "What isn't right? Is she planning to convict the rest of my family? She just said that she's not interested in small—"

"You," he says quickly, forcing out the word. "You're her Plan B. If you work your dad and come up empty, she's wasted thousands of FBI dollars on this operation. Again. If she at least got another big player to convict, she'll stay on the director's good side."

My chest tightens. It feels like I've just fallen flat on my back, the wind knocked out of me. Then I remember something important. "I signed an agreement as an informant. I have immunity."

Sharp lifts an eyebrow. "Did you read that agreement?"

"Of course I read it," I snap. Plus Aidan and Harper read it. "I'm not an idiot."

"What did it say?" Sharp prompts.

"That as long as I follow FBI undercover protocol, I can't be charged for any crimes related to this New York City con." Hearing it out loud eases my nerves a little.

"You can't be charged for anything related to *New York City*," Sharp repeats.

"Yeah, that's what I said—" The words get lodged in my throat, panic crawling up my insides. New evidence surfaced against my mom, tying her to the Dr. Ames con. I was right by her side during that con. The loyal rehabilitated daughter. "But...I'm only seventeen."

The words come out in a whisper. I don't trust my voice to hold steady.

"It isn't right," Sharp says. "If I thought it was okay, I sure as hell wouldn't be here, risking my job. Sheldon's crossing a line I didn't think she'd go near. But she's got a case. Maybe a good one. And you need to know what's at stake when your dad's hovering over a confession and you're afraid to close the deal...think about Plan B."

Sharp turns quickly, and before I can get another word in, he heads off in the direction he'd pointed earlier, the way to Penn Station. I fall back against the wall and scrub my hands over my face, wishing I had cold water to splash in my eyes, to wake me up from this nightmare.

How could I be so stupid? How could I walk right into this? I begged for it, actually. No wonder Sheldon got so uncomfortable when we were bouncing ideas around like teammates. Like equals. Nobody wants to arrest their teammate. Not even Sheldon.

For a few long, dark minutes I debate waving a white flag, giving myself up now and hoping for the best. Or disappearing down these tunnels and never coming out again. But the low point doesn't last long. Soon it's clear what I need to do. Exactly what Sharp and Sheldon told me to do.

Get my dad to confess.

CHAPTER
34

My pen hits the hardwood floors of the agency for the third time in the last hour. I scoop it up quickly, hoping no one noticed. But before I'm upright again, my dad pauses his conversation with one of the potential affiliates we're pitching ads to—scamming—today to glance over at me. He gives me this look that clearly says, *What the hell is wrong with you?*

What the hell *is* wrong with me?

For starters, I'm wired up with Sheldon and Sharp listening in. Then there's that whole Plan B thing looming over my head. Nothing to be nervous about. I check my phone for new messages, hoping the lack of drama outside this building will calm my nerves, but I end up rereading Agent Sheldon's text from more than an hour ago.

SHELDON: today's the day. Let's get this done fast. In and out, got it?

Yeah, that's not helping my nerves at all. Besides, fast isn't gonna win me any confessions. If I push too hard for information, my dad, the expert conman, will see right through it, and his guard will be permanently up.

"Is there a full-page option?" a woman asks me.

The question forces me to refocus, to remind myself that
at this moment, I'm no longer Ellie Ames, and I'm also no
longer playing the British Broadway performer. Today I'm
an administrative assistant for the Johnson Whitman Agency.
I've aged up quite a bit and have the charcoal Armani
pantsuit to prove it. I scan the table of materials in front of
me and quickly realize that full-page ads aren't an option,
which seems like a huge mistake. The actual brochure design
is of no importance to my dad or anyone working this con.
"No, there isn't actually an option for a full—"

"That's ridiculous. What if I'm willing to double half-page
prices?"

Based on the pinched look on this woman's face, it's
clear she will likely take her checkbook and go if I simply
remit my original answer. Experience with investment cons
has taught me how to recognize a Gold Star, my family's
code name for a subject who wants, more than anything else,
to feel extra special about their willingness to invest their
money. Since no one seems to have planned for Gold Stars
in attendance today, I have to improvise a bit, quickly coming
up with a subject-specific tactic. "Research conducted by our
advertising agency has shown that full-page ads are skipped
over in brochures and program materials nine times out of ten."

The woman's eyes narrow, but she says nothing, allowing
me to continue.

"What we recommend is sharing a half page with crucial
program material such as our audition prep tips. There's also
one other option." I stop abruptly, leaving a dramatic pause
hanging in the air. I've managed to grab my dad's attention
yet again, and he's now moving closer to the table. Beside me,
both Bruno and Uncle Milky are listening in.

"What?" the woman demands. "What's the other option?"

I look her over, pretending to deliberate something important. "Did you say what type of business you're promoting?"

"I'm a stylist," she says, then abruptly adds, as if she'd expected me to ask, "Clothing, hair, and makeup if my full team is involved. Fashion is my personal specialty."

"Huh." I hesitate, leaving her hanging again. "That could work out really well…"

"A full-page ad for my company?" she asks, looking confused.

"Think you could write an advice piece? Maybe something in the realm of dressing for musical theater auditions?"

"How to dress for your dream role," Milky suggests, chiming in from my right side.

"Audition styles 101," I say.

Dad is beside the woman now, offering his own ideas. "Bow-to-toe Broadway styles."

"That has potential." I glance at Dad, who has surely picked up on the Gold Star vibe by now. He offers me a tiny nod of approval. I turn back to the woman. "Of course, if that isn't what you had in mind, I'm sure we can find someone else to fill the slot. I've been debating reaching out to a few editorial friends over at *Vogue*. I interned there right after graduation. Good times."

"No, no," she argues, the skepticism falling from her face. "I minored in journalism, so this is well within my skill set. *Vogue* isn't relatable enough; those writers are out of touch when it comes to everyday fashion, like audition wear."

"I agree completely." I flash her a grin. "If we like your piece, then we'll give it good placement in the brochure and include your half-page business ad below the advice piece."

The woman looks momentarily ecstatic, and then a flicker of worry sneaks into her features. Her eyes sweep over the table materials. "Which pamphlet has information for this option?"

"None of them." Dad rests a hand on the lady's shoulder and lowers his voice. "This agency is committed to offering every resource possible to our clients, but only high-quality information gets past my desk and into the program material. Writing a feature isn't something we can put a dollar amount on."

"Right," the woman says quickly. "I get that."

"So you *are* interested in this affiliate ad package?" Dad prompts. "And you'll keep it between us for the time being?"

For that lengthy moment between Dad sending the runner on third sliding into home and the stylist woman's response, it feels like old times again. That brilliant moment when we know we've sealed the deal, usually before the subject even verbally confirms this. The *yes* is there hovering in the air. Thank God Sheldon and Sharp can hear only what's happening around me and not inside my head. I'd be out of an informant job faster than—

Informant. For the FBI.

Turning in my dad to save my own ass and hopefully free my mother.

The bubbling nostalgia twists and tumbles in my gut, making me feel sick to my stomach. What if I can't do this? I'd asked Sheldon that same question, but I had meant more along the lines of: What if my dad sees right through me and won't speak a word about Jojo or anything valuable? Now I'm wondering if I'm still vulnerable to my dad's infectious influence? What if loyalty to my family rises above self-preservation? And I think it could. If it weren't for my mom's freedom, balancing out the other side of the scale. It's her *and me* in exchange for him, I remind myself.

Another business owner wanting to advertise in the Johnson Whitman Agency material bombards me with questions, and I'm stuck playing this part for the remainder of the informational lunch.

Later, while my dad is walking the last potential affiliate out the door, I get a text from Agent Sharp.

SHARP: Sheldon is antsy. Don't let her get to you. Take

your time, don't force it. Use those great instincts of yours.

A tiny hint of relief washes over me, knowing that I at least have one person rooting for me, but then I scroll back and read an earlier missed text from Sheldon, and the relief is short-lived.

SHELDON: Get your dad alone and get him talking asap

I glance at my dad, who is watching the elevator doors close on the last affiliate. What would he say if I told him I'd been working for the FBI that day in the bank when my mother was taken away? What would he say if he knew I'm doing the same thing now?

"Guess who's getting that employee of the month plaque?" He flashes me a grin that I recognize as the kind reserved only for his real family. "Didn't know I raised such an overachiever. No full-page-ad option? Easy fix. Double the half-page ad price. But no, not good enough for my little girl. She doesn't quit until that woman writes a check for four times the cost of the half-page ad."

I hate how much I enjoy his praise, his approval. Especially considering the fact that I'd been so sure I'd moved past caring what he thinks. "I learned all my tricks from my father. I'll let him know you were impressed."

My dad laughs. It's the most honest sound I've heard from him over the last couple of weeks. He looks at me and then nods toward the elevator. "Come on, let's blow off these idiots, leave them to clean up the place. We'll go somewhere fun."

And there it is. Handed to me on a platter, didn't even have to work for it. That's because the hardest part is in front of me, maybe even out of my reach.

A minute later, after I've got my coat on, Sheldon sends me a new text.

SHELDON: here's your chance. Take it.

Mentally I fill in the implied *or else…Plan B.*

CHAPTER

35

"Look at that, a soul food truck!" my dad says, pointing at a row of colorful trucks parked near the famous Washington Square Park arch. "Just when I'd really started missing the South. Perfect timing."

Yep, perfect timing. Should be an easy conversation segue. From soul food to blackmailing city council members.

"Oh wait. False alarm." He stops at a spot closer to the truck and squints at the sign. "Seoul, like the city. In Korea."

"Those are two very different cuisines." Cold wind whips me in the face. I reach up to fasten the top buttons on my jacket, but my jittery stomach appears to have traveled to my hands, so I tuck them quickly back into my pockets to hide the visible shake from my dad.

"Different indeed," Dad mumbles while eyeing the menu. "Pho...that's like soup, right?"

"Isn't Pho Vietnamese?"

"Yep, I've moved on. Next truck over. Try to keep up, sweetheart," he says, flashing me the con man smile. "So pho?"

"You're right, it's like soup," I tell him. "Really hot soup. So my answer is yes. I'm in."

While we wait in line and then cart steaming bowls

toward a vacant table partially covered in ice and snow, I form a plan to at least attempt to lead the conversation toward the desired.

"My boyfriend asked me to go see about a boy for him," I say, and then instantly regret the out-of-the-blue approach. That never works. I know better. "He's been texting all morning. Wants to know if Bruno asked where he was today."

Dad leans over his steaming bowl, allowing it to warm his face, and I follow his lead, doing the same. "Did he skip out on the job today just to see if Bruno missed him?" Dad shakes his head and laughs. "Amateur."

"He 'says' he had something to do." I use air quotes and add an eye roll for believability. "Bruno didn't ask me anything."

"Nor me." Dad takes a bite of steaming soup and immediately drops his spoon. "Damn, that's hot!"

"Exactly why I haven't touched my spoon." That and the fact that my churning stomach likely won't accept this food. I turn my gaze from Dad and watch a woman in bright-blue earmuffs and matching blue gloves being dragged past our table by a gigantic black Lab. "Do you think Freddy is okay hanging with Bruno?"

"Why wouldn't he be okay?" Something that looks a lot like nerves crosses my dad's face but quickly vanishes, and he picks up his spoon again. "I'm giving it another go. Hopefully my taste buds will remain intact after."

"Dad." I level him with a look. "We've already had this argument. Mobsters are, no matter what you say, something to worry about. Pretty much always. Remember that was one of Mom's favorite sayings? 'At least we're not the mafia.'"

My mother's words spilled out effortlessly without any planning on my part. Words I'd forgotten until now. Dad's spoon pauses over his bowl, but then he dunks it right back in, gulping another bite, probably scalding the back of his throat.

"Huh," he says all casual. "Well, your memory is probably better than mine."

Okaaay? No, probably not. "Really? You don't remember?" I press and earn a *whatever* shrug from my father. "She said that. All the time. And we both know Mom's instincts and judge of character were better than either of ours."

"I guess." He stirs his soup and then points to a piece of meat floating at the top of my bowl. "The beef is amazing. Give it a try."

I study him, trying to guess his angle. There's no way he doesn't remember those things. But then again, he is the man who wrote off his firstborn without a second thought, the man who dove right into planning this New York City con practically seconds after Mom was hauled off to prison. "All her sayings turned out to be true, you know? 'A lie is so much better when it's wrapped in truth.' Do you remember that one?"

My phone vibrates in my lap but I don't stop to look at it. I can guess Sheldon's text without even looking: *What are you doing? Where are you going with this?* And the truth is I don't know where I'm going. Definitely not anywhere near Jojo and his many dark political corners. I just want my dad to say that he remembers. Or maybe even to snap at me and tell me to give it a rest, because it's too painful to think about Mom. But none of those things happen. He's too busy pointing out floating meat in our Seoul Food.

"Maybe," he says. "But you know me, I reserve my memory space for storing the words of drunken literary rogues."

I shove my soup away and lean back in my chair, arms crossed, eyes narrowed at him. My game face is long gone. "You're right. I do know you. I know *that* about you. Because you're my family."

I wait expectantly for him to say something, apologize

or backtrack or at least acknowledge the point I'm trying to make. But as I fume more and more inside, he grows more relaxed. Which pisses me off royally. "You know about her sentencing, right?"

"Oh." He finally looks up from the soup, giving me an ounce of hope that he cares. "Has that happened already?"

"Has it happened already?" I repeat. "Seriously? I know you're off the grid by choice, but how could you not—"

"Look, Ellie," he states, straightening in his chair. "It is what it is. Your mom of all people wouldn't want me dwelling on details like number of months—"

"Months!" I suppress the urge to toss my bowl of pho at him. "Try years, Dad. Ten, to be exact."

And if you keep that wall up, I may be joining her, too.

His eyes dart to the right and then shift to the left as if checking to see if I've created a scene. "Like I said, your mother wouldn't want me dwelling."

My cheeks burn with anger even in this cold temperature. How can you pledge to love someone forever, have children with them, and then not dwell on their ten-year prison sentence? Is this how Miles does it? How he can just be with me one day and not the next? Like, "Okay, we can't be together, guess it's time to get on with the next big job"? If only it were that easy for me. I wouldn't have to worry about my thoughts drifting to Miles or constantly fighting the desire to sniff the sweatshirt he loaned me way back in November. If I were like Dad, I wouldn't even be here right now. I'd still be back at home with Harper, enjoying some corny—and free—Holden Prep January session course. But based on the fact that he's barely given Mom a second thought while I've been obsessing over how to get Mom out of jail, I'm not anything like my father. My heart beats a painful bloody rhythm, oozing guilt and love and hurt while his seems to be made of steel or ice. Something that shields him against all these feelings I can't keep at bay. Maybe that's why I can't shake that admiration for him. Maybe I just wish my heart were cold like his so I didn't have to care.

But I'm not built like him. And I do care. Far, far too much.

"Did you ask her?" I challenge. "Did you ask her how she's doing? If she can survive ten years— " My voice catches; my throat is clogged. I swallow back tears, determined not to shed any in Dad's presence.

"I can't ask her that," he says quietly. "You know I can't go and see her."

"Because it's you they really wanted to catch," I blurt out, and finally earn a reaction from him. I flinch slightly as the words hit him and turn over in his head.

Those were definitely not the right words. Sheldon is probably having a heart attack. But it's not like it isn't common knowledge. The plan had been for him to walk into the bank that day. He has to know I've thought about that, even if he doesn't know I'm the one who tipped off the FBI.

Instead of denying or commenting on my accusation, he pushes his chair back and grabs both our bowls, not even bothering to ask me if I'm finished. While he's striding toward the garbage can, the anger bursting and fighting inside me like a caged animal evens out into a more controlled, deliberate rage offering the potential for premeditated use. I flip over my phone in my lap and punch a quick text to Sheldon.

ME: only him. Promise?

The answer comes less than ten seconds later, my dad still on his way back from tossing our barely eaten lunch.

SHELDON: yes. Only him. U have my word

I push my chair back and stand right in front of my dad. "If it were you…instead of her," I say, watching his face for signs of some remorse, but he looks like he might attempt a joke any second. "She would be a wreck and would do anything to—" I stop, my voice about to crack. I close my eyes for a split second and breathe. Maybe he doesn't deserve to know what she would be like if things had gone as planned that day in the bank. I'm done hoping for the best with him. I'm always disappointed. "Mom would have never let our family partner up with mobsters. She'd never want the risk or to put anyone in danger. She definitely wouldn't approve of threatening and blackmailing an important political—"

His eyes widen in surprise. He grips the sleeve of my coat, tugging me closer, and then leans in, his voice low. "I didn't have a choice."

"No?" The thick scent of confession rises into the cold air, offering an insatiable high, and soon any remaining doubts I had about today's plan are long gone. "The Zanettis made you come up with this talent agency con? They made you take compromising photos of a New York City council member? That's surprising, considering the fact that planning for the Zanettis usually doesn't go much further than carrying an extra magazine and silencer."

"You're right," he says in a low voice, looking stricken, his eyes checking the perimeter again.

Clinging to that high, I hear Sheldon's voice inside my head: *More, we need more.*

"About which part?" I say, and coat the words in as much teenage sarcasm as possible. "The fact that it's your fault I won't have a mother again until I'm nearly thirty? Or that the Zanettis are too gun-happy to come up with a multilayered blackmail plan?"

"Keep your voice down," he orders. "You're right about the plan. It was my idea to get those pictures of Jojo. But as for your mother? It needed to be her. Not me. Because we both know she isn't strong enough to lead this family, to hold everyone together, to make the tough decisions."

For a moment I'm paralyzed by shock. I did it. I actually freakin' did it. And then his words hit me like a smack across the face. I stumble back, wanting nothing more than distance between us. I let the anger take over, mask the hurt. "You know what? I don't need this. Maybe you can just move on, decide to cross lines our family swore to never step over, but I can't. I definitely don't want to be around when this giant bomb you've so carefully built explodes."

It all makes sense now. The mixed signals from him, the way he let me join the team but kept me in the dark about the biggest parts. He's okay with me being around if it's easy, if I don't ask much of him. But when things get too hard for my dad—like keeping in touch with a wife locked up in federal prison or accepting a daughter who wants a different life—he moves on to the next location, the next con.

I'm not about to let him know how much he hurt me. Not about to watch him walk away. Without another moment's hesitation, I turn my back on him and walk away. The phone in my hand vibrates. I take half a second to glance at it.

SHELDON: that's a wrap.

SHARP: Nicely done.

My second successful job as an informant. And this time, I'm not carrying even a drop of guilt. I did exactly what I came to do.

CHAPTER
36

Dominic drops into the empty space beside me on the subway. I stare at the pole in front of me and count the fingers wrapped around it. For several moments Dominic says nothing, but we both know what's coming.

"You okay?" he offers eventually.

I shrug. "Why wouldn't I be?"

The train jerks to a stop, and Dominic waits for the "stand clear of the closing doors" announcement to finish before saying anything else.

"So do you know when they'll..." He glances at me, possibly waiting for me to finish the rest. I don't. "You know, go after them?"

"Him," I correct. "They promised me—only him. And no, I'm not an agent or even a credible citizen. Just an informant. I'm not privy to that information."

Around me, my classmates—Holden blazers, complete with the school crest poking out from beneath heavy winter coats—talk quietly, the early morning hour forcing everyone into a temporary calm.

"What about your mom?" Dominic asks. "Do you know how long it will take?"

To what? Get her out of prison? Get her sentence reduced? I'm not sure which will happen.

"I imagine those things take time," I tell him, and turn to him with a smile. "Hopefully less than ten years, right?"

Despite my attempt to make a joke of this, Dominic doesn't return the smile. "Was it that bad? Setting a trap for your own father and luring him into it?"

"When you say it like that…"

He levels me with a look. "I'm being serious."

The grin drops from my face. I turn my attention back to the fingers and the pole. The anger from yesterday afternoon rises up in me like a disease that laid dormant. Tangle that with Sheldon's Plan B and it's a no-brainer. "It was easier than I thought it would be."

Easy to lure him in, not so easy to think about why it was easy. Because he doesn't care about his wife. Not enough to face the hard stuff. What had he said yesterday? That she would have wanted him to move on. Jesus Christ, she's not dead. But I get that people look up to him. They look to him for leadership. It isn't so much that he's chosen to take care of the "family," it's that he's changed the rules. The second my mom was out of the picture, suddenly the principles, the very tiny yet essential moral compass I was raised with, vanished from their daily practice. It's almost like those ideals were never his. Makes me wonder who my father really is, at his core.

"I don't think I would have been able to go through with it," Dominic says.

The train rattles, and Dominic slides into me, smashing me against a large man smelling like a gallon of freshly chopped garlic. I hold my breath and attempt to earn back the inches between us while turning over Dominic's words in my head. It doesn't take long for me to conclude that he isn't questioning my character. Or putting angel wings on himself.

"You like them," I accuse. When I look at him, he looks away. With a sigh I say, "It's fine. I get it. Their life probably seems fun, exciting even. And sometimes it is, but when it's your whole life, when you can't escape it…" The garlic man seems to be listening in on us. I lower my voice. "I'm just saying that they're easier to like when they aren't *your* family."

Dominic leans forward, resting his arms on his long legs. He glances at me for a split second, a storm in his eyes. "At least your family spends time together. Your parents actually taught you things, made you read books, learn multiple languages—you've hardly been to school, right? They single-handedly educated you. You know that my parents have never taught me a single thing? Not even that knives are dangerous or the stove is hot. They hired people to do that. My entire life."

I almost can't believe what I'm hearing from him. I mean I knew how he felt about his own family, but I hadn't expected this reaction. I thought he could handle being around them without this happening. Without buying into the illusion.

"You have definitely been drinking their Kool-Aid," I groan. "My parents taught me accents and how to *appear* to know another language. Also how to pick locks, manipulate people, capitalize on someone's weakness. Definitely in the running for parents of the year."

"Your family…they know one another. My parents don't know anything about me, and I can't remember the last time we were all in the house at the same time, awake. But your dad, he looks at you for two seconds and he's got everything figured out."

"No he doesn't," I argue. "Don't let the glitter deceive you. He doesn't know anything about me. Everything I've told him since we've been in New York was a lie."

He shakes his head. "I can't explain it. I just know that

he knows you. He knows what you're capable of, what you can and can't handle. He knows exactly how to hurt you." He shakes his head. "My parents think taking away my credit cards will hurt me. They have no idea that I don't give a flying fuck about money."

The train comes to another abrupt halt, and Mr. Lance calls from the front that this is our stop. I spring up from my seat and turn to Dominic. "Look, I agree your family sucks, but that doesn't make mine great. The likely answer is that they both suck. Differently."

I follow the herd of khaki pants and red plaid skirts from the train, up the steps of the subway station and back out into the cold, dreary morning. We walk a little ways before Lance and Geist group us together in front of an old but beautiful building on the campus of Columbia University. Ms. Geist gives yet another lecture on unofficial admissions interviews, and I tune her out.

Justice finds me and hooks an arm through mine. "I asked Mr. Lance if I could take you with me to that brunch my dad arranged, asked him if he thought the connections might be good for you."

"And?" I prompt, wondering why she would want to include me, especially if this was giving her an advantage for admissions.

"He just shrugged and said that was up to you," she says, and then gives me this worried look. "What's up with him? You were his Golden Girl."

My stomach twists for a whole new reason. I want to not care that I've somehow ruined things with my favorite teacher, but lately I don't seem to have much luck getting what I want. Is this the downfall of attempting the honest life? Finding even more things to accidently care about?

"I don't know what his deal is," I say, trying to sound evasive. I'm not interested in analyzing this. "What time is that brunch? Can it get me out of sitting in on Introduction to Sustainability and Environmental Science in the Eastern World?"

Justice's response is completely lost in the space between us, because my father, who appears to be lurking behind a giant statue, has given a familiar signal of two short, soft snaps to get my attention. Only I'm not alone in noticing him, which is not what he intended, I'm sure.

Justice glances at the spot where Dad disappeared from to hide behind the statue again, and then she turns to me, one brow lifted. "Please tell me that isn't another ex. There's older and then there's *older*. Let me be the first to tell you that something is very wrong inside your head and you need help."

Some of yesterday's anger returns along with some internal panic. I'm caught between two undesirable choices— facing my dad again or ignoring him and allowing more than Justice to notice his presence. I release a deep breath and whisper to my friend, "He's my dad."

"Your dad—" she starts, confusion all over her face. Probably because she and I have never talked about my parents. Ever.

I wave a hand to cut her off. "It's a long story. Messy, complicated divorce. Regulated visits."

"Are you…?" Her eyes widen. "Is he dangerous? Should we tell someone?"

"He's not dangerous." I glance at the group and then back at the statue. "Give me a minute, okay? Text me if anyone is looking for me."

With quiet feet and hopefully unnoticed movement, I make my way to the statue and slip behind it, where Dad is waiting impatiently. I don't know what he wants or how he even found me, but my best option is to let him speak and then get rid of him. Shouldn't the FBI be on their way to arrest him anyway?

For a moment I have this urge to warn him. But then I remember Sheldon's Plan B, and every hurtful thing he said to me, and soon I'm hoping to actually witness the handcuffs go on him.

Dad immediately grips my shoulders with both hands, holding me in place. "Thank God I got you alone," he says, sounding so incredibly relieved.

"What?" I demand, putting a bite to the word.

"Yesterday..." He glances around, checking, then checking again. "I need you to know the truth and then I'll leave you alone."

"Considering you've had eighteen hours to come up with a beautiful lie—"

"Yesterday was a lie!" he says, and then exhales, leans in closer, and speaks in a low voice. "The Zanettis tailed me; they were right there. And your mother is the one thing that I haven't let them near—"

"Yeah, because she is in prison," I remind him. What the hell is wrong with him?

"You think they don't have connections in every federal prison?" he says, his eyes wild with fear. "You think they couldn't make an accident happen?"

My heart sinks down to my stomach along with the realization of where he's going with this. "But why? Why get involved with them?"

"It's a long story. I only have a minute. You'll have to take the short version." He drops his hands from my shoulders and leans against the statue. "Right after the FBI took your mother, I went a little bit crazy, looking for every and any way possible to get her out. I researched judges in South Carolina, started following one I thought had the potential to be useful. He's got a gambling addiction worse than any I've seen before. Bookies were on him day and night. He told me he'd likely be assigned to your mom's case if there were an appeal to her sentence. I fronted him some cash to keep him alive—those bookies were dangerous as hell. He promised a short sentence if I paid him a hundred grand. I said that was insane; we'd never earned that kind of cash from any con. He told me the Zanettis were looking for someone like me to expand their revenue operations. I wasn't going to go there," he pleads. "I never would have gone near those mobsters, but then Sally got cancer…"

He pauses, watching me closely, waiting. I work hard to catch my breath, to keep each inhale and exhale even, but I can't believe what I'm hearing. "You're making money to pay off a judge and get Mom out? Why didn't you tell me?"

"I'm sorry, honey." He gives my shoulders a squeeze again and sympathy fills his face. "I was scared it wouldn't work out and that I'd let you down again. Plus it seemed like you were happy with your sister and that agent—"

"Whoa, whoa," I say, shaking my head, needing a quick reverse to five seconds ago. "How do you know about Harper?"

"How do I know?" he says. "You think I'd just let my little girl run off and not check up on her? God knows I was way too bullheaded to do that with Harper. Couldn't make the same mistake twice."

"You…you went after me? Oscar must have followed you," I conclude, putting pieces together. "That's how he found me."

"He didn't follow me all the way to you." Dad grins. "I did manage to lose him near the end. That way he didn't know exactly where you were."

"You knew this whole time that I was lying." I mull that over, hardly able to believe it.

Dominic was right. He does know me.

"I just want you to be happy," he says. "I don't care where or what that is. And it's your secret to tell."

Reality hits like a cold punch to the gut. Oh God, what have I done? "Dad, I need to tell you—"

Something over my shoulder catches his attention, and suddenly he looks at me, panic-stricken. "I have to go. We'll be off the grid, but I'll be in touch. Okay?"

He steps around me and ducks into a crowd of students and parents on a tour. I don't know who he's hiding from, but I can't help it—I run after him.

"Dad!" I call once I'm far enough away from the Holden group.

Sprinting now, I keep my eyes on him while he hops from group to group, but like Oscar, he's gifted at becoming invisible. I lose sight of him for a while, and then when I finally spot the black tails of his coat again, we're outside the campus and he's all the way across a busy street, preparing to duck into a subway station. I'm out of breath, my chest burning from running in the cold. I hit the button in front of the crosswalk ten or twelve times as if it might change sooner. I step off the curb, debating darting into traffic, and my entire foot sinks into a puddle of ice-cold slush. I shake water from my boot and after spotting a small opening, I take off across the road. The slush under my shoe, combined with a tiny patch of ice on the road, sends me flying forward, landing on my hands and knees, barely keeping my face from making contact with the hard pavement. Pain radiates through my body, and for a moment I'm afraid I can't move.

Tires squeal. I look up and go completely deer-in-headlights as a large truck slides forward. I brace myself for impact, but the tires roll to a stop inches from me, and I scramble to my feet, my heart all the way in my throat. I'm shaking from head to toe, but I manage to get myself to the other side of the road. The three cars that hit the brakes to avoid hitting me send a wave of icy gray slush from the road right at me. Little pellets beat at my skin, chilling me to the bone. I close my eyes and take the last step up to the curb.

"Dad!" I shout again. I've lost him. I thunder down the subway steps, earning some looks at my soaking-wet uniform and hair dripping with gray slush. As I'm digging my Metro card from my skirt pocket, I catch sight of him again just as a train is slowing to a stop. The doors open, and I push through dozens of bundled-up New Yorkers, quickly swiping my card and pushing through the turnstile.

He steps onto the train—I'm still fighting my way in—and turns halfway, as if he heard me approaching. But about twenty feet from me, a man I don't recognize and Agent Sharp step onto the train, stand right behind my dad. Sharp whispers something.

I halt right outside the doors, unable to breathe or move. Oh God, this is it. It's happening. Right here. Right now.

Because of me.

The doors slam shut and the train lurches forward, carrying my dad and the FBI agents preparing to arrest him. I stand there in the station, watching train after train go past, carrying only strangers, until an old woman taps my shoulder.

"Are you all right, dear? You look lost."

Tears bubble in my eyes. I want to scream: *I take it back! I take it all back!* But it wouldn't do any good. Nothing would change the fact that I single-handedly put both my parents in prison.

The world my dad built around himself since we reunited in New York has all been an illusion, hiding his real feelings, his fears, his love. All the things that would have stopped me from doing what I did.

And for a few seconds, I finally understand what it feels like to be conned. To be the people on the other side of all the jobs my family and I have done. To believe one reality so wholeheartedly only to have the curtain drawn back, revealing a completely different reality.

The old woman taps me again, and I know I have to move. I have to go somewhere or she's going to form some conclusions about my mental state and take action. But I can't just walk back to Columbia, to my Holden classmates, and pretend everything is okay. I need...I need someone who can...

Someone who puts loyalty above self-preservation.

CHAPTER
37

Miles takes one look at me shivering on his doorstep and wordlessly ushers me inside, bolting the door behind him. "What happened?"

I shake my head, not able to speak. I can barely remember how I got here. The subway mostly, but a lot of walking in the freezing temperature. And somehow, between watching the subway doors close on my father and Agent Sharp, and getting to Miles's apartment, I lost my jacket. Lost my will to look for it, too.

"I just— My dad—" I try to pull myself together, but hot tears roll down my face before I can stop them. "It's done. I did it. Got the evidence. And then I tried to warn him, but Agent Sharp got there before I could…"

Miles's face is full of a million questions. But he seems to set them aside when a sob escapes despite all my efforts to hold it in. And even though we hadn't left things on the best terms last time, Miles doesn't hesitate for a second. He wraps me up in his arms, holding me tight, his hand running over my hair. I bury my face in his shirt and keep crying. I can't remember the last time I broke down like this. Definitely never in front of Miles. But I think deep down I need his approval. I need it to be okay that I feel like this, even if it's about my dad.

"Are you hurt?" he whispers against my ear after a few minutes. "Did anyone follow you here?"

I lift my head and look right into a pair of concerned, kind blue eyes. *Kind and loyal,* I admit to myself, though painfully. How can I fault him for his bravery, his relentless determination? "No to both."

"Good." He leans forward and rests his lips against my forehead. "What exactly happened?"

I close my eyes and briefly explain about my dad and the judge in South Carolina and the evidence I'd already handed over. When I finish, I open my eyes to see his reaction, and I don't even need to ask if he knew about the judge. He didn't.

"I did this, Miles. I'm the one who got him to confess to bribing the city council guy. I did this." The tears overflow again, my chest tightening with each breath.

"Shhh, it's okay." Miles wraps strong arms around me again, both hands rubbing up and down my back. "Relax. Breathe."

"I just wanted to help my mom," I whisper. "And he had a plan all along and I—"

The words are lost in the back of my throat, but neither of us needs them anyway: He gets it. Miles just stands there holding me, saying nothing but comforting words until I'm calm again.

"You're freezing, Ellie." He tilts my chin up; his thumb brushes over my bottom lip. "Your lips are blue. How did your clothes get so wet?"

"Slush," I say, a shiver running up my spine. "Dirty New York City slush. I stepped in a puddle, and then I slipped and fell and there was a truck—" I glance down, looking myself over for the first time. "God, I'm a disaster."

"You're beautiful." He tries to run a finger over my hair

but ends up tangled in it. "But you do have icicles in your hair."

"Dirty icicles. And I can't feel my feet."

Miles releases his hold on me and takes my hand. "Let's fix this. Before you end up with pneumonia."

I'm so cold and exhausted and confused that I don't protest when he leads me into the small bathroom. I lean my back against the wall, unable to fully support myself while Miles turns on the shower. Despite his previously admitting to being driven crazy by a fully clothed version of me, Miles is all business while his fingers work their way through the buttons on my shirt. His own T-shirt is now soaked from my leaning against him, and in this small bathroom, there's hardly enough room for him to back away and prevent the freezing material from brushing my now-bare skin. He immediately reaches for the hem of his shirt and then, after glancing at me, hesitates for a beat as if forgetting his all-business mentality. But seconds later, he tosses the soaking, dirty shirt into a laundry basket right outside the bathroom door.

His gym shorts sit low on his hips, causing the St. Felicity's mark to peek out above the waistband. He catches me staring at it, and the concern on his face turns to guilt. I close my eyes again, not wanting to think about any of that. Wishing that I hadn't stormed out of here last time, wasting days. Days I could have spent with Miles, not pushing him away. Soon I'm freed of my own soaking-wet shirt, and only for a moment do I feel a hint of embarrassment and nerves watching a shirtless Miles dutifully locate the button and zipper on my pleated skirt. The rest of my life is so overwhelming that Miles seeing me in my underwear, not even for the first time, holds little concern.

"Lift your foot up," he says gently while bending down, his fingers wrapped around my right calf. I obey, and he tugs off my boots and wet socks one at a time. He stands upright again and opens the shower door, testing the water temperature. "It'll probably sting. A lot."

I nod but make no move to get in. Miles grows more worried by the second. "Ellie, you really need to—"

"Give me a minute, okay?" I glance warily at the water. Odds are it will let me down. Maybe turn to ice the second I step under it. "How long does the hot water usually last in this place?"

Miles answers by giving me a gentle shove from behind until I'm standing under the shower, the stall too tiny to escape the stream of water. The hot water hits me—and yeah, it does sting—and I jolt to life. I look down at my body and then back at Miles through the still opened shower door. "I have my underwear on."

He shakes his head, looking embarrassed or guilty, I'm not sure which. "They were already wet."

I glance down at my chest, a hint of nerves creeping up now. "This bra is cold-wash only."

Miles's mouth forms a half smile. "Want me to turn the water cold?"

"No!" I step farther under the stream. The hot water beats against my back and runs down to my feet, thawing them. "I'm never going near cold water again. I don't care if my bra is ruined." I close my eyes, tilt my head upward, allowing hot water to hit my face and wash the dirty slush from my hair. "Do you have any shampoo? Soap?"

He had been about to leave the bathroom but stops to retrieve a plastic shower basket from under the sink along with a couple of towels. A few minutes later, I emerge from the bathroom, a towel secured around me, another I'm using to dry my hair. Miles, still shirtless and barefoot, hits a button on the coffeepot, causing it to whir and hiss.

"I'm making coffee in case you want—" He's turned around now, staring at me. He clears his throat in a way that makes my face warm. "Are you— I mean do you— How was the shower? Hot enough?"

My hands pause in their efforts to blot my hair dry. "I can feel my feet again."

"That's definitely good." He stares a beat longer, causing more heat to flood my face, then he jumps into action, crossing the room to dig in a bag near my feet. "You need something to wear, don't you? And after you're dressed, if you want, I can go back into Manhattan with you. I need to figure out what's going on anyway."

Panic and guilt hit me all over again. For a moment, with Miles staring at me in a towel, I'd forgotten all of that. When he stands with neatly folded clothes in his arms, the words spill out: "I don't want to go. Not yet."

The all-business, helping-a-friend version of Miles seems to vanish when his eyes meet mine again. He sets the clothes on the bed, takes a step closer to me until only inches separate us. His hands move to my face, holding it gently. "Tell me it's okay to kiss you because—"

My heart takes off in a sprint. "It's okay," I say without thinking. But then when I do think about it, when I ask myself why I turned him down before and just as quickly invited him back…it becomes clear that last time we were together, self-preservation won. Today, loyalty wins. And a strong desire to not waste any moments with Miles. Because he does have things to do, and those will likely involve leaving me. But today he's here and I'm here.

"It's okay," I repeat.

Miles's mouth meets mine, his hands drawing me closer. One kiss turns into many, and soon I can't think about anything but the single towel and pair of gym shorts that separates us from being completely naked.

And I stop thinking about my dad and anything and everything but this boy who is, in this moment, perfect in every way. I know that the truth will resurface, the challenges that sit between us won't resolve themselves today or likely even tomorrow, but part of me can't help but think that we've given so much of our selves to these big things and maybe we need this. Time alone to think about nothing else but us. Otherwise we might lose the good parts of ourselves in the jobs we're doing, the mistakes we make—some of them intentional—we might lose hope in the human heart and all its potential.

After both of us are breathless, our hearts racing, Miles releases me, peels back the thick comforter on the bed, allowing me to climb in first. The sheets are cold, and a shiver immediately runs up my spine. Then Miles slides in beside me, peels away the wet towel, and brings his warm skin in contact with mine.

He kisses me again, his hands gliding perfectly up and down my back, then his mouth makes its way from my lips to my neck, shoulder, collarbone—everywhere. When his lips press against my forearm, I wince, and Miles pulls back to take a look. His index finger gently trails over a spot that has turned black and blue. "You said you slipped and fell?"

"Yeah, in the road. In the middle of traffic." My heart picks up all over again, hearing those tires screech, barely stopping in time. "It could have been a lot worse."

Miles closes his eyes briefly, as if picturing what "a lot worse" might look like. Then he plants a much more gentle kiss against the bruise, travels the length of my forearm to my wrist and then my palm, which has scrapes I hadn't even noticed until now. When his lips return to mine, our kisses turn from slow and careful to more urgent, more intense. My fingers drift south, beneath the covers, and wiggle his gym shorts and boxer briefs down below his hips. He quickly kicks them off the rest of the way.

Unlike my previous experiences being naked with

someone, the tension, the feelings, seem to bubble from the inside out. Miles presses his fingers behind my knee, wrapping my leg around him, and I'm floored by how effortless this seems for him, so much that I blurt out, "Aren't you supposed to be the inexperienced one? Shouldn't you be nervous or something?"

He laughs, his lips vibrating against my skin, then he lifts his head and our eyes meet. He holds a trembling hand out for me to see. "Nope, not nervous at all."

I'm not sure which is more endearing—the fact that he's nervous or the fact that he so willingly admitted this. Both factors make me want him even more, like right now, because I'm not letting myself think about later or tomorrow or any similar words. After I ask him to, Miles produces the condoms I suggested he buy a while back. His fingers shake so much opening the package that I gently pry it from his hands and do it for him. Not that I don't have butterflies in my stomach, ones with gigantic wings flapping rapidly. But I guess one of the realities about sex is that there really is more pressure for him, being a virgin, than for me. Despite my reassurance that there's no need to feel any pressure, it still sits there between us until eventually we're joined together and nothing else seems important.

Miles's lips rest near my ear, whispering beautiful words, asking me if I'm okay at least half a dozen times. And all I can think is, if we didn't have these obstacles between us, this dead friend who had very big goals and high expectations, I could love this boy. I know I could because my heart already hurts thinking about leaving him again.

A while later, I'm lying perfectly still, perfectly perfect in Miles's arms, enjoying the feel of his fingers moving through my now-dry hair, his warm body pressed up against mine. I close my eyes and wish for everything outside to pause. Just for a day or two.

"Do you need to get back soon?" he asks.

"Not yet." I tighten my arm around his midsection.

"Ellie?" The way he says my name stirs warmth and emotion inside me. "I'm sorry about your dad."

"Really?" I mumble. "He is still a criminal. He did do the things he was arrested for."

Miles is quiet for a long time, probably replaying all the lectures on criminal versus noncriminal he's given me over the past several months. But eventually he says, "I guess it's not as simple as that, is it?"

"Who are you and what have you done with Miles the Great?" I scoot up high enough to plant a kiss on his neck. "But thank you for not saying he deserved to be caught."

"It wasn't fair that you had to make a choice without all the information." His fingers roam the length of my back. "If I'm being honest, that's the part that bothers me the most."

A lump forms in my throat. He's right. That really wasn't fair. But maybe I didn't have enough faith in my family, in my father.

"You're okay?" Miles asks for the tenth time, a hint of nerves still in his voice. "I mean, everything was okay?"

I laugh. I can't help it. I lean on one elbow and look him over. "What's with the constant questions? Do you want a performance evaluation or something?"

"Constructive feedback can be very useful," he says, and then he lifts his head and steals a kiss. "It seemed fast... maybe too fast?"

"I don't know, it's not like I had a stopwatch running." I smile at him. "You know that's a problem that can be rectified."

Catching my hint, his eyebrows lift and then he pushes himself upright before leaning over me again. "Practice makes perfect, right?"

. . .

Late afternoon sunlight streams into the small Brooklyn apartment when I peel my eyes open after having dozed off. I feel around for Miles and find an empty space beside me, already turning cold. I hear movement in the room and roll over in time to see him tossing items into the large duffel on the floor.

He smiles when he sees me awake. "Hey."

"Hey." I sit up and reach for the clothes he picked out for me earlier.

Miles steps into the bathroom and emerges with my underwear and bra. "They're dry now."

I dress beneath the covers and when I toss them back, Miles sits at the end of the bed, pulls thick socks over my feet, and shows me the fan he turned on pointed at my wet boots. Hopefully those will be dry, too. Then he hands me a thick fleece jacket that zips halfway. I tug it over my head and inhale the scent of Miles.

My head emerges in time to see him adding two books from beneath the bed into the bag. A thought nearly as terrifying as my father being hauled off to prison hits me. "You're leaving," I say.

"So are you," he counters, but there's concern in his eyes again. "Four more days, right?"

"You wouldn't pack a bag four days early. You're leaving now," I argue. "The FBI has my dad; that means you're done here. Where are you going? Back to school?"

He stares at me, then looks down at his hands, saying nothing.

"Right." I choke out the word. "You can't tell me."

Miles slides in front of me, resting a hand on my arm. "If I can, I will. Swear to God."

I open my mouth to tell him that I get it—it hurts like crazy but I get it. His phone rings, and soon he's on his feet, answering it. I sit there hugging my knees, listening to this one-sided forty-five-second conversation. When he hangs up, the sympathy returns to his face. "I have to go out for just a little while. But I wanna talk about this, okay? Justice says she'll cover for you, everything is fine, so can you stay here? Please?"

My heart melts again, and I feel myself nod, earning a sigh of relief from Miles as he tosses on his jacket and reaches for the door. "I'll be right back, okay? I'll bring food. Something really good."

For about five minutes everything is fine. I sit there on Miles's bed, waiting for him. But then a sense of dread rolls over me. Miles is focused. He's driven and doing something so very scary and important. And I'm a master manipulator who loves shaking his focus. What if I change his mind? Or what if I don't? How much damage have I already done today?

I squeeze my eyes shut, willing that thought away. Being with Miles wasn't a con; it was realer than anything I've ever done. And it still might be goodbye.

I climb out of the bed, put on my boots, and write Miles a quick note, letting him know that I had to get back to the Holden group.

And he needs to get back to his mission.

CHAPTER
38

Dominic finds me the second I enter the hotel lobby. "What the hell happened to you today?" He looks me over, taking in the baggy borrowed sweatpants. "And where's your uniform?"

"It's a long story." One that he, of all people, deserves to know. Especially after I snapped at him this morning. But the wound is still fresh, so I give him a condensed version. While I talk, we walk toward the ballroom where the recap-our-day session is supposed to take place.

"Wow, that's..." Dominic trails off, appearing to be rendered speechless.

"Yeah, I know," I say bitterly.

We round the corner and are soon in sight of some of our Holden classmates. Dominic speaks in a whisper. "Are you going to tell the FBI about the judge in South Carolina? Seems like it would be a subject of interest to them."

I stop dead in the middle of the hallway, unable to move. "That is a great idea..."

Dominic turns to me, a look of skepticism on his face. "Why do I get the feeling we're not talking about the same thing?"

"Definitely the same thing," I say with a nod. "But maybe not free information. A bargaining piece. Those seem to work well with the FBI."

"You want to work out another deal?" he says. "To help your dad?"

"It's worth a shot, right?" For the first time since my dad ran from me this morning, I feel the tiniest glimmer of hope. "Now how do I get out of this recap session so I can get a hold of Sheldon ASAP?"

Bret Thomas, who has just appeared in the hall outside our temporary classroom, stalks right up to me. "We need to talk."

"Sure," I tell him. "How about tonight? I've got something I need to—"

"No," he says firmly. "Now."

With that, he grips my arms and gently leads me farther down the hall. Dominic jogs to catch up to us, though I'm sure he'd rather bolt than be part of an intimate discussion with his ex–best friend.

Once we come to a stop, I tug my arm from Bret's hand and spin to face him. "Seriously, what is your deal?"

"This." He holds up his phone, showing Dominic and me a picture.

A picture of Agent Sharp and me talking in one of the hotel stairwells. It's taken from half a dozen floors up. "Where did you get that?" I demand.

So he hasn't ditched his creepy photo blackmail habit. Great. What else has he taken pics of during this trip? Me sneaking away from the group? Me conning stage moms out of their money?

"I got it from Justice's phone. She's worried about you and wanted me on the lookout for *your ex*," he says, emphasizing the last two words. "The real question is what the hell are you doing with this guy?"

Beside me, Dominic shifts, looking extremely uncomfortable. I roll my eyes and fake annoyance. "I've already been over this with Justice and Chantel. It was a mistake. He and I are over—"

"Cut the bullshit, Ellie!" Bret says, surprising me so much that I flinch at his raised voice. "Do you know who he is?"

I can feel Dominic's eyes on me, waiting for a new lie to spill out of my mouth. But I can't think of anything.

Slowly the anger falls from Bret's face, and his eyes widen. "Oh shit. You don't know who he is, do you?"

"You mean the FBI agent part?" I say.

Bret now looks panicked. "He's also one of Jack's cronies."

For a moment everything feels out of place—Bret saying Jack's name, telling me I'm in danger. I've hardly spoken to the guy in weeks. But then I remember that Bret knew Jack. He bought a gun from him in exchange for some compromising photos of Dominic and Simon. God that feels like an eternity ago.

As the pieces click together in my head and I'm good and panicking, Bret adds, "He's in the league of dirty agents, Ellie."

CHAPTER
39

I reach out to grip the wall as if the floor were tilting beneath me. "Are you sure?" I ask Bret.

"More than a hundred percent," he says.

God. Sharp. All this time I'd been around him—

I shake off the thoughts and work hard to form a plan. "What about a woman with that guy?" I ask Bret, pointing to the phone. "She has dirty-blond hair, usually tied up in a bun and um…"

"Black dress pants and blazers," Dominic adds emphatically. "Stiff as hell. Seems like she's got a stick up her ass."

Bret shakes his head. "I don't think I've seen anyone like that associated with Jack, but it's not like he invited me to a meeting with the whole group. Doubt I was ever meant to figure this out."

I turn to Dominic. "I don't think Sheldon is in that group. She's too by the book, doesn't fit the profile."

"Agreed." Dominic nods vigorously. "Now go find her or call and see if she's still in the city."

A disturbing thought occurs to me right then. "She wasn't there this morning. On the train. With my dad. It was Sharp and some guy I didn't recognize."

I've already got my phone out, preparing to dial Sheldon's number. It's very possible she's working with a dirty agent and has no idea. I'm about to hit call when I notice a newcomer approaching our little trio—Mr. Lance.

"It's five minutes past start time," he says expectantly. Dominic and Bret exchange looks, but none of us moves. "Start time as in you should all head into the designated room now."

"Ellie has a family emergency," Dominic blurts out.

Bret chimes in as if the two of them haven't been mortal enemies for more than a month now. "Her sister's appendix ruptured."

I stand there unmoving on the outside, and on the inside everything is on high speed, my pulse, my thoughts.

Mr. Lance looks at Bret and Dominic, then he crosses his arms. "Can you boys give Eleanor and me a minute alone?"

It's clear he knows we're lying, and Dominic and Bret, who have likely guessed this fact as well, look completely torn until I nod for them to take off. I just need to go. I don't need them at the moment. I'm perfectly capable of making up my own lies. And I absolutely wouldn't have gone near ruptured appendix. It's way overused.

"Look, Ellie," Lance says, giving me the same disconnected look from the other night. "I know you disappeared this morning during our Columbia tour. Justice tried to cover for you, but I know you weren't in the class you were scheduled to sit in on or the admissions interview, and you certainly weren't at the brunch Justice said you attended with her. So I'm having trouble buying your sister's appendix story."

Lucky for me I've acquired the skill of texting without looking. I hide my phone behind my back and punch in a quick text to Sheldon.

ME: we need to talk. Where can we meet?

"If you'd like to remain in good behavioral standing during this trip," Lance continues, "it would be advisable that you join us for the recap session."

My phone vibrates in my hand, sending me into a full-on panic. Sheldon replied. I need to get to her. I spin several lies around in my head while Lance stands there waiting for me to say or do something. The longer I think on it, the more panicked I get. What if something happens to my dad while I'm here trying to get out of class?

Seconds later, it becomes clear that only one thing will get me past Lance—the truth. Maybe he deserves the truth. Isn't that what he asked of me the other night?

"You're right," I tell him. "I didn't stay at Columbia, and my sister's appendix is fine as far as I know. But my family, at least one of them, is in serious trouble right now, and I'm pretty much the only person in the entire world outside of the bad guy with him who knows this and can do something about it."

Lance opens his mouth as if to argue, but I lift a hand to stop him.

"If I tell you more I would be revealing confidential information regarding an ongoing FBI investigation—" I stop for a moment, putting all the facts together. "Actually, not just the FBI but a couple of other government organizations both with three-letter acronyms. I swear to you that someone will confirm this later. Someone with a badge and security clearance."

He waits ten full seconds and then wordlessly steps out of my way. I know we haven't resolved our issues and that I've broken Holden's field trip rules. But it can be dealt with later.

"I'm sorry," I say quickly. "About everything."

I race down the hall back toward the hotel entrance while checking my phone for a text.

SHELDON: at an unmarked FBI office not too far from

your hotel. I can give directions

An FBI office? Couldn't pick a better place to meet. Or safer.

ME: Yes! Directions please

I'm out the hotel doors and into the Times Square crowd, waiting to hear in which direction to go.

SHELDON: head west on 47th st.

I turn and head in the correct direction, preparing to cross the street.

SHELDON: there's a Toyota dealership at the corner of 47th and 11th ave

The journey is nearly a mile, and I run the whole way, weaving through all of the people. Luckily when I get two blocks from Times Square the crowds have thinned significantly. I get another text from Sheldon when I'm out of breath and nearly to 11th Avenue.

SHELDON: walk behind the building. Look for a sign that says "Office for Rent" and lift it away. Push the call button if I'm not outside.

It's nearly six thirty, and without the bright lights of Times Square, it's also dark, especially on this block with the dealerships already closed and their lights off. I find the sign with no problem, but before I can lift it, a door I didn't even realize existed opens and Sheldon walks out. This woman has been the bane of my existence for weeks, but I'm so glad to see her I nearly hug her.

"What's wrong?" she says, immediately reading my face, earning more of my trust just from that.

"Agent Sh-Sharp," I sputter, clutching the stitch in my side. "He's…" He's what? I hadn't exactly scripted this part. Does she even know about St. Felicity's or the rogue group of St. Felicity's members gone wrong?

"He's what?" Sheldon demands.

"Have you done it yet?" I ask her. "Arrested my dad?"

"We're still waiting on—"

Oh God, it really is true.

"Sharp took him," I say. "Sharp and some other guy. This morning. On the One train near Columbia."

Her forehead wrinkles, confusion all over her face. "What do you mean Sharp took him? He couldn't have—"

"Look, it's all really complicated, but Sharp is involved with the same group that murdered Simon Gilbert," I tell her, speaking as rapidly as possible. "Somehow they've got their hands in this con of my family's, probably working with the Zanettis."

She lifts both hands to stop me. "Okay, okay, I don't know what the hell you're talking about, but it sounds like we need to get you to a safe place and get a location on Agent Sharp and your father."

Relief washes over me. I shake my head and nod at the same time. "Yes, I mean yes let's do that."

Despite her flaws and disdain when it comes to me, she seems to take my concerns very seriously and acts quickly, getting on the phone with someone, requesting a car service ASAP. Then she calls someone else, probably an FBI boss, and relays some minimal details. I scroll back through my messages, trying to stay calm. My breath catches at the sight of a text from Miles. Sent about forty-five minutes ago.

MILES: where did u go?? Stick with your Holden group! Stay away from fbi agents!!!!

I'm attempting to process the meaning of that but am interrupted by a black town car with tinted windows. It pulls right up to the back of the building, despite the lack of actual road. Sheldon has her back to me, still on the phone. Two men exit the car, and I prepare to move toward it, but Sheldon, having likely heard the doors shut, turns. My gaze travels to her face, takes in her look of fear, and then my eyes shift to her right hand, which is now reaching for her service weapon.

I turn in time to see both of the men draw their own pistols, and then everything moves in slow motion. One second I'm on my feet, the next an FBI agent is flinging her body toward mine and I'm falling. I'm falling and watching one of the men as his finger moves to the trigger. The thud of my heart fills my ears and everywhere, but I watch the man jerk in reaction to the force of his gunshot. My back and elbows smack into the hard gravel ground, the weight of Sheldon on top of me only worsening the impact. Then the back of my head smacks against the ground and my ears ring, my vision blacking out then returning.

Sheldon is on top of me. Limp and unmoving.

Before I can even react, strong hands pull her off and leave her faceup on the ground. Red spreads quickly over the front of her white blouse, her eyes still wide open. *Ohmygod… ohmygod…they killed Sheldon. Oh. My. God.*

Come on, Ellie, focus!

The two men lean over her and, using Miles's surveillance techniques, I let my gaze quickly sweep over the two of them, taking in the most important details—both tall, more than six feet, one with dark hair, one sandy, aged between thirty and forty, black dress shoes, man who fired shot has V-shaped scar right above shirt collar.

I scramble to my feet, preparing to run, but suddenly a large hand wraps around my chest, gripping me tight. A male hand. A third man. Sheldon lies bleeding to death less than a foot away. They're going to kill me, too. Adrenaline courses through me, and I easily toss the newcomer over my shoulder and flat on his back. He lands with a *thud* and a loud grunt. The other two men both look up, surprised. One of them, realizing the likelihood of my running away, reaches out for the front of my shirt. I duck beneath his hand, dive for the ground, and roll sideways, springing back to my feet.

"You idiot," the other guy says to the one who just tried

to grab me. "Use your fucking gun!"

And soon a gun is pressed against my forehead and two more are aimed at me from a distance. Even if I used the disarming trick properly, it would do me no good, because two more weapons are on deck, ready to take the first one's place. I glance at Sheldon and her blood-covered shirt. My stomach rolls and fear mounts inside me. I'm not getting out of here alive.

The man closest to me, the one with the pistol at my forehead, steps behind me, and without warning presses a rag to my face. This is something I hadn't prepared for in any of my self-defense lessons. So I don't immediately grasp what's happening or about to happen. The chemical smell is revolting but enters my nostrils with incredible speed.

And moments later, my body turns limp, my eyes roll upward, and the world around me goes dark.

CHAPTER

40

"You've raised quite a talented little girl, Hayes," a familiar voice says.

My heavy eyelids seem sealed shut, my body throbbing in far too many places to move. I wiggle my arms but meet resistance in the form of a round object sitting between them. The giant beams. We're at the agency. How the hell—

"I'm not sure what your part in this operation is," I hear my dad say, "But it doesn't need to come to this. Let's chat like old friends, figure out a compromise. I don't see why this can't be a win-win situation."

Finally, I pry my eyes open, sit up slowly. Blink several times until the wide-open agency comes into view and then Sharp's face, ten or fifteen feet away, his gun pointed in my direction.

"That was the plan. Wasn't it?" Sharp says. "In fact, I was never supposed to be out in the open for this side. I needed that FBI job. But then you and your daughter had to betray us. Who are you working with? CIA? NSA? What did they offer you to give up names?"

My dad is handcuffed to the same wooden beam, right

beside me. I turn to look at him, and both relief and worry cross his face. "Look, I don't know anything about whatever names you're referring to. As a rule, my family and I steer clear of any organized government groups."

Sharp offers me a sarcastic smile, then turns to my dad. "Is that right? You and your family?"

My heart picks up, my body finally awake. *Please don't do this, Sharp.*

"Ellie's just a kid," my dad says, glancing at me. "Let her go; she'll vanish without a trace. Nothing to worry about. Then you and I can work out our issues."

Sharp leaves us, drags a chair across the beautiful wood floors, creating a screech all the way. He sits in the chair, looks us over with great interest. "Eleanor, maybe you should tell your dad what you've been up to over the last year? It's quite a story."

I shake my head, refusing. This is why Miles wanted me out of this job. He didn't want me taking the fall for his work. Miles…did he know about Sharp being in the league of bad agents? Was Sharp's one of the coded names on the wall in his secret lair? He wouldn't have kept that from me, would he?

My hands start to tremble. Dad must notice this, because he leans closer to me, his mouth near my ear, and whispers, "It's okay. He would have shot us already if that were the plan."

I turn my head, look at my father, whose expression is filled with the same guilt that fills my gut. "Dad, I'm sorry. I'm so sorry; this is all my—"

"So it's true?" Sharp cocks his head to the side, surprise on his face. "Your dad isn't involved?"

"No, he's not," I say in a rush. "Not even a little."

Sharp laughs. "Wow…you've got balls, Ellie. I'll give you that. Putting both of us on the FBI's wanted list—one teenage girl. And neither of us saw it coming. Like I said, talent."

Confusion fills Dad's face, but he says nothing.

I glare at Sharp. "You got yourself on that list. I trusted you!"

He holds his arms out wide. "And I trusted you. Even taught you how to disarm. Didn't know you were going behind my back, working against me."

"I could say the same thing," I retort.

Sharp waves his free hand toward Dad. "Go on...tell him. I can't wait to see this."

"Tell me what?" Dad says.

My face flames, and fear bubbles in my stomach. But I turn to Dad anyway. "It was me," I whisper. "With Mom. I tipped off the FBI. Got her arrested."

Dad shakes his head. "Did they—" His voice cracks. "Did they threaten you?"

"No one threatened me." I squeeze my eyes shut, lean my forehead against the wooden beam. "I wanted to see Harper, and Agent Sheldon told me if I—"

Just speaking Sheldon's name again, all I can see for a moment is her, lying face up, the red blood against her white blouse.

"We switched places," Dad says, his voice breaking a little. "Your mom and I. It wasn't supposed to be her."

I look at him again, my heart shattering, seeing his pained expression, like someone punched him in the gut. "I'm sorry, Dad."

"And here? In New York?" he asks, his voice flat as he turns back into the skilled con. "What was your game plan?"

I don't answer. I can't. I'm such a coward.

"Trading your mom for me?" he guesses, the pain returning to his face for a brief moment.

"I didn't know about the judge," I plead. "To me, it

seemed like you just forgot her, didn't care, and I couldn't stop thinking about her."

"Every man for himself," he says, staring over my shoulder, shaking his head. "Guess I had this coming to me, raising you like that."

The room blurs around me. A couple of tears trickle down my cheeks.

Dad just shakes his head. "Clearly my feelings are not the priority at the moment." He turns to Sharp. "Now that you've given us our Jerry Springer moment, mind telling me what your end game is?"

"I thought that was pretty obvious." Sharp checks his cell and then stands. "Miss Teen Informant is going to tell me exactly who she's been talking to, and then my friends are going to kill both of you. And lucky for us, the cleanup should be quite easy, considering you're practically invisible to the world."

I stare at Sharp, showing my fear, I'm sure. Beside me, I feel Dad move closer. He waits a beat and then says, "Friends? What friends?"

Just then, the stairwell doors open and two people enter the room—Faustino Zanetti and Miles Beckett.

CHAPTER
41

"Right on time," Sharp says, then he turns to Miles. "That's one benefit of military school, I guess."

Oh God, maybe he did know about Sharp?

It takes everything in me not to shout out loud to Miles. Even without him looking at me, I can see the command in his eyes, the thoughts in his head. *Stay calm. Don't give me away.*

But did you give me away? Did you just hand me over to Sharp, knowing he was in Jack's group?

My dad doesn't hear or see this at all. He looks at Miles, his face twisted in anger. "You're working with these guys?"

Miles looks at him and shrugs. "You're the one who told me you don't work with outsiders. Sounds like that rule should have stayed true."

Even I react at the venom in Miles's voice—it feels so real.

The office door opens and Bruno exits. His arms are filled with stacks of hundred-dollar bills bound with twine. "Thirty-five bank withdrawals, but I think we've got it all."

"Good," Sharp tells him. "Because thanks to Miss Informant, we've got to split sooner than planned."

"You sure the security override worked?" Bruno asks Miles. "All this money coming out of the bank will have the Feds on alert."

"Hear any sirens?" Miles snaps at him. "If you do, I'm sure it's because your idiot criminal family can't walk into a bank without setting off alarms."

I look from Bruno to Miles to Sharp, trying to figure out what each knows about the other. Sharp doesn't appear to be aware of Miles and me knowing each other. Which means he likely doesn't know about Miles's semester at Holden.

"All right, boys," Sharp warns. "Play nice."

"I didn't sign up for this," Miles tells him, gesturing a hand toward Bruno and Faustino. "I was told I'd work with respectable government agents, not mobsters."

Sharp is now busy counting a stack of bills. "And I wasn't informed of what a pretentious, entitled kid I'd be forced to partner with, but we can't always have our way, can we?"

"Why are you working with us now?" Miles asks Sharp. "What happened to Lewis?"

"Dead," Sharp says, his tone flat. "He was about to run—scared of those idiots apparently." He nods toward Bruno and Faustino. "I couldn't let him take off with all that information."

If this shocks Miles, he hides it well, taking a moment to scrutinize Sharp as if trying to figure out if he's telling the truth.

But this might mean that he didn't know about Sharp. If only I'd talked to Bret more; *he* knew about Sharp. We could have put things together sooner. My stomach churns with regret.

For several minutes, Sharp talks all of them through plans on moving the money silently, getting out of New York separately and without leaving a trail.

Dad takes advantage of this meeting and leans in close

to me again. "Got any hairpins? A pen?"

I shake my head. "They have guns, Dad. You can't just pick a lock and escape."

He's silent for a moment, and then he speaks in a different tone, a sad one. "Was it Harper? You think I should have gone after her? Is that why you wanted me…" But he doesn't finish.

There are no words that will make my betrayal any better, and I can't tell him I'd do it differently. New York, yes, but Charleston? I'm not sure. He did turn his back on Harper all those years ago. He took her from me, and I wanted her back. But I should have just asked. Should have trusted that he knew I needed my sister and he'd let me go.

"I'm sorry," I whisper again. Then I say, louder, to Sharp, "You're wrong about me. Being invisible. What about Holden? They know me; they know where I'm at. They're going to look for me, and unless you've cleaned up perfectly, all roads will lead back to—"

"True, true." Sharp nods. "And they'll uncover the truth. That you vanished with the mysterious boy who's been lurking around the hotel. Your teacher even spotted him calling your name the other day. Oscar, I think?"

Color drains from Dad's face. I know what he's thinking: He sent Oscar to that hotel to follow me. And this is a side of my dad I've never seen before—worried about me, worried for my life. It's so big it overpowers the hurt I saw moments ago.

"Five hundred thousand," Bruno says to Sharp.

"Should have been a million," Sharp tells him, then shoots me a look. "But it's good enough to grow. Overseas, of course."

"That's my area of expertise," Miles says. "Want me to get started on that?"

"Hold your horses, rookie." Sharp lifts a hand. Then

he nods in the direction of Dad and me. "First order of business…"

He doesn't finish. Doesn't need to. The lighting is dim in this room, but I swear I see Miles go pale. Dad shifts even closer to me, his side brushing mine. A gun lifts, the barrel aimed at Dad or me, it's hard to tell. But it's all familiar, too familiar.

Except this time, instead of sitting beside me, Miles is the one pointing a gun at me.

"Doing okay?" Sharp says, taunting Miles. "You know there is nothing I love more than a straight-as-an-arrow CIA operative with a kid willing to wade in the murky water. Especially one from Marshall Academy. But time is money, kid, prove you're worth the trouble."

"Wait," Dad pleads. "Ellie will give you her word; she won't speak of any of this to anyone. Just let her go."

Sharp attempts a sympathetic look. "It's hard for me, too. I like her. Most of the agents in my organization feel the same way. But it's too messy, letting her back out into the world." Sharp spins to face Miles. "Him first. The save-my-daughter plea is getting to me."

Dad swallows, tugs pointlessly at his hands cuffed around the wooden beam. "Ellie…"

"I should have trusted you," I tell him. It feels like I have to.

"I should have told you my plans," he says. "Should have gone after your sister. Or given her my blessing to leave."

Miles's hand is steady on the trigger, but he hesitates. Sharp releases a groan. "Ten seconds, rookie. Or Faust will do the job for you, and that's not great for your rep."

My fingers find Dad's, our pinkies linked together. And I think about Dominic and his family, how little they know their son, how they've not taught him anything, how little parenting there is in that relationship. And even though

I don't want my family's way of life anymore, I can't say truthfully that my father doesn't love me, doesn't know me better than I know myself, because it's clear on his face, in this air between us.

My eyes meet Miles's, and I think the words I can't say aloud. *Don't do it. Let someone else. Not you. Anyone but you.*

"Come on, Beckett!" Sharp barks. "Five, four, three..."

Faustino Zanetti raises his gun.

Dad squeezes his eyes shut, squeezes his finger tighter around mine. I stare hard at Miles, my insides frozen. Then I watch his gaze flick for a second toward the giant window to my left. My heart gives two quick beats. Miles's finger presses against the trigger. A shadow falls over the window, and suddenly two black shoe soles appear. I suck in a breath.

"Now!" Sharp shouts at Faustino.

Miles's arm swings right. And he pulls the trigger.

CHAPTER
42

The shot rings loud in my ears. Glass shatters everywhere. A second shot follows. Then a third. A sob builds in the back of my throat, but I quickly realize that Dad is still squeezing my finger, still very much alive. Faustino Zanetti falls to the ground. Agent Sharp clutches his chest and falls over the chair, his body landing less than five feet from me. And Bruno's back hits the wall and he slumps over. Miles shot one of them but what about the other two? Why are they down? How—the ringing in my ears feels like an object between me and the rest of the room. I blink. Shake my head. Then Miles sinks to his knees in front of me, sets his gun on the floor, his hands now trembling as they fumble with the cuffs linking my wrists together.

Seconds later, the metal gives, freeing my hands. The cuffs *clank* to the floor. I'm not sure if he grabs me first or I fall in to him first. Or we both move in synch, but before I can even take a breath, I'm clutching Miles, tears streaming down my cheeks, his face buried in my hair.

"I'm sorry, Ellie, I'm so sorry. I swear to God, I didn't know about Sharp. I didn't know," he murmurs. "That was too close."

"You didn't know, either?" I ask, though it's not really a question. I believe him. "But who shot...I mean how..."

Briefly, I glance behind Miles, watch Agent Beckett Senior shake off shards of glass. Okay, that's who shot the other two. The black shoe soles against the window.

My knees dig into the hard floors, but I don't move to sit or stand. Instead, I pull back enough to look at Miles's face, to take in his now-haunted eyes. I lay my hands on his cheeks, steering his eyes to meet mine. Then I take in the body lying not far from us. This one dead by Miles's hand. When I turn back to him, he's pale.

"Hey...are you okay?" I ask him.

"I couldn't do it," he says, his voice hoarse. "I couldn't shoot all of them at the same time and that meant one of them might—"

He stops short and buries his face in my hair again. And I remember what Clyde said, that night in the cabin with Jack—*you're just a boy; you aren't ready to kill someone*—and wonder if he was right. If he's still right.

"It was self-defense, Miles," I say, hoping to reassure him.

He lifts his head, draws in a breath, and nods. "I know."

His warm fingers slide across my cheeks, drawing me closer. His mouth meets mine, and we're both a hundred miles away, alone in our own universe.

I hear someone clear his throat, and the moment bursts. Miles and I break apart, him climbing to his feet then holding out a hand to me.

"So I'm a little confused." Considering my dad has never seen anyone shot before, he's putting on a stellar performance of acting calm. "How do you two know each other?"

One look at my dad, and the fear and loss from only moments ago returns, and I'm fighting tears all over again. I squat down in front of him, attempting to unlock the cuffs, but footsteps sound behind me, and a hand touches my wrist, stopping me.

"No, Ellie," Agent Beckett Senior says.

There is a hint of regret in his voice but also a firmness, reminding me that orders from a CIA operative are to be followed. He moves toward Miles, grips his shoulder, and silent words seem to flow between them before he says to Miles, "You did what you had to. You'll be okay."

And even I can see how much those words help Miles; the color returns to his face and he offers a firm nod.

"Eleanor," Agent Beckett says, turning to me again. "In a few minutes, a team of agents will arrive, and it's imperative that you aren't here when they do. We're still overturning names of dirty agents in Jack's rogue group, and all of them seem to know you."

"Me?" I ask stupidly. "Why?"

"It floated around with Jack and then emerged, probably with Sharp's silent partnership in this job."

"So you want me to go back to the hotel? With the Holden group?" Suddenly I remember the events before I was brought here to the fake agency. "Sheldon. She's…she's dead."

I never really had an emotional connection to the woman, but seeing her die like that, my throat is thick with unshed tears.

"You can't go back to the hotel," Agent Beckett says. "Until they've been taken out, you need to lay low. Preferably out of the country."

"Wait, wh-what?" I sputter, hardly believing this.

"Listen to him," my dad says, as firmly as Agent Beckett. "He's telling you that you aren't safe, that this is going to happen again."

Agent Beckett nods, a look of respect on his face. Respect for my father the criminal. "Clyde will meet you at JFK with everything you need. Understood?"

I look among my dad, Agent Beckett, and then at Miles. "What about you? They know who you are, too. Aren't you in danger?"

Miles offers a sad smile. "Always."

He doesn't say it. Doesn't need to. Simon left him a job, and he intends on finishing it. Even without me. My heart breaks into a million pieces, but I don't let it show. He's made his choice, and what am I supposed to tell him? It isn't important? Run away with me? Loyalty is Miles's middle name.

"Ellie," he starts, looking as torn as I feel.

But I shake my head. I don't want to hear it. Not unless it's him saying he'll stop this endless fight.

Agent Beckett glances at his son and then says, "We'll give you a minute with your dad."

They both disappear into the office, and my dad immediately reverts to his sarcastic self. "Think the Feds will let me share a cell with your mom?"

I expect to feel guilty all over again, sad even, but instead adrenaline rushes through my veins. Adrenaline and a plan. I wait for the office door to close, and then I snatch up as many stacks of bills as I can hold from the floor where Sharp dropped them. I quickly tuck them into my dad's jeans and then grab the tool Miles used to free me and uncuff my dad. He wordlessly watches me, guessing my plans.

"Go," I order. "Before I change my mind. Find that judge and get your wife back."

He's on his feet in half a second. "You aren't coming with me?"

"No," I say, glancing at the office. "I'm following orders. And I can't tell you what to do or force my new right or wrong on you, Dad, but think about doing something better, something important with your skills."

He hugs me, plants a kiss on my forehead. "Bye, honey. Be careful."

"Tell Mom I love her and…" My voice breaks. "That I'm sorry."

Three minutes later, when Miles and his dad walk out of the office, my eyes are dry and my dad has likely disappeared into a New York City crowd. CIA operative or not, I know better. They won't catch him. And I doubt Agent Beckett will work too hard trying to, given his speech the other day about me still having time to back out of turning my dad in. I hadn't wanted to back out then, but now, now everything is different. My dad redeemed himself in my eyes through all his effort to get my mom released. And I redeemed myself for attempting to turn him in by letting him go just now.

We're even. Squared up in all the ways possible.

"What—" Miles starts when he notices the missing criminal.

Agent Beckett just stares at the spot my dad had occupied and the open handcuffs lying by the wooden beam.

"I turned my back and he was gone," I say simply, knowing full well Agent Beckett can hear the lie in my voice. "I think he took a pin from my hair when I hugged him."

"She needs to go," Miles reminds his dad, worry all over his face again. "Like, thirty seconds ago."

Agent Beckett shakes his head, hands me a fifty-dollar bill, and points to the door. "Grab a taxi to the airport."

I chance one more look at Miles, the loss of him doubles, and I can't bear to get any closer. I say the same words my dad said to me. "Be careful."

And then I turn my back on him and thunder down the steps, taking them two at a time, hoping he hadn't seen the tears fall.

Goodbye, Miles, I think, for me. For closure.

CHAPTER

43

Clyde is already at the airport when I arrive. He doesn't call out to me but instead turns his back and leans against a luggage cart. I brush up beside him and allow him to set an envelope in my hand. I slide it up my sleeve until it's concealed.

"Everything you need is here," he says. "Someone will be in touch soon."

And then he's gone. Just like that. Leaving me alone.

I've never been inside an airport, never flown on a plane before, but I manage to get myself into a bathroom stall and examine the envelope. Inside I find a passport with my photo and the name Helen Henry below it. She's twenty and from Buffalo, New York. There's a new cell phone, several thousand in cash, and boarding passes for a flight to Fiji.

Numb, with my head hazy, I stumble through the airport security, find my way to a gate, board the flight. It's when I'm sitting still, my head resting against the seat, that I nearly panic. Am I going to see my sister again? What about Dominic? Or Justice or… What the hell am I doing here?

A flight attendant walks by, and I tug at her sleeve, gripping onto it. "Have you locked the doors yet?"

She studies me for a moment and then smiles. "First time flying?"

I release her and nod.

"Don't worry—it's easier than it looks." She pats my shoulder and then moves forward to stuff a bag into an overhead compartment.

I sink back in my seat, filled with a million thoughts, with unshed tears. I want to go back. To Holden, to Harper. To Miles. I close my eyes and try not to think about earlier that morning, of Miles and me tangled together in his bed. It was everything it should be, the start of something wonderful and new between us, and yet it was also goodbye. I knew it deep down in my gut but ignored it. I lean my head against the window and allow the weight of this broken heart wedged between my ribs to steamroll over me.

A warm body lands in the seat beside me and I breathe evenly, attempting to not seem like a depressed broken-hearted teenage girl.

"Helen, right?" a voice says from the empty seat.

A familiar voice.

My eyes fly open and sure enough, it's real. He's real. Miles. "What are you doing here?"

He glances over one shoulder and then leans his head close to mine. "I was just thinking about how much I hated that feeling of missing you…seeing you again and not knowing for how long. And when I told my dad this, he just said to leave."

I'm confused and hopeful and way too many things to speak at first. I tangle my fingers in his. "Can you, though? Leave?"

"I should have done this in the first place," he says, kissing me quickly on the mouth. "Should have left the grown-ups to take care of things."

Despite my shock, I can't help but say, "You might be a

kid, but I'm twenty."

Miles laughs, kisses me again.

The plane rumbles beneath us, and I stiffen. "What was that?"

"Relax, it's just the engine." He straightens in his seat but keeps our fingers laced together.

We pull away from the gate, and I watch the airport grow farther away. "Will we be able to go back?"

"Yes." Miles lifts our linked hands to his lips and kisses my knuckles. "I promise."

"And we're going somewhere safe?" I ask.

"The safest." He looks at me again, holding my gaze until my face heats up.

"What?" I demand.

"I love you," he blurts out. "I should have said it before."

"Me, too," I rush to say, and then I kiss him long enough to get a look from the flight attendant. Once the cabin is secure, the plane finally lifts into the air. I squeeze Miles's hand until it's numb, I'm sure. I watch the world get smaller and smaller below us and wish that I could talk to my friends, my family one more time. I lean against Miles, feel his arm wrap around me. I glance up at him. "Promise you won't jump out of these windows?"

He laughs again. "I promise. You get to keep me around for a while."

"A long con," I say. "This should be fun."

ONE MONTH LATER

I trudge down a long dirt road, trying to keep up with the group. The solid ground beneath my feet is unfamiliar and I sway a bit before finding my balance again. We pass a man and woman dressed in designer clothing, looking so clean and polished. I do a double-take, turning halfway around to look them over. It's been so long since I've seen anyone dressed in nice clothes. Many in no clothes at all. I glance down at myself, run a hand through my tangled hair, and for the first time in weeks I feel self-conscious.

I've been awake for nearly thirty hours, haven't showered in five days, and my clothes are torn and filthy. Also, my mouth tastes like stomach acid in the worst way, probably because I've spent about twelve of the last thirty hours barfing.

As if reading my mind, Miles tugs a water bottle from the side of his hiking backpack and offers it to me. With a sympathetic smile, he says, "At least now you know that you get seasick."

I nod and take a sip of the water, rinsing my mouth before spitting into the grass lining the dirt road. "Yeah, it was a real educational experience."

The bottle gets stuffed back into Miles's bag. I'm afraid to drink much until I'm sure it'll stay where I put it. Miles remains at my side, allowing some distance between the two men we're supposed to be following. I glance sideways at him a couple times while walking, surprised by the peaceful, even excited look on his face. He's been awake even longer than I have. But grunge definitely looks better on Miles than me. He's rocking the tanned, scruffy, rolled-up sleeves and pant legs look. Me, on the other hand…

Despite my protests, Miles removes the heavy backpack from my shoulders and tosses it over his own shoulder, causing the two bags to bump together. Without the extra weight I'm able to close some of the distance between us and the two guys in front of us. They are speaking rapid French to each other, too fast for me to translate all of it, but I do catch one guy asking the other which hut we've been assigned.

I look at Miles, raising an eyebrow. "A hut? I guess that's a step up from a tent. But I do recall you promising me a hotel when we got off the boat. One with hot water and real beds."

He laughs but doesn't meet my gaze. "Not a word of complaint from you for an entire month about traveling off the grid, sleeping outside —"

"Parasite infested water," I add. "And I'm just saying it's pretty shitty to promise me something and then not deliver. I'll be fine, no worries."

But he isn't wrong. I haven't complained at all. I figured we were doing what had to be done, so what was the point of griping about it. Plus, it's been kind of fun, Miles and I working together again, trying to figure out how to move from country to country without leaving any trail behind us. This meant cash only payments, eating, sleeping, and shopping in places with little technology, no surveillance equipment. Some of what we've done is similar to my family's way of life. Just expanded to many countries—Uzbekistan, Nepal, Bangladesh, Indonesia, and a whole bunch more I can't think of in my exhausted state.

A hut appears out of nowhere, and for a second, I'm thrilled that we've reached our destination, hot water or not. But then I see the sign on the door—in French—and quickly translate it as "office." We're led inside, and Miles converses with a woman behind the desk before producing a large envelope the captain of the boat we were on before had handed him over thirty hours ago. I watch in silence, hiding my surprise when he hands over a credit card and two passports. The passport Clyde gave me a month ago is tucked into my bag. This is a new one.

The woman behind the desk smiles at us, then opens the passports, flashing a photo of me above the name Kaley Carrington. Well that's new. Looks like I'm sixteen now. I catch sight of Miles's passport, too—Brian Carrington. Same last name. We're related now? I lean forward against the counter to see more. Same birthday, too.

Not just related but twins? Gross.

"Your parents will be joining tomorrow?" the lady asks us in broken English.

Our parents?

Miles's face reveals a flicker of surprise, but he hides it well. "Yes, that's right. Tomorrow."

He answered her question in French, which appears to excite the woman. She flutters around, gathering items until we've both got keys in our hands and the men who led us here are taking our bags, leading out a back door. Realizing that at least one of us speaks French, the men switch to what I can only assume is Tahitian.

Behind the office hut is something so startling I blink to make sure I'm not imagining things—a golf cart. It looks so out of place in the middle of nowhere. In no time, we're cruising down that dirt road again, expelling very little energy this time, passing rows of doors to huts.

The ocean is visible once again and it's magnificent, blue in places, green in other spots, and crystal clear. I'd hated it when we were on the boat, rocking constantly with no end in sight, but seeing it from solid ground I can finally appreciate the beauty. Finally the golf cart stops in front of what looks like a small hut held on stilts over the water. But when I step inside, a whole different image is revealed. A giant gorgeous living room opens in front of us. Across the room is a deck with a small pool that seems to filter right into the ocean somehow. I walk farther inside and stop before my feet cross over a square glass panel in the floor.

"Oh my God," I whisper to Miles who is now beside me, both of us admiring a school of fish swimming beneath our feet. "What is this place?"

"A resort," he says simply, and then he leaves me to tip the guy who brought our bags inside.

When he returns and we're alone, I have a sudden surge of energy despite my lack of sleep and recovering seasickness. I sprint up a spiral staircase and gasp when I see the second floor loft. The biggest, most beautiful bed covers about half of the room. Off to the left is a mega big bathroom with a shower big enough to fit a dozen people comfortably.

"Are you seeing this?" I ask Miles.

He's trailing behind me, flipping through the resort brochure. "Hot water every day, it says."

I spin to face him, nerves fluttering in my stomach. "Your parents sent us here, right? What do you think this means? That things are better or worse?"

At first we talked constantly about where everyone else in our lives were, what they were doing, if they were worried about us (I've been able to send Harper a few postcards luckily) but eventually we just stopped. There was no point in worrying beyond making sure we were doing everything we could to stay out of anyone's sight.

"I'm not sure what it means," Miles admits. "But yes, they sent us here."

"Do you think they're really coming tomorrow?" I ask, and he shakes his head, unsure. I glance longingly at the giant bed and then the big bathroom. "If they do, they'll probably want this room, right? We should take the two small rooms downstairs."

Miles steps closer, hooking an arm around my waist and tugging me closer. "All I know is they won't be here tonight. So..."

Not needing any more prompt, I hurry to the shower. "Dibs!"

I wake up with a start, sitting up quickly and blinking in the dark. It takes me a minute to remember where I am. The soft bed is so unfamiliar, as is my squeaky clean body and new clean clothes I bought at the gift shop earlier today...or maybe yesterday?

"Hey," Miles says from beside me, and I immediately sigh with relief. I've gotten so used to waking up beside him. "You okay? Still feeling sick?"

I hadn't eaten any dinner, not wanting to chance another puke fest, but now my stomach rumbles with hunger. "I'm good. Just forgot where we were."

"Quite an upgrade, huh?" he says.

I return to lying down, but this time with Miles's arms around me, my cheek resting on his chest. "Definitely. It's weird. Like your parents knew we were in desperate need of a real shower."

We fall silent again and something feels different than all the nights we've spent together since leaving New York. It feels like an end, but I don't know that for sure. "Are you glad you came with me?" I ask, and then immediately regret the question. "I mean do you wish you could be there hunting down more of Jack's group?"

He tightens his hold on me, kisses my hair. "I'm exactly where I want to be."

Truth. I can hear it loud and clear. All the time I've spent with Miles has reduced his ability to lie to me. Probably vice versa, too, but I'm okay with that.

I remember something from weeks ago and start laughing. "Remember the fight we had over mystery meat in Nepal that first night?"

"Yep," he says, and I can hear him smile. "I thought we were doomed after that."

"Me, too." I laugh again. "I was sure we'd get tired of each other after a while."

But I'm even more in love with him than the moment he sat beside me on that flight out of JFK airport. We've had some nervous moments, times when one or both of us was sure someone had followed us. But overall, we worked well together, we usually want to see the same sights, try similar foods. Which is weird because I used to think Miles and I were so different. Turns out when both of us are being open-minded and traveling in a new foreign country, we have a lot of common interests.

I lift my head, scoot up a bit, and kiss Miles in a way that hopefully shreds any doubt that I don't love his company all hours of the day—and night. He responds immediately, kissing me back and then pulling me on top of him.

His mouth grazes my ear and then he says, a whisper, light as the ocean breeze right outside of this room, "I love you."

I rest my hands on his face, holding his gaze below mine and letting myself really look at him. He's different than the boy I met outside the apartment pool months ago. I'm different, too, I'm sure. But if I look hard enough, I can see traces of that boy, qualities and pieces of him I didn't know or couldn't back then. I can't imagine not getting to see this face, these eyes, every day. But whatever happens, we'll deal with it. We've dealt with so much already. I touch my mouth to his again and whisper against his lips. "I love you, too."

Neither of us end up going back to sleep. Instead we put the master loft bedroom back together again with the skill of two people who have made invisibility a career—just in case anyone is actually going to show up today. Then we stand outside and watch the sun rise over the water, Miles's arms around me, the air outside tropical and perfect.

After the sun is fully in the sky, when we contemplate going for a swim, both of us turn at the sound of a golf cart rumbling down the dirt road. Miles and I look at each other for a beat and then dart inside, across the living room. The door to our "hut" opens and sure enough, Agent Beckett and Agent Beckett enter. I watch Miles as a grin spreads over his face. And then I look at them and laugh. They're decked out in vacation wear, Hawaiian shirts and all.

Mrs. Beckett spreads her arms wide. "My two beautiful children! I'm so happy to see both of you."

Before embracing them, I toss Miles a disgusted look. Not loving this whole twin cover. Ew. I'm hugging Mrs. Beckett, nearly as glad as Miles to see these two very amazing adults, but over her shoulder, I catch sight of someone else clambering through the door, dragging a giant suitcase.

Someone with blond hair and feet identical to mine. "Oh my God," I whisper under my breath. I abandon Miles's mom and rush toward the door, but stop short taking in another newcomer.

Harper.

And Aidan.

My sister is here. I can't even speak. Or move.

Harper sees me and I can tell it's not easy for her to hold it together, either, but she glances back at the golf cart driver and then looks at me and Miles and shouts, "Surprise! Family spring break with Aunt Harper! Who's excited?"

There isn't any room in my head or heart to process her words. I stumble to the door and hug my sister harder than I did when we saw each other after five years apart. Soon I'm crying and so is Harper. Even though the golf cart driver is still here. Miles skillfully hands over a tip big enough to send him on his way.

When I finally break away from Harper, I just look at Miles's parents and say, "How?"

"Took a while to create our family's identity, but it came together a few days ago," Mr. Beckett says.

I reach for Harper again, squeezing her way too hard. I can't help it. There were times when I was sure that we'd never see each other again. After I release Harper and rush over to give Aidan a hug, we all sit on the couches, listening to Mr. Beckett explain how he put this "family" vacation together.

Miles sits beside me on the loveseat, his fingers combing through my hair while his dad talks. He keeps turning to stare at his mom and then his dad and then Harper. And I know how he feels. It's just been the two of us for what feels like an eternity. We've barely spoken to anyone along our journey, often because of language barriers, and sometimes for security reasons.

Finally when the energy settles from our reunion, Miles asks the very question that had been at the forefront of my mind. "So what now? Are we done running?"

"Almost," Mr. Beckett says, exchanging a weary look with

his wife. "I'm sorry, I'd hoped for better news, hoped to bring both of you back with us, but we still have some stragglers in Jack's group."

"But we were able to make some travel plans for you," Mrs. Beckett assures us. "We thought Europe might be safe now that you've been off the grid. There, we were able to arrange places for you to stay, real homes, not a tent in the wilderness."

"We should be able to visit in another month or so…" Mr. Beckett adds. "Probably Switzerland because communications are easier there."

"Will it be terrible for you?" Harper asks tentatively. "To keep going like you've been?"

I feel Miles's warm fingers rest on my leg, and then he laces our fingers together and gives my hand a squeeze.

"We'll survive," he says, all serious. "Whatever needs to be done, we'll do it."

I match his serious expression, silencing the voice inside me that's chanting, *Europe, Europe, Europe!* "Whatever we need to do," I agree. "If that involves suffering through a month in where…France? Italy?"

"Definitely the Alps," Miles says. "Oh! And Morocco! We are totally going to Morocco."

Both Miles's mom and Harper roll their eyes at the same time. His mom says, "Okay, so apparently it's not the big sacrifice we thought it'd be."

Miles's eyes meet mine. "Definitely not."

After a few seconds too long, I tear my gaze from his. "Not that we can't enjoy a week in this tropical heaven."

"Yes, as twins," Mr. Beckett reminds us, gesturing for the two of us to scoot apart. "I should hope you can manage a week as siblings without blowing our cover?"

With a sigh, Miles puts a couple of inches between us. But as everyone gets up to check out the place and unpack, he leans in and whispers in my ear, "Now we have even more reason to look forward to Europe next week."

Despite the explicit directions, I lean forward and kiss him. "Last one for a week, I promise."

And he kisses me back, making it worth the wait ahead of us. Sometime hopefully I'll hear from my own parents, find out when my mom will be released, and maybe even get back to my life and Holden Academy. But for now, I have a week to spend with my sister and Aidan, a sturdy backpack, a couple of passports...and Miles.

And that's enough for now. Maybe forever.

ACKNOWLEDGMENTS

Thanks a million to my agent, Nicole Resciniti, who I could not survive without. Liz Pelletier for her continued support of and love for this series as well as my other Entangled books. Lydia Sharp and Stacy Abrams for nudging me along inch by inch with this book. Melissa Montovani for always making publicity easier than it seems—mostly due to her hard work and help at every stage. Heather Riccio for publicity help and those weekly morale-boosting Entangled Bestseller List emails. Thanks to Curtis Svehlak for a great job getting this book through the final stages of production. Thanks to my family and friends for their continued support. And of course my readers who I've dedicated this book to.

Grab the Entangled Teen releases readers are talking about!

Pretty Dead Girls
by Monica Murphy

In Cape Bonita, wicked lies are hidden just beneath the surface. But all it takes is one tragedy for them to be exposed. The most popular girls in school are turning up dead, and Penelope Malone is terrified she's next. All the victims have been linked to Penelope—and to a boy from her physics class. The one with the rumored dark past and a brooding stare that cuts right through her. There's something he isn't telling her. But there's something she's not telling him, either. Everyone has secrets, and theirs might get them killed.

Lies that Bind
by Diana Rodriguez Wallach

Reeling from the truths uncovered while searching for her sister, Anastasia Phoenix is ready to call it quits with spies. But before she can leave her parents' crimes behind her, tragedy strikes. No one is safe, not while Department D exists. Now, with help from her friends, Anastasia embarks on a dangerous plan to bring down the criminal empire. But soon she realizes the true danger might be coming from someone closer than she expects…

entangled teen

an imprint of Entangled Publishing LLC